Praise for The Sam Austin Chronicles:

"Impressively well written and thoroughly entertaining from beginning to end, *Target Citadel* is the anticipated sequel to *Destination Citadel*, the first installment of Robert Adrian's Sam Austin Chronicles."

—The Midwest Book Review

Checkmate Citadel: "Another terrifically entertaining science fiction novel from a consummate master of the genre."

—The Midwest Book Review

Titles by Robert Adrian

Destination Citadel

Target Citadel

Checkmate Citadel

Countdown Citadel

COUNTDOWN CITADEL

—

ROBERT ADRIAN

ISBN: 0990610438
ISBN 13: 9780990610434
Library of Congress Control Number: 2016905475
Cambrian Park LLC, San Jose, CA

PROLOGUE

Two men and three women stood in a nondescript room, where they faced multiple displays. One of the men made a gesture, and an image of several asteroids appeared.

"Not long ago, we were a bunch of neophytes when it came to mining among the asteroids," he said. "No one took us seriously back then. They said we didn't have any experience, we weren't looking in the right places for precious materials, we didn't know how to run a mining operation, we would be eaten alive by the competition, we'd be broke in six months, and so on." He turned to one of the women and asked, "Where do we stand on our goals, Georgia?"

She stood near a display and brought up a new image. "It has taken some time, Lazarus, but we've finally achieved the success we needed with our mining activities to support the next step of our operations. Not bad, considering the competition, the lack of experience, and everything else about us that was wrong. The same people who couldn't think of enough things about us to criticize are now calling us geniuses."

She shook her head and continued. "It's amazing how blind most people are about such things. It's not that hard when you know what to look for, which we do. We've done very well with the new strikes we discovered, but others have had similar success. Where we've really made a lot of people look like chumps is by going back to places where the professionals had already gone but had abandoned as barren, and we've shown them that they were wrong. With that kind of blindness, it's hard to believe people ever got into space."

Another woman spoke. "There are plenty of other things it's hard to believe people can do. That's a good thing for us, since we'll show them we can do everything better than they can."

Lazarus nodded his agreement and turned to the other man. "Speaking of doing things better than others, where do we stand on taking the next steps, Heph?"

"We're just a few months away from having the team and resources in place to expand our operations into space, throughout the solar system and beyond," the other man said. "It took humanity a hell of a lot longer to do it the first time than it'll take us. We're going to show people that Citadel is no longer the gold standard when it comes to building ships and going places. There's no reason so far why we won't be rolling out our new technology as planned."

Lazarus's eyes gleamed with anticipation. "Sam Austin and Citadel have had everything their way for years, what with special trade deals, protection by political allies, and monopolies on key technologies. That kind of situation usually leads to complacency, and I'm counting on that complacency being their undoing. Finally, Sam Austin and Citadel are going to have some competition. We'll be able to keep them guessing about us until it's too late and we have everything we want."

CHAPTER ONE

As he took a stroll through the Mall in Washington, DC, J. W. Preacher III considered himself to be truly blessed. Although his full head of snow-white hair was a reminder that he'd never see eighty again, he was in the vigorous autumn of his life, despite having put on some weight since the day, more than a half century past, when he'd married the love of his life. There were numerous Preacher children, grandchildren, and great-grandchildren to remind him what was really important.

He had lived in Washington for many years after joining the law practice his great-grandfather had originally established more than a century earlier. The practice had stayed in the family, and in time, he'd taken over the firm from his own father.

For virtually the entire existence of the Preacher law firm, one of its most prestigious clients had been Sam Austin. Preacher had fond memories of being introduced to Sam for the first time by his grandfather, John S. Preacher. The old man had been proud of his grandson, and the boy and Sam had warmed to each other immediately. Preacher was still amused all these years later over the notion that his grandfather was considered the "old" man in that meeting, when it was Sam who was the senior by over half a century.

It seemed that the walls of every Preacher office at the firm contained images of various meetings with Austin, with the passage of time measured in the changes in fashion and the amounts of gray in everyone's hair—everyone's except Austin's. His hair, as always, remained dark, and his face was mostly unlined. Time hadn't caused his tall, lithe frame to become stooped, made him any less light on his feet, or dimmed the sharp intelligence within his vibrant blue eyes. He had stayed in exceptionally good shape, with a firm grip that could make the recipient wince if that was his intention.

Austin's immortality had been considered unremarkable for many years, but it hadn't always been like that. Preacher's grandfather had talked about his own father, the first J. W. Preacher, who had been born after Sam had walked on the moon as an Apollo astronaut. As the first J. W. Preacher had grown up and pursued his dream of becoming a lawyer, he'd noticed, like so many other people, that Austin seemed to have defied the passage of time. Although Austin had remained a member of the astronaut corps, he had eventually returned to his career in the US Navy.

As the years passed and stars appeared on his broad shoulders in acknowledgment of his advancements in rank, Austin looked increasingly out of place whenever groups of Apollo astronauts gathered for reunions. People unfamiliar with his exploits sometimes even mistook him for the son or even grandson of one of his colleagues instead of a fellow pioneer. He had stayed current with his status in the astronaut program and returned to space several times in the decades following his historic moonwalk. As a mission commander, he'd looked younger than most of his fellow astronauts, some of whom had only been children when he'd made his first appearance in space.

Eventually it became known to the public that he'd been exposed during a moonwalk to an unusual beam of intense blue energy that had originated from deep space. Although there was no definite proof, people assumed that his lack of aging started from that point. None of the information that NASA had preserved at that time could shed any light on *why* he'd stopped aging, and numerous medical tests hadn't provided any further insights. Later events from history that exposed the uglier side of human nature, such as the Bio War, had convinced him that continuing to seek answers may not be in the best interests of humanity. As a result, for many years he had been adamant about refusing to cooperate with any requests for further tests.

Preacher's thoughts moved to the more recent past. It seemed that he'd hardly taken over the Preacher firm before he found himself grooming his son, J. W. Preacher IV, for the day when the older man would step aside. Several years ago, he'd known it was time, and he'd given up what had been a second home for so many years.

Preacher hadn't simply gone into a comfortable retirement, however. While still in charge at his firm, he'd helped Austin set up an incredible new venture to reach and colonize the planet Citadel, located impossibly far away in another star system. Austin had not only headed the venture, but had led the first group of colonists as they'd headed out. Preacher remembered well the images of the departures of their spaceships, which could warp the very fabric of space-time to get there faster than the speed of light itself.

After the Citadel Group had spent years not knowing whether the colonists had even arrived, let alone whether they had survived, the technical brain trust on Citadel itself had finally perfected the technology for communicating between the two systems. Everyone was delighted to hear that the colony was thriving, although this delight was tempered by the news that one of the ships had never arrived, and so three hundred people were considered lost in space. The Earthlings' delight had also been cut short when they found themselves on the receiving end of a savage attack by an unsuspected race of aliens that had already tangled with the Citadel colonists, nearly destroying the fledgling settlement.

Preacher thought back with sorrow over the news that the Mars settlements had been devastated, and he recalled the tense moments when the aliens had launched a similar attack against Earth. Just as the planet's defenses had crumbled under the onslaught, Austin had showed up with the weapons that were able to destroy the alien invaders. Earlier, he had declared that Citadel was now its own nation, and a grateful Earth and Mars were happy to recognize Citadel as such.

A new nation needed an ambassador, and Austin had called upon Preacher to serve as Citadel's representative to all nations in that solar system. Since no one else had the technology that enabled the members of the Citadel Group on Earth to make the journey to Citadel and return, there would be no embassies on the distant planet itself. Thus, all diplomatic activities would go through Preacher, who now worked from the stately residence he had acquired on Embassy Row in Georgetown.

Although the Citadel Group, which was based in Earth's solar system, operated somewhat separately from the Citadel embassy, it was still considered to have diplomatic status as well. Astrid Henkel, the head of the Citadel Group, worked closely with Preacher. Such was Preacher's relationship with Austin that Preacher could act on behalf of all of Citadel's operations in Earth's solar system if necessary, especially in an emergency. A few years earlier, a dire situation had compelled Preacher to exercise that authority, helping to save Citadel from ruin. The situation had been called "Harrington's War," after the disgraced former US president who had sought to use her powers to wage war against Citadel in the vain hope of being reelected. The Preacher law firm, of course, continued to work with Citadel's ambassador as needed.

Although Henkel usually talked with Preacher remotely due to the distances involved, she found herself sitting in a comfortable chair in the Citadel embassy, seated near Preacher and his son. Earlier, they had joined the older Preacher during one of his walks around the historic city.

"For someone who wanted to talk, you're kind of quiet today, Dad," the son commented. "You hardly said a word during our walk."

The younger man bore a striking resemblance to his father. In addition to having similar facial features to his father, he had the same dark-brown skin, and his full head of hair was already streaked with broad patches of gray. His dark eyes had the same sparkle that his father's had, and people warmed to him right away, just as they did with his father. So far, the son had managed to avoid most of the extra weight that his father had accumulated.

"Did I?" Preacher replied. "I guess I'm not quite certain how to begin."

Henkel turned to the ambassador with an amused look. "That's never been your problem before, J. W. Why not start with the fact that you wanted both of us here in person?" She looked away for a moment, facing toward the famous Smithsonian building even though it wasn't visible from the embassy. "Not that I mind a chance to visit a beautiful city. It's quite different from my hometown of Penzberg."

Now it was Preacher's turn to look amused. "I've visited Penzberg, Astrid, and it is quite charming." His expression became serious. "However, as much as I enjoy reminiscing about places I've visited, we aren't together just to walk through this town to admire the view. I'm concerned about a new group that's been in the news, the one that claims to be putting together an operation that can venture into space the way the Citadel Group can. They call themselves Phoenix. What can you tell me about them?"

"Not nearly as much as I'd like, which is unusual in view of the technological expertise they supposedly possess," she replied uneasily. She walked over to a display and brought up several images. "They've become very wealthy in a short time due to some incredible finds from their prospecting activities among the asteroids."

She pointed to several rocks, saying, "Somehow, they seem to know where to look for the richest lodes with the most precious substances, even if others have already passed over the spots." She brought up some new images showing construction in space. "They've been converting their wealth into the development of a space-based infrastructure that looks like it could rival ours."

"That part isn't secret," Preacher replied. "What seems to be a secret is the identities and backgrounds of the people involved. They couldn't have simply appeared out of nowhere. You must know at least some of them, by reputation if nothing else."

Henkel shrugged. "That's part of what worries me, J. W. No one at the Citadel Group has ever heard of anyone associated with Phoenix."

"Where did they study? They couldn't have picked up that kind of advanced technology on their own." Preacher's expression darkened. "Lord knows, people have tried and failed. The best they've managed before now is to steal from *us*."

She shook her head before he could ask the next question. "No, there's no way they could have stolen anything from us. Our security is far advanced from what it was years ago when Brittel stole key files and sold them to others. Once I heard about Phoenix, it was natural to look into it. I'm certain that nothing has been compromised."

"What about those files, Astrid?" he pressed. "There's no way to know *everyone* who has seen them. Couldn't someone have studied them over the years and figured out the same things we did and then made his or her own warp-field generators, ones that are viable for repeat interstellar trips?"

"It can't be done," she said emphatically. "That original technology was—and is—a true dead-end. It got most, but not all, of the original ships to Citadel, but barely, and it wouldn't get them back here. While we'll never know for certain, we've always assumed that the reason the one ship didn't arrive was catastrophic failure of the generators. Even *we* couldn't work out the solution, and we're the ones who came up with it. If Bret Yabuno and his people on Citadel hadn't figured out the solution, we'd probably still have no idea whether they'd even survived the trip. Only a fool would place any trust in the original technology.

"Getting back to the question of where these people studied, we have contacts with all of the major universities, and none of these people attended any of them. Besides, something like this would be highly prestigious, and the word would get out from any university they attended. Right now, they're an enigma."

Preacher turned to his son. "What can you tell me about this enigma? While we may not know how they got the necessary training to get into space, they had to have come from somewhere and gotten some backing. Who are they?"

The younger man chuckled. "Good thing we know each other so well, Dad, because once I heard about these people, I figured you'd want to know about them. They're pretty good at maintaining their privacy, but we've been able to figure out that they probably don't number much more than fifty members. While they haven't announced a formal hierarchy, there seems to be a group of five people who are the leaders."

He walked over to a display. Moments later, an image appeared, showing five people standing near each other. A window revealed a background of stars, with a couple of asteroids off in the distance. "This picture was taken eighteen months ago. The first man, who looks to be in his late thirties, calls himself Lazarus. The other man, who calls himself Heph, appears to be in his late forties, or possibly early fifties."

"That's an unusual name. How does he spell it?"

"He spells it *H-E-P-H*. We have no idea if that's a given name or a nickname. The first woman is Georgia, and she looks to be in her late forties. The next is Pandora, and she appears to be the oldest, probably in her late fifties. The last is Diana, and she is probably in her midthirties. If they have a leader, it is probably Lazarus. He seems to be center stage for most announcements, and he doesn't appear to just be a figurehead."

Preacher gazed intently at the faces for several minutes, his eyes shifting from one set of features to another, before he concluded, "I don't recognize any of these people. They're all adults, and we know they weren't born out there among the asteroids. Where else have they shown up, and under what names?"

The younger man frowned. "For all the background we can find, these people may have been born eighteen months ago. The mining community is famously relaxed when it comes to worrying where people are from. This wouldn't be the first time that someone disappeared and reappeared within that community, to start over from whatever problems they had. For all we know, they've altered their appearances."

"What about matching them with others who vanished around the same time these people showed up?" Preacher asked. "The disappearance of fifty people would have been noted."

His son nodded. "True, but there were no matches with reported unsolved disappearances from around that time frame. In fact, we can't even find *five* people who vanished without being accounted for, at least not five with the technological knowledge to do what they've done so far."

"Prospecting out there isn't the kind of activity where all you need is a pickax and a pack mule," the older man said with a slight chuckle. "They couldn't have started out without significant resources to support their mining operations. Who's been backing them financially or logistically?"

"We don't know. There are a few unsubstantiated rumors that they were seen on Mars eighteen months ago, just before the mining started, but we don't know if the backing came from any of the interests there." He grinned. "As you know, the people on Mars are adamant about maintaining their privacy. I doubt even Amelia Gordon could help us much on that score, despite the fact she's their president."

"I'll check with her anyway, just in case," Preacher said. He looked at Henkel. "What have they said about when they had the epiphanies needed for advanced space travel?"

"They claim that they only figured everything out within the last three months, when they finally had time to engage in advanced research after striking it rich with mining."

"They're saying they figured everything out in three months?" Preacher asked in disbelief. "What are the chances this is all a bluff and they don't really have the technology they claim?"

Henkel brought the images of the space construction back up. "Seeing is believing, of course, but what we've seen so far about their activities in space shows they know what they're doing."

"The Space Command and the rest of the mining community all know how to build space facilities, but they can't visit Citadel," Preacher scoffed.

"That's true," she admitted. "While they've been tight-lipped about themselves and their operations so far, they'll have to open up when they demonstrate their technology if they want anyone to take them seriously."

Preacher gazed at the images for a moment. "I think it's time to let Sam know what's happening. He'll want some advance notice if there's any possibility of these people doing what they say they can do. Having some uninvited visitors there could make things pretty awkward with the people back here."

CHAPTER TWO

Two ships faced each other just outside the Citadel system, each taking note of the other vessel's position. Both brought their weapons online, a sign that combat was imminent. There was little room for maneuver, suggesting that brute force rather than tactics would decide the matter. In that contest the smaller ship would be at a disadvantage, as it lacked the full array of weapons found aboard its adversary.

A countdown was underway aboard *Pathfinder*, the smaller ship, while the larger vessel waited patiently, as if certain of the outcome. The only option available to avoid extreme damage or worse was for the smaller adversary to run, hoping it wouldn't be caught from behind by the destructive power of the other ship's weapons. As the countdown approached zero, the ship neither launched its weapons nor ran. In an instant, it was simply gone, without a shot having been fired.

Although *Pathfinder* had vanished from the view of *KT-2*, the Keith Thomas–class transport nearby, the larger ship could be seen in ghostly silhouette on the main display of the tough scout ship's bridge. *Pathfinder* captain Alicia Shaw watched the display calmly. A new countdown appeared on another display as a member of her bridge crew called out, "They'll be launching their weapons in thirty seconds, Captain."

Aboard *KT-2*, Captain Frederick Washington, known as "Wash" to everyone, including his crew, gazed at the display; he noted the disappearance of *Pathfinder* as well as the commencement of the new countdown. "Lock the torpedoes onto *Pathfinder*'s last position," he ordered dispassionately. "It isn't going anywhere."

Pathfinder's captain continued to read the countdown before turning back toward the image of *KT-2* on the main display. She and her crew watched with fascinated expressions as the transport deployed its fully loaded torpedo launcher. Moments later, the torpedo was launched directly toward *Pathfinder*'s position. With so little room for maneuver, it seemed impossible that the weapon could miss them, but it appeared to slide around their position, the image distorting as it moved, until it was past them and heading toward deep space.

The view from *KT-2*'s display was different. Wash noted with interest that at some point, the space around the torpedo seemed to distort slightly, but the weapon itself didn't. They never lost sight of it as it passed through where *Pathfinder* had been located and ventured beyond. Eventually, the device was deactivated remotely to avoid creating a hazard in space.

"It's time for something bigger," Wash ordered.

Back aboard the smaller vessel, as if on cue, another countdown appeared on a display, and the crew watched as the torpedo launcher was replaced by the transport's rail gun. A large rock, which was really a very small asteroid, was loaded into the rail gun, and the action paused as the countdown approached zero.

When the countdown reached the magic number, the new weapon launched its payload down the same path the torpedo had taken. This time, the extreme speed at which the payload was launched prevented anyone from getting a good view of it as it rushed toward its target. As the rock approached the scout ship, it gave the impression of no longer traveling in a straight line, but of seeming to stretch and slide around its target. The aft display confirmed that the rock was heading out along a path that might continue for eternity.

The people aboard *KT-2* watched as the rock raced through space. The speed was so great that all they saw was a faint distortion that seemed more imagined than real, and then the rock continued on its course without having caused any damage. Again, Wash showed no emotion as he ordered, "Let's see if we can fry them."

By now the image of a countdown on a display aboard *Pathfinder* was familiar, and they waited to see whether they would survive an assault by another weapon. They watched as the rail gun was demobilized and the larger ship's electromagnetic-pulse (EMP) weapon was deployed. Right on cue, as the number reached zero, they saw a faint glow in the eerie setting of their warp bubble, but the image was unchanged otherwise. The pulses had no more success in reaching their target than the solid objects that had preceded them.

Shaw had noted without apparent emotion the failure of any of the larger ship's weapons to reach the scout ship, let alone to actually cause any damage. A hint of an amused look appeared on her face as she took in the ghostly image on the display and said, "Now it's our turn."

Back aboard *KT-2*, a new countdown appeared on a display. Moments later, they saw *Pathfinder* reappear, still in its original location, making it seem impossible for the transport's deadly weapons to have failed to destroy the target. Not only was *Pathfinder*'s adversary undamaged, but the crew found themselves facing a torpedo launcher as it was brought online. The distance and size of the larger ship made it impossible for the scout ship's newly deployed weapon to miss.

"Now it's our turn," Wash said with an edge in his voice instead of any hint of amusement. He never took his gaze away from the display as he spoke into his link: "Take us away, Chief."

Pathfinder's captain kept her gaze locked on a display as well. Impossible as it had seemed for the transport's weapons to miss their target, it seemed equally impossible for a ship that large to simply vanish.

Aboard *KT-2*, the image of *Pathfinder* disappeared from the display, but only for an instant. It reappeared a moment later, this time as a ghostly silhouette against a dark background, with no stars to be seen. The weapon was still deployed, however, and the countdown told them they would be under attack in just a few seconds.

"Any lateral movement, Chief?" Wash asked.

"No, Wash," came the reply. "We're steady right where we are."

The conversation was cut off as the countdown showed zero, and the torpedo seemed to burst out toward them; they had no way to avoid it. Because of the transport's much greater size, the torpedo appeared to distort more quickly than the one that had approached *Pathfinder*. It took just a moment for it to stretch around and past its target before continuing harmlessly on its way toward deep space.

Wash didn't bother to ask for an update on the status of the ship; the display had told them everything they needed to know. A new countdown appeared, and they watched as their adversary deployed its own EMP weapon. Regardless of the circumstances, one could never face an EMP onslaught without being aware of the potential for catastrophic damage. Although he appeared calm, Wash's hand maintained an iron grip on the arm of his chair.

No one said anything as the countdown went toward zero. The seconds passed, and still the bridge was silent. Normally an EMP attack wreaked havoc with display images, making it nearly impossible to see what was happening. Although there wasn't anything to see, the best news was the fact that the ghostly image on their display stayed steady.

Wash contacted his chief engineer. "Any signs of damage, Chief?"

"Nothing," she reported. "They may as well have been huffing and puffing at a brick house for all the difference it made," she added.

To everyone's relief, no new countdowns appeared on the display. Wash relaxed his grip on his chair, and the tension that had been building ever since the first encounter with the scout ship finally dissipated.

"That's great news, Chief," Wash said in an easy voice. "Time for us to return to the real world."

"Coming up, Wash."

A moment later, the ghostly silhouette and the eerie darkness surrounding it vanished, and they found themselves once again facing the real *Pathfinder*.

Wash faced a display as he spoke to *Pathfinder*'s captain. "Well, you dodged a bullet or two today, Alicia. Good thing you're able to hide in that rabbit hole!"

Shaw shrugged and then grinned. "Old news, Wash. *Pathfinder*'s been able to find that rabbit hole for a long time."

Wash grinned back. There was a gleam in his gaze as he said, "Well, then you ought to be ashamed of yourself for the lousy aim; there you were, at practically point-blank range with a big target, and you couldn't even find it!"

There was laughter on both bridges as the scout ship captain replied, "Good thing that rabbit hole was big enough to hide that big target of a luxury liner you drive, or you'd have been history!"

———

There were plenty of people linked in to the review of the latest conflict between *Pathfinder* and *KT-2*, including Sam Austin and several of the guests at his comfortable residence. Austin's home, which had been expanded over the years into a series of buildings enclosed within the extensive protective walls surrounding the property, marked the boundary between the farthest west the planet's settlers had managed to reach from the Town Square and the beginning of true wilderness. Outside Austin's compound, there was no civilization to offer any protection to the unwary traveler. Large swaths of wilderness abutted Austin's planted acreage, and the native predators known as "cheaters" still lurked about in hopes of an opportunity to make a kill.

One of Austin's guests was Bret Yabuno, who stood near a large display that prominently featured images of the two combatants. Yabuno gestured toward *KT-2*'s chief engineer. "We've all seen the preliminary report, Lisa, but it helps to walk us through some of the findings."

Lisa Benning stepped up to the display and pointed toward the image of the smaller vessel. "First of all, as expected, *Pathfinder* had no trouble staying outside of normal space-time in its own warp bubble. It never moved or drifted out of position. Now for the amazing news."

She pushed aside the images as she brought up a ghostly image of the smaller vessel. "This is one of the images we were able to capture of *Pathfinder* while *KT-2* was in its own stationary warp bubble. As you can see, the ship stayed in a fixed position, without drifting. Otherwise, we'd never have gotten these images, since they never appear when a transport is in 'motion' in a warp bubble."

"They can appear when *Pathfinder* is in motion," someone pointed out.

"True," Yabuno acknowledged, "but we all know that the principles behind *Pathfinder*'s bubble are somewhat different, to accommodate the different size and configuration of a transport." He turned toward Benning. "Please continue, Lisa. How did the warp-field generators perform? Any problems with any of the readings?"

She brought up an image from her engine room. "The generators worked fine through all of the countdowns, with no anomalies reported."

Her brow furrowed slightly. "However, it's what happened after the countdown, before we reappeared in normal space-time, that's cause for concern." She brought up another image of the scout ship as seen from within *KT-2*'s warp bubble. The analysts in the room with Austin watched as the countdown expired and were puzzled when nothing unusual happened. As the *KT-2* crew made ready to leave their bubble, the phantom *Pathfinder* became less distinct than usual, nearly dissolving completely, even though the dark background reminded them that the transport was still outside of normal space-time.

"What the hell was that?" Shaw asked. She looked around the room. "Honest, we weren't playing any games with *KT-2*. We didn't do anything after the countdown expired."

"We know that, Alicia," Yabuno replied with a touch of humor in his expression. "Besides, it wouldn't have mattered. There wasn't anything you could have done anyway." He looked back at Benning. "What do you think it means?"

Benning placed an image of the generators next to the image of the ghost and gestured at some of the readings from the sophisticated hardware. "You can see that the generators began to have problems right before the images started to lose focus. I think it means that the generators can only maintain a motionless status for so long before things start to fall out of phase."

Her expression carried a warning. "This was the longest test we've done to date. We were lucky that the tests were over when they were, since we might not have been able to stay out of the line of fire if the bubble had collapsed at the wrong moment. While these results tell us that we've made incredible progress from where we were a couple of years ago, we still haven't resolved every problem."

Benning's warning had changed the jubilant mood into a somber one.

For the first time Austin spoke. "Your words are well taken, Lisa, and a reminder that we shouldn't be resting on our laurels. However, let's keep sight of the fact that there may be circumstances where the amount of time that this most recent test lasted may mean the difference between success and failure in an emergency." He looked at Yabuno and Alan Turner and chuckled. "I guess that means that while the test results are a hell of an accomplishment, it's not yet time to declare victory or even talk publicly about what we've been doing."

Yabuno's grin was a bit lopsided, while Turner was more philosophical as he replied, "Three years ago, we couldn't even begin to figure out how to do what we've done within the last few days. Perhaps in another three years, we'll be saying much the same thing about these challenges."

CHAPTER THREE

I t was a good thing there was plenty of room at Austin's lake to accommodate all of their guests. They were celebrating a major milestone for Citadel, as the first wave of settlers had been there for ten years. *That would be ten Earth years plus an extra hundred days*, Austin mused to himself, since Citadel years and Earth years, although close, didn't quite match up. Each year on Citadel was about ten days longer than on Earth, although the days were nearly the same in length. The anniversary was important because the land grants for those first settlers had now become permanent, meaning those settlers wouldn't lose them even if they pulled up stakes and returned to Earth—not that anyone had expressed an interest in leaving.

Austin surveyed the people in and out of the water and was pleased to see so many people from the first group of settlers. Bret and Donna Yabuno were there with their four kids, romping around a shallow section of the lake. Bret was Austin's oldest friend among the settlers; they had formed a strong bond over common interests in technology back when they were trying to get the Citadel Group launched. Bret and Donna had become good friends as a couple with Austin and his wife, Liz.

Joe and Sara Albretti were there with their two children. Although Sara wasn't an original settler, Joe was; he had stayed on even after his first wife, Gina, had died in a sacrifice that had helped save Citadel years earlier. Sara and Joe had met later when she was visiting as the captain of a Keith Thomas transport. He had finished with his grieving over his first wife's death, and he and Sara had gotten married and decided to build a life together as settlers. They had named their first child Gina, after his late wife.

Alan Turner and his wife, Dawn, were also first settlers and were there with their three children.

Of course, Austin himself and his wife, Liz, were first settlers, with Austin leading the first group of twenty-five ships to their new land, and Liz supervising the offloading of settlers and equipment to the planet. Austin had continued to lead the settlement even after it became a nation recognized by other nations. He looked around, delighted to see their third child, Anna, already taking to the water even though she was less than two years old. The two older kids, Matt and Luke, had long since become accustomed to the water. Austin was touched to see that they watched over their little sister with care.

The younger boy, Luke, had been born while Austin, Liz, and Matt were visiting Earth years earlier, although Luke had no memories of the planet of his birth. Matt remembered Earth and had kept in touch with the relatives he'd met during their visit. Anna had never known any home except Citadel.

Thanks to a steady stream of settlers bound from Earth, as well as many births on Citadel itself, there were now over fifty thousand people on the planet, with more than seven thousand of them having been part of the first wave. Although Austin felt a connection with all of the settlers, he had an especially strong bond with the first ones, since they'd gone through the first hardships together. They had survived what was then a twelve-month voyage and had found out about an unforeseen technological problem that meant their ships could not return them to Earth, even if they wanted to quit. In addition, they had kept trying to make their communications system work so that they could at least communicate with Earth, but without success.

For several years they'd continued the hard task of building and sustaining their homes, including cooperating with each other in building the enclosures that protected them from the deadliest predators on the planet, which they called "cheaters." They'd been ecstatic when Bret and his people finally found the breakthroughs they needed to enable them to build new ships that could travel between the two star systems. No one had objected to the fact that the new ships they called "transports" could make the trip much more quickly than the first voyage's ships. They'd also learned to bring to life the communications network between the two systems, and had finally solved the problem of generating artificial gravity in space.

The challenges hadn't all arisen on Citadel either. They'd had to fend off attacks by enemies from Earth and from beyond both solar systems.

Austin's friends had gathered in his home that evening for a lively discussion about some challenges facing Citadel. "How much longer are we going to accept as full partners in Citadel people who want to come here from Earth's neighborhood?" Yabuno asked. "Though we still have vast amounts of land available, we're becoming even more spread out than before, thanks to the large parcels that each new settler receives as a temporary grant."

"That's not really a problem, is it?" Turner replied. "We're all linked in throughout the planet anyway."

"We're linked in, but there isn't much of a physical connection, since people are spread out so much," Albretti said. "Makes it hard to see where things like cities will arise over time."

"I think that's already happening," Liz said. "There have been regional groups coming together for common purposes, such as local infrastructure improvements, cooperative agricultural and mining activities, and so on. Give them more time, and you'll see cities arise."

"In that case, we'd have to redefine what it means to be a city. Right now, the only way for those regions to become cities is through taking in huge tracts of land that are thinly populated, even assuming that settlers continue to have children. To me, that barely qualifies as a town."

"I'm less concerned about whether we have cities or towns than in developing a specific character to Citadel that won't be diluted by people from else-where," Yabuno said.

"That's why we do such thorough screening," Liz replied. "We make sure the people that we accept as potential settlers share a common set of values with us, in addition to having the skills needed to succeed with our way of life."

"The screening has been effective," Yabuno acknowl-edged. "However, at some point we need to focus more on raising our children with the Citadel values and less on whether a new batch of settlers really fits in here. I want to be sure that there is land available for our chil-dren that doesn't require traveling to the far side of the planet to reach. If we keep on granting large parcels to people who may or may not work out, we may be short-changing the children of the people who are already here. The only other solution is for parents to subdivide their parcels to leave to their children, which leaves them in a worse position than what is available for new settlers. Add another generation or two to the equation, and it looks even worse, with plots of land that are too small to sustain a family."

He looked around the room as he continued. "It won't be very many years before we have to face these issues with our own children as they become old enough to start their own lives. I'd rather see the land grants go to them than to strangers."

"What's the solution?" Turner asked. "If we start grant-ing parcels to new settlers who are based completely in the wilderness, we'll isolate them in a way that isn't good for anyone and set them up for failure. By expanding out from existing parcels, the newer settlers get the benefits of a certain amount of civilization, instead of having to do everything the hard way. The only other solution seems to be to stop the influx of settlers, which has led to a prosperous world that benefits us all."

"Eventually, the latter approach probably is the solution," Yabuno replied. "That doesn't mean giving up prosperity; it just means that it will be mostly homegrown. For now, I think we should consider scaling back the scope of the efforts to bring new settlers here so that we can focus on nourishing in our children a specific character that is Citadel. It's one thing for adults who have developed their values elsewhere to come here and adapt to our values, probably with their own interpretations as to what those values are. It's another to have Citadel consist primarily of people who have grown up here, where the values are already established."

"Your comments remind me of something Ben Franklin once said," Austin said. "He said words to the effect that the generation that brought the revolution to America would eventually die, and the next generation, which had been born there, would grow up as Americans. In a sense, that's what you're saying. So long as the population growth comes primarily from immigration, we delay the growth of a society that is truly Citadel." He laughed. "Of course, part of what you're saying is that at some point we'll all need to die out to make way for the first generation of native-born Citadel citizens. I think I'll wait a while before yielding my spot."

"One thing no one has really addressed is what to do when we feel things are crowded enough that we can't grant huge tracts anymore," Sara said. "That applies regardless of whether we are primarily a nation of immigrants or of people who were born here."

"Even if we remain a nation primarily of immigrants, we can keep up with our current land grants for a long time," Turner said. "If we remain a nation primarily of people who were born here, then we can go on much longer, since the rate of increase in the population would go way down."

"Still," she persisted, "we'll reach a point where we have to deal with the issue. What do we do then?"

Austin looked at Yabuno and grinned. "Reminds me of conversations we had over a dozen years ago, doesn't it?"

Yabuno nodded and walked to a display. Images of their solar system came into view. "If Citadel were the only habitable planet in this solar system, it would have been worth the effort to reach the place. However, one of the really attractive things about this solar system is the fact that there are three planets in the habitable zone of our star. While Citadel is in the sweet spot, both Shiloh and New Harbor aren't bad prospects either. Shiloh, in particular, is a good candidate for future exploration, since it is closer to our star but has avoided the hell that is a Venus-type environment. Instead, it has an atmosphere quite similar to the one here, with temperatures well within the ranges acceptable for human habitation. It is virtually the same size as Citadel, and, like Citadel, it has a moon that helps keep things stable from a rotational and climatic perspective. Although the Shiloh year is shorter due its closer proximity to the star, the day is almost the same length as the day on Citadel. While the same figures for New Harbor also look promising, we would probably want to do some terraforming in order to bring the temperatures up a bit. That's why we called it New Harbor, since it will serve us well as another harbor once we've done that work. For now, that makes it a clear third choice for colonization after Citadel and Shiloh.

"Sam and I have long considered Shiloh to have the potential for being something of a safety valve, both in the case of the need for accommodating the expansion of the Citadel population and in case of a planetary disaster involving Citadel."

Austin moved to a different display and images of life that was alien—even by Citadel's standards—appeared. "This information was obtained from probes that were sent over some time back. While the images are interesting, we don't know enough about Shiloh or New Harbor to be able to confirm that humans can even live there, let alone thrive in these places. Having basic information, such as atmospheric composition, gravity, length of day and year, axial tilt, and so forth, is a good start, but still doesn't tell us if either of these planets can sustain human life. We haven't had the luxury of spending the last ten years on anything except learning about and defending Citadel. The reason we were laughing is that this conversation has served as a reminder that it's time to investigate Shiloh in more detail now, while there's no sense of urgency, instead of later, when we're facing a crisis.

"We've already sent a more elaborate set of probes over to Shiloh to study the place in far greater detail, to give us the kind of information we need. Assuming for the moment that the information is promising, then we'll send over some teams to do on-site assessments." Austin's expression became somber. "Let's hope that they don't have the same fate as the first scouts who visted Citadel long ago. As we know, not all of them left this planet alive."

CHAPTER FOUR

Austin had been especially proud of the fact that he'd finally been able to get something more akin to a government established on Citadel, although it wasn't nearly as complicated as the governments on Earth. As J. W. Preacher had explained years earlier to the first group of colonists, Austin had been entrusted with enormous power to make decisions on behalf of the settlement that would have seemed almost dictatorial if exericsed by others. Characteristically, Austin's exercise of those powers had been wise and effective. Although he had wanted to ensure that there were limits on his power as the leader of Citadel, his fellow citizens had turned the tables on him by insisting on keeping things mostly as they'd been before. As a compromise, there was now a council to help advise him, although it met at his discretion. While the citizens had accepted some institutional limits on the power of his office, they insisted on those limits only applying to the next person to be president after Austin was done with the job.

Austin had tried to get things moving by setting up a convention to establish a new government, to be governed by the consent of the people, as documented in a written constitution. At the first session, he'd tried to turn over the meeting to someone else to act as the president of the convention, but he had been overruled by multiple voices declaring that he'd been elected to the job and should get on with it. A great deal of discussion later, Austin looked at a display. "This is how the proposed Citadel Charter now stands after having been amended by the convention on several points, not all of which I think are the best approach," he said with a raised eyebrow.

"Face it, Sam," Yabuno said, "Citadel is populated with people who agree with you that we don't need a lot of government in the first place. As you've pointed out, this is a society that doesn't even have lawyers to tell us how our lives should be run; we can figure it out for ourselves. That's one reason why we refuse to call the document a 'constitution.' If we did that, then lawyers from another planet would start telling us what a constitution means and how to do things, instead of leaving it for us to figure it out. Calling it a 'charter' is part of a fresh start for us."

"That may be a fresh start, but you're willing to let me figure a lot of it out for you," Austin replied. "How is that a good thing?"

"If that's what we are doing, and you were a different man, I'd worry about it too," Yabuno replied. "The reality is you're where you are because you're honest, intelligent, a good leader, and willing to make sacrifices for the good of all, even placing your life on the line for us. Just as important, you don't meddle in our private affairs. If we're going to have a government at all, then you're the man to make sure it only does what it's supposed to do."

"What about the day when I'm no longer in this job?" he asked. "You may not have the same confidence in the next person."

"We probably won't," Yabuno admitted. "That's why some of the limits on the president's authority don't come into play until after you leave office, which we hope won't be for a long time. Every person here has read the history lessons about the Second Constitutional Convention and your role in it when you were the US president. What other leader would seek to reduce portions of his power as part of trying to reduce the overall scope of the federal government's powers?"

Austin thought back on that time, more than a century earlier, when he'd been the US president and played a major role in making the Second Constitutional Convention both a reality and a success.

Twenty-First Century
"I think we are ready for your appearance at the Constitutional Convention tomorrow, Admiral," said Captain Janice Harris, US Navy, who was President Austin's chief of staff. "People are more interested in what you'll say at the convention than in listening to any of the usual crap that passes for mass entertainment. I can't count the number of people who have asked me for some inside information on your speech." She smiled as

she said, "I probably shouldn't repeat some of the words I used to tell them to stop bothering me and to wait for the speech along with everyone else."

Austin grinned. "I'm sure they were fine words, even if I won't be quoted using them."

Another man was in the room. He was in his sixties, with gray hair and dark-brown skin; he had the air of a man who enjoyed his life. He had been a lawyer for more than half of his life and was an expert in many areas of the law, including the US Constitution. His name was J. W. Preacher, the ancestor of several men with the same or nearly the same name, and Austin had entrusted him with reviewing the constitutional amendments that Austin had written. Austin was planning on submitting them to the Constitutional Convention to propose that the state legislatures ratify them.

He turned to Preacher and asked, "Any further word on the proposed amendments, J. W.?"

"Nothing further, Sam," Preacher replied. "I followed your instructions to leave your language alone unless there was a specific issue relating to the Constitution or other laws that needed to be addressed. The few changes that I have already suggested address those issues. Otherwise, I think your words do a fine job of saying what you mean them to say." He chuckled. "You must have done some research on your own, since the amendments were better than what most of my staff attorneys could write."

Austin looked at Preacher with eyes that were warm with appreciation as he asked, "How were you able to prevent leaks regarding my proposed amendments? In Washington, even lawyers often seem unable to resist the urge to tell *someone* about something that is supposed to be confidential. Although there have been some interesting comments in the press regarding what I may have in mind, it's pretty clear that people are just making guesses at this point."

Preacher's expression became slightly more serious. "First of all, while I can't speak for all of my Washington colleagues, I take very seriously my obligations as a lawyer, one of which is to keep my mouth shut regarding the business of my clients. Heaven help the foolish man or woman in my firm who doesn't act likewise. However, it doesn't really matter in this case; I did all my own research, so the support staff and other lawyers from my office don't know that you engaged me for this assignment. Private citizen Sam Austin, rather than President Austin, hired me, so even Congress can't get its hands on my work. Besides, I should be thanking you for giving me the honor of doing this service for our country."

———

The next day, Austin looked out among the delegates to the Constitutional Convention and marveled at the people who sat before him as proof that the republic was still capable of correcting flaws with its governance.

"Thank you, ladies and gentlemen, for inviting me to your convention," he began. "I say *your* convention because this convention belongs to you, the people. I have always felt that it is the people themselves who are in the best position to decide how they are to be governed and to create institutions to carry out those wishes.

I stand here in awe of the fact that the people have chosen to convene this convention in order to reassert their rights under our Constitution.

"Regarding the original Constitutional Convention, which took place over two hundred forty years ago, we know the members of that convention had a difficult task ahead of them. They had to consider how to revise a system that had become unworkable and was no longer responsive to the needs of the country. Does this purpose sound familiar? It should, since that is why the states have brought together this new convention.

"The result of the original convention was an amazing document—the Constitution of the United States of America. That document has, on the whole, served the country well. However, several points need to be kept in mind.

"The first is that even that amazing document was understood to need changes, which is why the states ratified the Bill of Rights some two and a half years after the Constitution went into effect. The issues were both complex and simple in nature. They were complex enough that a single amendment was not sufficient to address the concerns of the people. At the same time, the issues were simple in the sense that the purpose of the Bill of Rights was to ensure that the liberties of the people were safeguarded against the actions of the federal government.

"We now find ourselves facing a situation with some interesting parallels with, and differences from, the one faced by the founding fathers. As a result of actions taken by various parts of the federal government over a number of years, we find that some of the liberties that were intended to be safeguarded from encroachment by the federal government are no longer safeguarded. Not only do we find that there is a lack of willingness by the federal government to acknowledge and correct the problem, there is even an attitude that is, in some cases, hostile to the people's exercise of these rights.

"How to address this problem is, ultimately, for this convention to propose and for the people to decide. I would like to caution the people at this convention to keep in mind that they have been entrusted with a great responsibility. Change should not be undertaken for the sake of change and should not be made lightly. However, change should not be avoided simply because it *is* change. People are often pressured to do nothing, in order to avoid offending anybody. If this convention does nothing, then it will have failed in its purpose. If that happens, you will be answerable to something far more important than the judgment of various self-appointed experts; you will be answerable to the judgment of the people who sent you to this convention. I have confidence that when the time comes, you will be able to say to all people that you had the courage to do what needed to be done, without regard for the 'political correctness' of those actions.

"This convention will consider various amendments to the Constitution to address the concerns raised by the people. I offer several amendments for this convention to consider as part of that process. I would like to mention that others may propose amendments that do a better job of addressing the subjects of the amendments I wish to offer. If that happens, then I will yield gladly to the better amendment. Likewise, if it is the judgment of this convention that some or all of the amendments that I offer are not appropriate for consideration, then I again will yield gladly to your judgment.

"I propose that the convention issue a new document with a series of proposed amendments to the Constitution, entitled the 'Second Bill of Rights.'" Austin spent some time summarizing each amendment.

He then paused to let people catch their breaths before continuing. "I will conclude my comments by stating that this is the greatest opportunity that we have had in many years to bring our federal government back to the balance that is needed to ensure that our rights are preserved. The highest branch of government is the people. I have every confidence that you will take full advantage of this opportunity and produce a document that will enable you to look the people in the eye and say, 'We did our best to do what was right.' Thank you. God bless you, and God bless the United States of America."

Twenty-Second Century

"One of the challenges of my unusual life span is that I know I will be judged for actions not just by the people who are around at the time, but by future generations," Austin said to the people assembled as the Citadel convention.

"The Second Constitutional Convention was definitely a situation where I expected to answer to future generations for my actions, as well as for any failure on my part to act," Austin said. "One lesson from history is that the president always needs to have significant authority when it comes to foreign affairs, as well as to the security of the country. Another lesson is that men and women in our government can commit and get away with all sorts of mischief if the other men and women in government don't have the courage to do their jobs," he reminded them.

"While this should have been an obvious lesson, there weren't enough people ready to remember and act on it when Courtney Harrington committed and nearly got away with an appalling list of crimes as the US president. I want to be sure the people of Citadel never have to go through something similar."

"Point taken, Sam, but again, our structure of government is quite different from that of the US," Yabuno replied. "The original organizing documents setting up Citadel included some significant protections for the settlers, and the new Charter does much the same thing."

Austin shrugged, then grinned. "OK, if anyone ever wonders whether I always get my way, consider this as proof that I don't. Let's have a vote on whether to adopt our new Charter."

The chorus of sound made it unnecessary for Austin to insist on a formal count. They had their Charter.

—————

Austin viewed it as a start and planned on getting the people to agree over time to having more say over their government. The irony of the situation wasn't lost on him. Later that evening, he and Liz had talked about it as they were getting ready for bed.

"It's interesting," he said with a chuckle, "that the more I fight to ensure the people have a proper say over their government, the more they want to entrust that same power back to me."

"Not so amazing, really," Liz replied, laughing lightly. "While you insisted initially on broad authority as the leader of Citadel, no one worried about it, because they already knew from history that you wouldn't abuse that authority. You haven't, of course, although you've some- times had to make some tough decisions that probably no one else would have been able to. You've combined that authority with an equally broad moral authority, and people know you're the right person to be our leader and make those decisions."

She leaned close to him. "We've been married for over eleven years now, and you've been the husband I've always hoped to have and a wonderful father for our children. Every day, you are a living reminder of how a strong, moral man lives his life and sets the best kind of example for others."

She pulled back for a moment, the covers falling away to reveal her naked body. "Although the years haven't left their mark on you as you have outlived several prior wives, I can't claim that there aren't some wrinkles and lines that weren't here a decade ago. I just know that I am yours, body and soul."

Austin reached tenderly toward her and brushed away a long strand of her dark hair. "My previous wives, God rest their souls, are in the past, and I've tried to live in the present. You've always been an extraordinary beauty, and you've never looked more beautiful than now, as you've grown into the stunning woman before me. While there are plenty of beautiful women on this planet, I only have eyes for the most beautiful one of all, whose bed I am delighted to share."

She took hold of Austin's hands as she murmured, "Glad to hear it, lover."

CHAPTER FIVE

Austin had reviewed the latest message from J. W. Preacher with interest. Preacher was an extremely shrewd judge of people and events, and Austin had learned to take seriously any concerns raised by his ambassador. He linked Yabuno and Turner into his home, where Liz joined him as well. She often had insights into people that others might not catch.

Preacher was not alone on his end, being joined by Astrid Henkel and Dan Bacas. Bacas was the head of the Citadel Group's space yard and knew as much about building faster-than-light vessels as anyone. The message was, of course, prerecorded, since there wasn't yet any means of achieving instantaneous communication between the two star systems.

After the usual greetings, Preacher began on a positive note. "Before I talk about the main purpose of my message, I want to say I was delighted to receive your report about Citadel now having an official Charter that sets forth its government." He beamed. "The document does a masterful job of laying out, in a straightforward fashion, everything that people really need from their government. I'm sure all of the Preachers before me who have been privileged to give you advice would be as proud of what you've accomplished as I am. I think the first J. W. Preacher, who advised you on the amendments you wrote for the Second Bill of Rights, would be especially pleased by what you've done. It will be an honor to report this wonderful news to the international community."

Preacher continued. "Now that I've acknowledged that good news, I need to move on to the main reason for my message. We all know that others have claimed to be able to design and build ships that can travel between stars. Those who have tried have all failed; even Captain Card's trip to the outskirts of Citadel was with technology his backers stole from the Citadel Group, not with anything they developed on their own. Fortunately, that technology turned out to be a dead-end, and Card and the rest of his would-be visitors are long dead, victims of their own folly and greed.

"In the case of this new group of people, they seemed to come out of nowhere eighteen months ago. They've claimed to have developed their new technologies within a three-month period after they made a fortune in mining and devoted those resources to their research."

He nodded toward Bacas as he continued. "Dan can give you his take on the space yard Phoenix has been building."

Bacas moved toward a display and brought up several images. "Sam, these are some images we've acquired of their operations." A hint of professional admiration crept into his voice. "As far as building a first-class yard is concerned, they seem to know what they're doing. It's clear they don't give a damn about our knowing about it either, since they've made no effort to restrict our ability to keep tabs on their progress."

His expression darkened. "They've also made it clear that they can keep us in the dark when they want." He brought up other images. "As you can see, once they were ready to build ships, they erected barriers that serve to mask what they're doing. We've tried all sorts of long-range techniques to assess their activities, with only limited success. In short, we can't tell if what they're building is a real alternative to our transports, or if they're just messing with us." He snorted. "That would be a hell of an expensive way of messing with us, though, if that's what they're doing."

Henkel spoke. "I'm sure you want to know what else we've been doing to learn about them, Sam." She brought up several images and gestured toward them as she said, "Out of a group of approximately fifty people, we still believe that most decisions are made by five of them. Here are images of each of them. To the extent they have a leader, we believe that person to be their chief spokesman, a man who calls himself Lazarus. He doesn't use a last name. In fact, most of them don't. He appears to be in his late thirties and is articulate, without giving away anything he doesn't want to give away.

"We assume that the name Lazarus isn't his given name, although we haven't ruled it out. We can't find any record of this man anywhere from before two years ago, whether under that name or any other name. We've been hampered in our search by the fact that privacy principles on Mars and elsewhere within the space community have limited our access to various records. In addition, he has declined all attempts to get him to reveal anything about his background.

"Assuming that we aren't being manipulated, our experts believe there is an unusual dynamic between Lazarus and one of the women in that group of five leaders, who calls herself Pandora. They may be in a relationship and may even be married. We've checked all of the marriage and partnership records and can't find anything to confirm this assessment, although the same privacy principles have made our search incomplete."

An extra bit of color appeared in Henkel's expression as she continued. "Interestingly, our experts also believe that another woman in that group, who calls herself Diana, has a strong attraction to Lazarus and resents having to keep it under wraps. At least some of the time, he seems to be aware of the attraction.

"I'm sure everyone has noticed the significance of the names Lazarus and Phoenix," she said. "Both are names associated with death and rebirth. We don't know why those names have been chosen. For all we know, they could be references to their having decided on new identities as they undertake a new venture. What we do know is that they claim they'll be ready to start trial runs of their ships, with all of the technology that makes our transports unique, in about a month or two." She looked at Bacas, who shook his head.

"That's about as arrogant a claim as I've heard in a long time," he said. "There's just no way that someone who's never built something that complicated can do it right the first time, without much more extensive troubleshooting and trials than they seem to have planned. No matter how bright they think they are, it doesn't work that way. Even our people, who know more than anyone about building these ships, still do shakedown trips before we certify a transport, although we take far less time to do it than we used to.

"The other thing that is interesting is the fact that they've talked, at least in general terms, about what they plan on doing, but have been unwilling to explain to anyone how their technology works—they haven't even let people see any examples of it. In a sense, the secrecy is understandable; hell, we protect our technology pretty fiercely. However, we've already proved that our technology works, so the onus is on them to prove that someone else has figured it out as well."

Preacher provided the conclusion. "While they haven't gone into a lot of specific details over their plans, they seem interested in proving that they are as good as the Citadel Group, perhaps even better. They plan on being a major player in this solar system, and they also plan on making their own trips to Citadel. While we've declared Citadel closed to further colonization, there's an interesting question over whether any of the other planets in that solar system can be colonized. So long as our people are the only ones with the ability to get through the radiation field surrounding the system without being harmed, we effectively control access to the rest of the system."

A worried look crossed the old man's face. "However, there are still two other planets in the habitable zone around the Citadel sun. As we know, Planet Shiloh, which is based on a name once proposed by your old friend and moonwalking buddy from your Apollo days, Sam, is viewed as a particularly good prospect for colonization someday. If these people can get into the Citadel system, the colonization may happen sooner than expected, and not on our terms.

"We've talked more than once about the importance of being the only ones holding the key to the Citadel system, so I don't need to spell out for you the implications of another society having access to the interior of the Citadel system. Among other things, your security may be fatally compromised as far as your ability to protect yourselves against any further mischief from outside forces is concerned. I, for one, don't want to see an end to the grand experiment that has been Citadel.

"We will keep in touch with reports on the progress of Phoenix. Watch your backs, Sam."

The message ended, and Austin's gaze took in the faces still on the display, as well as his wife's face. "Thoughts?" he asked.

"We've heard these types of claims before," Yabuno noted in an unimpressed tone. "I'm not sure we need to start worrying just yet. Even Dan can't find any direct evidence in support of the claims by Phoenix, and he knows what to look for. Also, I agree with another of his points; even if they've somehow managed to solve the problems associated with putting together a viable warp-field generator, there's no way to put together something as complicated as a counterpart to a Keith Thomas transport and have it work perfectly from the start."

Turner nodded. "Besides, there's been nothing in the scientific literature even remotely hinting at any of the breakthroughs they've claimed. I just don't buy the notion that a group of natural, untrained geniuses could focus for a few months and solve problems that have bedeviled some of us for years."

"Do you think this is all just an effort get publicity for something?" Liz asked.

"I'm tempted to say yes, except I can't understand why anyone would go to all the expense and trouble without a damned good reason," Yabuno replied.

Liz looked at Austin and said, "You've been quiet since we saw J. W.'s report, Sam."

His expression focused intently on the images of the five leaders of Phoenix. "I keep wondering who these people could be."

"Do you recognize any of them?"

He shook his head. "No, I don't know any of those faces. I wonder why it seems so personal with them to beat the Citadel Group and Citadel itself."

Yabuno shrugged. "There are plenty of people who are envious of what we've done. We solved problems that no one else could, such as creating warp-field generators that can travel to and return from other star systems. We developed artificial gravity and came up with a communications system that can send messages to and from our two systems in a month. We've also solved lots of other problems related to founding and sustaining a viable colony on another planet. There are others who want to prove they can do those things."

"They're also envious about the fact that we control access to the derelict spaceship that wandered into our system," Turner said. "They keep assuming that there's a treasure trove of technology that we're gleaning from it." He chuckled. "They still have trouble believing that all we've been able to learn is how to refine some concepts relating to warp-field generators. If we hadn't done our own work first, we wouldn't have been able to understand their information anyway."

"I think more than just envy is in play," Liz said. "The fact that they've gone to such lengths to obscure any information about their pasts suggests that they have something to hide."

"That makes sense, but it may be as simple as they've gotten into bed with some of the less-than-savory operations out there when it comes to mining, and they don't want to acknowledge it," Austin reminded them. "However, this is a lot of speculation at this point. What they've accomplished to date won't mean much if they can't deliver what they've promised. The next message from J. W. should be interesting.

"In the meantime, we should consider the results that have come back to us from the probes we sent over to Shiloh." He chuckled. "We sent practically anything that was possible to send, with the result that we have far more data that we ever had when trying to decide whether to visit Citadel."

Yabuno laughed. "I remember those conversations well."

"Let's talk about what we've learned from this data."

Yabuno walked to a display, and images of their sister planet appeared. "We know that the atmosphere can support unaided breathing by humans, with an oxygen content slightly richer than on Citadel." New images of colorful alien foliage appeared. "The place is teeming with the kinds of life that we want to see on a planet we want to colonize. The soil seems to be fertile, so agriculture is possible. We don't know whether humans can consume anything that grows there, but we can do sampling and testing if we decide to visit. We did the same thing when we arrived on Citadel. None of our biological screenings has revealed any microorganisms that we believe to be dangerous to humans, although we need to keep in mind that we had the same results from our on-site screenings on Citadel.

"Shiloh, like Citadel, is active tectonically, meaning that the core is still at least partially molten and the crust isn't so thick that everything inside stays trapped and heats up the planet uncontrollably, creating a greenhouse effect. It also means that all sorts of minerals and metals are likely being moved around the planet, so mining is also a possibility. You can look at the data for some information on likely substances we can mine.

"Even though Shiloh is closer to our sun than Citadel, the temperatures are very similar. For want of a better description, Shiloh does a more efficient job of avoiding excess heat buildup than Citadel, without sacrificing the type of climate important to humans. Obviously, the year and the seasons are shorter, since the orbit is shorter. The seasons are probably still sufficient to support agriculture, although we're not yet certain about the impact of the climate on crop yields. For all we know, local plants may have adapted to the shorter growing season in ways we don't yet understand. We also don't yet know enough about the climate to be able to predict the amount of instability relating to events such as storms."

"What do you think our next steps should be?" Austin asked with a grin.

"We decided to visit Citadel with less hard data than we have here, so I'd say it's worth visiting Shiloh. A team of experts is already on its way from the Citadel Group to explore some extreme environments on Citadel that are well off the beaten path. Shiloh is a hell of a lot farther off the beaten path, so we should have the experts review the data, and if they think it makes sense, they should change their itinerary and visit Shiloh."

"Interesting that you should make that suggestion. I've already spoken to Dr. Hall to make preparations for the Citadel Group team to visit Shiloh. She's working with Curly to set up a module that will be placed in orbit around Shiloh, to serve as a combination medical facility, test lab, isolation environment, and home base. Hall and her people would stay aboard the module, in support of the Citadel Group team that would be based on the surface. By the time the team arrives, they should be able to go straight to Shiloh, assuming they agree that the trip is justified. Think they will?" he asked.

Yabuno chuckled in response, knowing that no team would be able to resist the chance to visit an unexplored planet.

CHAPTER SIX

While Phoenix had demonstrated the skills necessary to build a space yard, the group still needed people to make it happen, even in an era where much of the construction in space was highly automated. Jeff Coffey had been working in space on special projects for decades and was available when asked to sign a contract to provide his services. The pay was good, and he didn't have any family, so the long hours on the job weren't any kind of hardship.

He'd been surprised at the capabilities of the people running the construction projects, particularly the man in charge of construction, who called himself Heph. Coffey had never heard of him and knew the community of people handling these projects well enough to know the man had never been involved with anything similar, which meant he didn't have any field experience. However, Heph seemed to have the technical knowledge relating to what he wanted to accomplish, and with veterans like Coffey, that was fine.

Coffey had never been involved in a major project that went as smoothly as this one, especially once some of the basic structural elements for the vessel had been put together. It seemed impossible, but areas that should have needed a lot of extra work turned out fine the first time.

Heph had kept a tight rein on the technology used in the construction of the Phoenix ships. While the overall design of the ship was not unfamiliar to someone like Coffey, there were large areas that were simply off limits to anyone not a part of Phoenix. After the basic structure of the engine room had been put in place, no one was ever allowed back into that part of the ship unless he or she was a part of the mysterious organization.

While Coffey understood that Phoenix wanted to guard against others stealing its technology, the man's curiosity was piqued. Despite his years in space, he'd never worked on a Citadel transport, so he'd never even seen a warp-field generator up close. He knew he'd never have a better opportunity to see one than while the construction was still underway.

The long hours on the job offered him the excuses he needed to keep an eye on the engine room and wait for his opportunity to gain entry. Although the designations of day and night in space were often arbitrary, late one night Coffey found himself alone near the engine room. While there were security protocols designed to keep people out from restricted areas, Coffey had plenty of experience in getting around those protocols in order to do his job.

He liked to keep a record of his projects, which was for his private enjoyment and not to share with other employers or workers. He held something in front of him to take in the view as he entered the forbidden area, floating in the microgravity environment and moving along by grabbing handrails. It wasn't his regular link, as private links weren't allowed. He also wasn't stupid enough to try to use the official link Phoenix had issued him, as he knew it would be monitored. The item he held looked innocuous, suggesting it lacked any technology.

He'd been careful to have the images transmitted directly to a remote location without retaining anything on the device itself. That precaution had saved his ass a few times, as he'd nearly been caught checking out things on other jobs that his employers thought he didn't need to see. Since his official link appeared to be clean and he didn't appear to have any other communication or recording devices with him, he'd avoided any problems.

At first, nothing seemed out of the ordinary, and he felt a bit disappointed. His attitude changed once he looked toward the far end of the compartment. He saw another hatch and approached it. He had little difficulty in getting it open and passed through with increased interest.

He wasn't disappointed by what he saw this time. He stared at the device in amazement, never dreaming that something like that could place a ship outside of normal space-time, literally in another world. There were other devices as well, which he assumed controlled the artificial gravity the ship was claimed to possess. He knew even less about that area of technology and realized he could never have guessed at its purpose if he'd encountered the device in another setting. Currently, the devices looked completely dead, although he wasn't sure what they'd be like if they were online. While he was tempted to yield to one of the oldest of human desires and touch them, he knew it wouldn't be a good idea. For all he knew, the devices could be brought online by touch, which would probably set off various alerts. He didn't have any way to explain his presence there that wouldn't jeopardize his paycheck.

Reluctantly, he put away his recording device, putting it into an inert mode, which made it indistinguishable from a solid piece of stone. He took a last look around the place before heading back toward the open hatch. He drifted through and closed it behind him. The place was as still as a tomb, and he made his way toward the outer hatch carefully, leaving no sign that he'd ever been there.

As he turned back to seal the last hatch, he had a brief sensation of bright lights and a flash of intense pain, and then everything was gone.

Diana hovered over the limp figure floating near the hatch, to check on his condition while glaring furiously at the man standing nearby.

After a moment, she moved away from the motionless body. "You idiot!" she hissed. "He's dead, which means we can't interrogate him to find out why he was inside the engineering section."

"Isn't that obvious?" the man replied. "He was spying on us to learn about our technology."

"No kidding," she replied sarcastically. "What we needed to know was whether he was just curious for his own sake or working for someone else. If we've been penetrated by someone outside, we need to know by whom."

———

Five men and women stood near a display, staring at an image of the dead man. "Before we get into the question of how the hell he managed to get that far into the engineering section before we knew about it, have you inspected the engineering section?" Lazarus asked with some heat.

"Yes," Heph said. "We went over everything in fine detail. Nothing's been disturbed, and nothing's there that shouldn't be there."

"That's a good thing, for the sakes of several people," he warned. "Now, back to the question of how he got inside." He looked at Diana.

"He's been around long enough to know how to keep his eyes open and override security to be able to do his job," she answered. "His work assignments gave him the perfect opportunity to hang around places without arousing suspicion." She looked around the room. "That one's on us, since we've been demanding that these guys work those hours. Guys like that often just want to be left alone, which makes it tough for us to monitor them all the time."

She held up a link. "While he was smart enough to know that we can use these things to track everyone's movements, he didn't realize that it was still tracking certain biometric signals. He thought he'd deactivated those features, but we'd slipped some things into these links that he didn't catch. He never had a clue that we received an alarm when biometric signals were transmitted from a restricted area when none of us was there."

"Why did you kill him, instead of capturing him so we could do some questioning?" Pandora asked.

Diana looked at Lazarus. "That was due to the brilliant insight of the fool who joined me to intercept Coffey." She looked at Lazarus skeptically. "Are we sure he wasn't a village idiot in a past life?"

"I think that's been pretty well established," he said coldly. "He'll be reminded to leave the thinking to us." He looked at the items shown on the display. "Is this everything he had with him?"

"Yes," she said, nodding. "He had his tools, some personal items, and his clothes."

"Did he have a link other than the one we gave him?"

"No, nothing like that," she said. "We've confirmed that our link didn't record anything. We've checked out his tools, and there's nothing there that could transmit anything."

Lazarus frowned as he pointed at something. "What's this?"

"That's one of those good-luck charms that a lot of the people in space carry around. It's supposed to be made from a fragment of an asteroid."

He considered it for a moment. "Did you scan it?"

"Yes, it's just what it looks like, a solid piece of rock on a chain."

Pandora spoke. "We have to decide what to do about the body."

"Yes, *I* do," Lazarus said pointedly. "We'll need to log him out and place a notice in his file to the effect that he quit, and then forward his outstanding pay to his personal account. Fortunately, we've been careful to keep all of our operations based out in space where there isn't much oversight of what happens, so we should be able to handle any inquiries by relatives or others."

"What about the body?" Georgia asked. "We know that the Citadel Group keeps tabs on what we do, and it isn't as if we can just weigh it down and dump it in the ocean. With our luck, their long-range sensors would catch us if we were to try to jettison his body somewhere in space."

Lazarus looked at Diana, who replied, "Space is pretty vast, and the odds are against anyone spotting something as small as a body that's been launched on a course that would take it out of the solar system many years from now. However, it isn't worth the risk. We can jettison the body into Jupiter, just the way the Citadel Group did years ago when they didn't want the Space Command to capture their transports in their yard. Once something goes down there, it's gone for good. We carry out operations passing close enough to the neighborhood that no one will notice something that small leaving one of our ships. Seems poetic," she said. "They did it to prevent others from getting access to their technology, and we're doing it for the same reason."

"That brings us to whether Coffey was working for anyone but himself," Lazarus said. "I don't believe in coincidences, and we know how much others would like to know what we're doing."

"I wouldn't put it past J. W. Preacher to have a hand in this," Pandora said with disdain. "He's clever and a lot more ruthless than he lets on. If Sam Austin wanted him to spy on us, Preacher would be glad to do it."

"While I agree that the Citadel Group should never be taken for granted, there are other interests around that would love to get in on our operation and push us aside for their own gain." He looked around the room with an amused expression. "After all, we've met some of them already; however, our own backers are tougher than anyone else and have provided us with incentives to stay focused. Otherwise, we wouldn't have succeeded with our mining activities."

He frowned. "The problem with all of these scenarios is that Coffey would have needed to record what he saw if he was working for someone else. We haven't found anything he could have used for that purpose. He would have also tried to get access to our restricted files, including trying to get access to the display on the generators. We know he never tried."

"We may have stopped him before he had a chance to try," Pandora pointed out.

"That's possible," Heph acknowledged. "However, we caught him after he had finished checking it out, which suggests that if he had intended to use the display, he would have done it. I would have expected a spy to have been sharper than Coffey was about 'sneaky' technology.

Frankly, the way that we caught him suggests that he was what he seemed—a nosy guy who was smart enough to figure out how to go through the wrong door, but not smart enough to know that he was in trouble the moment he did it." He looked at Lazarus. "What do you think?"

Lazarus paused in thought for a moment. "It could be everything you say," he concluded. "We'll probably never know for sure. The good news is, he didn't get access to our files and couldn't have recorded any images, so our technology hasn't been compromised."

He gave a hard stare to Diana and Heph. "You two will make sure no one else gets the chance to do what he did. Just because we were lucky this time doesn't mean spies haven't been planted here. The moment we are far enough along that we don't need any other outsiders, we will pay them off and get rid of them. We still have some things to prove, and nothing will stand in our way!"

CHAPTER SEVEN

It had been hours since the first Phoenix ship had left its yard, and it was nearly outside the solar system within which it had been created. The level of interest in the vessel was even higher than when the original *Pathfinder* had taken its maiden voyage more than a dozen years earlier. Many organizations, including the Citadel Group, had set up beacons to monitor the trial run. In fact, despite assurances by Phoenix that no assistance was necessary, a Keith Thomas transport was standing by in case there were any problems with the trial. Since travel through space was open to all, Phoenix dropped any further objections.

In view of all the attention, or perhaps because of it, Phoenix didn't bother trying to hide its creation from the rest of humanity. People weren't sure what to make of the new ship. While its design plans had looked vaguely like countless other designs for vessels intended to carry people and cargo, the actual result looked nothing like any other ship they'd seen. The contrast with the Keith Thomas ship that had joined the spectators was

pronounced. In addition, although size was often difficult to grasp against the vast backdrop of countless stars,
people were shocked to realize that this vessel was even
larger than the Citadel vessel.

The one thing that wasn't a surprise was the ship's
name. It was perhaps inevitable that a class of ships from
a group with the name Phoenix would be called the
"Firebird" class. This one would bear the name of the
class, with many more promised to come on line shortly.

Citadel transport *KT-12* was present for more than
just rendering assistance, of course. The Citadel Group
planned on using the vessel, along with the other Citadel
beacons that had been deployed, to obtain as much data
as possible about its self-proclaimed rival.

Aboard *KT-12*, Captain Hull and the rest of his bridge
crew watched the image of the new ship, which was
reduced in size to fit within the display. Back on Earth,
while Citadel's embassy was open for business as usual, its
ambassador sat in a comfortable chair and watched the
events with great interest. Not far away, US President Pete
Lee was sitting in the Oval Office while engaged in much
the same activities as Preacher. The interest extended
half a solar system away, where Mars President Amelia
Gordon was likewise observing the events. Thanks to the
Citadel communications array, the communications were
in virtually real time.

Firebird finally reached its destination and halted while
facing toward deep space. The countdown for departure
was broadcast throughout the system, so everyone knew
from a glance at a display just when the massive vessel
would attempt to depart.

To the great surprise of the spectators, Lazarus and several other members of the Phoenix inner circle had insisted on being aboard *Firebird* for its trial run. They broadcast directly from the new ship's bridge as the seconds ticked away. They floated around for a moment, pulling themselves along the rails before strapping themselves into their chairs.

"Greetings from *Firebird*," Lazarus said enthusiastically. He gestured around the bridge. "We've finished our tests, and we're sure you're about to see something extraordinary happen. In a few seconds, we'll be so far away that it would take a Citadel transport to rescue us if anything were to go wrong." His grin remained as his expression changed from lightheartedness to competitiveness. "Of course, in a few more seconds, we'll show that one of our own ships could just as well do a rescue of a Citadel transport." He signed off, since no transmission would be possible during any time within a warp bubble.

Preacher shook his head at the audacity of the gesture. While Austin might be nearby to observe an initial trial involving a Citadel transport, he had never been foolish enough to be aboard the transport itself during the proceedings. In addition to his concerns about his own safety, Austin realized that Citadel couldn't afford to lose its leader if something were to go wrong. Lazarus clearly felt differently. If this trial was a success, Lazarus's personal show of confidence would be a huge boost to the group's prestige. If the trial was a failure, they'd find out whether Phoenix was aptly named and could recover.

The seconds finally dwindled away, and the countdown reached zero. An instant later, the vessel vanished, leaving behind only a faint distortion to show that it had ever been there. More seconds passed, and then a message came through the Citadel network and was broadcast throughout the solar system.

An image of the Phoenix leader appeared, apparently unharmed. "This is Lazarus, reporting from *Firebird.* We have completed our first trial within a warp bubble, with no harm to anyone and a ship that is functioning perfectly. Obviously, we aren't where we were, and our friends at the Citadel Group can confirm that we are now well outside the solar system and are transmitting our message back to you through a Citadel beacon."

His gesture around the bridge was more pronounced this time. "As you can see, not only are we in no difficulties, but our artificial gravity is now functioning smoothly as well." For emphasis, Lazarus got out of his chair, and walked around his bridge. Other people made a similar show of striding around, their feet obviously staying on the deck without artificial assistance. There was no more maneuvering with a floating motion that required a near-constant use of rails or handholds.

Preacher was far too experienced to react openly as he saw that Lazarus's claims were true. For the first time, people were walking normally aboard a ship that hadn't come out of a Citadel yard.

Lazarus continued. "We have one other task to perform while we're out here, which is to deploy some of our own beacons. When we return shortly, Phoenix will have its own communications network up and running throughout this solar system." He couldn't help rubbing it in as he said, "There are other places to visit, including some in the Citadel system, and no place will be off limits to us. Everyone who wants to join our colonies is welcome to apply."

———

Later, Preacher faced a display as he discussed the events with Henkel and Bacas.

"That was a hell of a show today, J. W.," Bacas said.

"How much of it was just a performance, and how much was real?" the old man asked pointedly.

"It was all a performance, and it was all real too," he replied. He brought up several images and gestured as he continued. "There's no question that *Firebird* left our solar system in a warp bubble and reappeared right where their crew said they would, near one of our beacons. It's also clear that they moved around the outside of the solar system in additional warp bubbles and deployed multiple communications beacons."

"Why do they need their own beacons?"

"The obvious answer is that this frees them from having to rely on anyone else's communications network in this system. It also means that they have the beginning of a communications network that could, in theory, be extended all the way to Citadel," he said in a concerned tone.

"What about the claims of having artificial gravity?"

"That one's harder to prove," Bacas replied with a shrug. "Even a kid could create an image that made it look like they had artificial gravity on that ship. However, they've announced plans to have people come aboard

Firebird shortly, so we'll know pretty soon whether those claims are bogus. They don't need to be in a warp bubble for artificial gravity to work.

"I wish I knew where they got their training. The community of people who can do this isn't that large, and I know most of the top people." He chuckled. "In fact, a lot of them work for me. There shouldn't be that many unattached people of that caliber out there available to do this work, but there must be."

Preacher looked at Henkel. "What do our instruments tell us about what happened today?"

Henkel brought up some images as she replied, "They confirm what Dan has been telling us. They definitely left this system, moved around further, and returned under circumstances that had to have been achieved with the use of warp bubbles."

"What are the chances that they got their hands on Citadel's technology to make it happen?"

She shook her head. "Pretty much zero, J. W. First, it was a hell of a feat just to scale up the technology to accommodate larger size of their ship. While we could, in theory, do it too, we don't have a how-to manual lying around showing someone else how to do it. I've reviewed our security and confirmed that no one has had any access to our core technologies who shouldn't have that access.

"Second, and this is the most convincing part, the energy signature of *Firebird* is unlike anything from our ships that have warp-field generators. It simply isn't possible to scale up our technology to accommodate a ship like theirs, yet end up with an energy signature that is so different."

She sighed. "We have to face the fact that they've come up with completely new technology to do what our ships can do."

Bacas chimed in, "We also have to understand that their first ship in the class appears to have performed perfectly, which just doesn't happen, not even in our yards. If they're really that good, then they'll be able to launch a lot of ships pretty damned fast. That means that they'll be able to serve as an alternative to carrying cargo that needs to stay within an artificial-gravity environment. As we know, there's a market for that service, since we're the ones who have had it to ourselves. It also means that if they're serious about getting to the Citadel system, there isn't anything we can do to stop them. I'm not just talking about shipping cargo to Citadel either."

He brought up images of *Firebird* and *KT-12*. "The Firebird class of ship looks like it can carry a lot more passengers than a Keith Thomas transport can. While we have a hell of a head start as far as the population on Citadel is concerned, it may not take all that long for them to catch up with us on another planet like Shiloh, depending on how many of their ships they can build."

His face took on a worried look. "Friendly competition is one thing, but am I the only one who has the impression that Phoenix would like nothing more than to flood Shiloh with enough people to make things difficult for Citadel?" The equally worried looks facing him were his answer.

CHAPTER EIGHT

As *Firebird* continued to maneuver outside the limits of the solar system, the mood aboard the new vessel was celebratory, although not quite as festive as one might have expected, considering the circumstances.

"I'd give anything to have seen the look on Preacher's face as he watched us leave this system," Lazarus said, grinning.

"I'd give anything to see the look on *Austin's* face when he saw the look on Preacher's face," Pandora said. "Preacher is probably making a report right now about the new competition!"

"I'm sure he is, Pandora," he said. "Of course, there was never any question about the outcome today. Our technology was perfect, just like it always is. Now that we'll be allowing outsiders to come aboard our ships, we need to be certain our security is upgraded." He turned toward the youngest woman in the room. "Where do we stand, Diana? Can we let them aboard without having to kill them all?" he asked with a hint of amusement.

"We don't have to worry about anyone, Lazarus," she replied coolly. "We've learned from our encounter with Coffey. All points of access to our technology have been identified and blocked. We're still working on security for long-term passengers when that time comes, but we have some time before that happens."

"Not as much as you may think," another man warned.

"Tell us why, Heph," Lazarus said.

A man in his late forties stepped up to a display. Images from their space yard appeared as he said, "As we know, we started construction initially along a conventional, although ambitious, schedule. Now that we've confirmed the diagnostics anticipate every potential problem while construction is still underway, we can accelerate the schedule quite rapidly, even more than we anticipated. What's more, we can expand the use of automation to a level that is unprecedented. That means we'll have our fleet of Firebirds ready in a few months, at most."

"Having a fleet will take care of things in the Citadel star system, but we can't forget about this one," Lazarus said. He checked out another display. "Are we ready to deploy another beacon?"

Diana confirmed they were ready, and the beacon was launched. They watched the device as it took its place in space, another piece of the puzzle in place to free them from any reliance on the Citadel network.

"We're setting up a fleet of beacons to match our fleet of ships," she said.

"A fleet of ships won't do us much good without people to ferry," Lazarus remarked. He turned toward a woman in her late forties and asked, "What kind of feedback have we had regarding potential colonists, Georgia?"

Her expression was one of pleased disbelief. "The response has been practically off the charts. There have already been millions of inquiries about joining us as colonists to Shiloh. We shouldn't have any trouble narrowing that number down to the people we want."

"Let's just be sure we narrow it down to people who can pay for the privilege," Pandora replied cynically. "While we've done incredibly well, we'll be broke pretty soon if someone else doesn't start paying some of the bills around here."

"That's obviously not a message we want shared outside this circle," Lazarus reminded them. "As far as the rest of the world is concerned, we're still rolling in money after our lucky strike at mining."

"We all know that," she replied testily. "Just because you speak for us in public doesn't mean you're the only one with a brain."

"Don't forget whose brain it was that came up with this idea," he warned. "We'd be nowhere, with no future, without this idea." He took another look at a display. "I think that does it for the deployments out here, at least for now. It's time to head back to our solar system and to deploy more beacons. I want there to be so many of the things underfoot that the people will be unable to think of anything else. We'll have more reminders of our presence in time."

CHAPTER NINE

J. W. Preacher rarely ran out of patience, but dealing with Phoenix was trying even his legendary poise. He had practically worn himself out seeking to head off Phoenix by claiming that the group had no right to colonize Shiloh in the first place. While he wasn't particularly surprised that Pete Lee, the US president, wasn't inclined to step into a dispute about rights in another star system, he was disappointed to learn that his old friend, Amelia Gordon, the Mars president, wasn't able to offer him much more support.

"Amelia, we need your support in this matter," Preacher said with plenty of energy. "As the leader of a nation that was founded by settlers, you know all too well what can happen when an outsider tries to destabilize your society. It was little more than a generation ago that Mars itself nearly faced extinction when those rascals tried to start a war with Earth to get their way. They didn't care about the destruction it would cause; they only cared about what it would mean for their desire for power. Face it—if Sam Austin hadn't been the US president at the time, Mars might not even exist today."

Gordon held up her hand to cut off Preacher's next words. "Before you say it, J. W., I also know full well what Citadel and Sam have meant to the survival of Mars, Sam back then as well as following the attack by the aliens. We are and will always be immensely grateful for what you did. It is in the spirit of that gratitude that we will not break any of our commitments to Citadel in order to pursue opportunities with Phoenix.

"However, we live by a code out here: Earthbound governments don't get to decide things out in space. The people out in space do the deciding on their own. Like it or not, that means Citadel and Phoenix will need to resolve their differences by themselves."

"What would you do if someone tried to establish a new colony on Mars?" Preacher pressed. "Would you really try to work out things with that group, or would you kick them the hell off the planet?"

Gordon laughed. "You know full well what we'd do, but it's long settled that the entire planet is under our jurisdiction anyway, so the comparison isn't valid."

Her expression grew serious. "You might consider, instead, the earlier part of our history, when competing commercial interests set up their separate colonies on Mars. We went through a painful process of conflict before unification, which wasn't completed until after the crisis you speak of had passed. As you know, our official name is the 'United Settlements of Mars,' in recognition of how we came to be. Sam served as the shepherd over the negotiations that led to that recognition.

"The key thing is that while we accepted a certain amount of oversight from Earth on several matters as the price for independence, we didn't accept any interference from Earth when it came to settling our internal differences."

She sighed. "What that means, for better or worse, is that once colonists establish a foothold in the Citadel system, you may end up making a deal that you swore you'd never make, because that's sometimes the price that must be paid to ensure your survival. Sam Austin was the man who taught the people of Mars that hard truth during our negotiations, and it still applies today."

———

The five people who faced Preacher on the display all had calm, confident demeanors. Lazarus had a smile that bordered on arrogance. "We were delighted to hear you wanted to speak to us, Ambassador Preacher," he began. "Something like that would only happen if Phoenix has become important." He waved at the images of multiple Phoenix ships in the background. "I'd say we've become more than just important, wouldn't you?"

Preacher's expression remained politely neutral. "Anytime someone achieves the technological breakthroughs that your people have achieved, it is important, Lazarus. What I'd like to discuss is the uses you have in mind for these breakthroughs."

"Is this an official inquiry by Citadel and Sam Austin, or is this a private conversation?" the Phoenix leader asked, enjoying the sparring.

"I am Citadel's eyes and ears in this solar system," Preacher replied. "I have many conversations with people without the need for calling something official."

"It doesn't matter, Ambassador," Lazarus said easily. "We figure that this will go back to Sam Austin anyway. Why don't we talk about what you think we want to do with our technologies?"

"You have in your hands what people rarely have, which is an opportunity to do enormous good with something precious. I won't try to call your technologies 'gifts,' since I'm sure they were the result of significant creative effort on your part." Preacher's gaze became more piercing. "You've made it clear that you want to reach out to the stars with your technologies, which is understandable. What is less understandable is your desire to reach out to the Citadel star system with these technologies instead of to another system where you can establish yourselves as true pioneers."

"Where would you suggest we go?" Lazarus countered. "No other system has been detected that has the same promise as the Citadel system, with multiple potentially habitable planets in a stable system with valuable resources to exploit. I can see why you like it so much."

"You're playing with words, Lazarus. Other systems have been detected that show promise; there simply hasn't been the same level of analysis that there has been with respect to Citadel. It took years of study of data from multiple sources before what was eventually called the Citadel Group settled on Citadel as its first destination for interstellar travel. If you had the patience to perform the same analysis, you may well find another system with similar promise. Why wouldn't that appeal to you?"

"Why dedicate ourselves to years of searching for something that may not be out there when we already know about something that is within our reach?" His words took on a slightly mocking tone. "Besides, you should be flattered that we want to emulate what you've achieved by founding our own colony."

"You seem less interested in doing the hard work of founding a colony than in trying to compete with Citadel," Preacher said pointedly. "We spent a great deal of time and effort ensuring that the people we selected for settlers shared a common set of values with us, were well suited for the activity, and would have the support needed to make the effort successful. On the other hand, you seem willing to accept anyone who can pay for the privilege, without ensuring that these people would even make good colonists."

One of the women spoke. "Your standards are arbitrary, even elitist, Ambassador. If someone wants to become a colonist and is willing to take the risk, why shouldn't he or she? While individuals may fail, the colony itself will benefit from having such people. Your concern about the fact we want to make money is interesting, when that's been a motivating factor for virtually every venture in space for over a hundred years. Although you've claimed an almost exalted status for yourselves, even calling yourselves a nation, Citadel has never been shy about the fact that it wants to make money."

For the first time, the smile on Lazarus's face faded, although his tone remained even. "I've been remiss in not introducing my colleagues." He gestured at each of the individuals as he called out their names. "This is Georgia, this is Heph, this is Diana, and my colleague who has just been speaking so eloquently is Pandora."

He glanced over at Pandora briefly as he continued. "Face facts, Ambassador; Phoenix is going to Shiloh, and we're going to establish a colony."

It was Preacher's turn to radiate a confident smile as he spoke. "That's getting somewhat ahead of things. The only 'fact' is that your ships can leave this solar system. They *may* reach the outer portion of the Citadel system. However, no one has ever gotten through the radiation field without Citadel's permission. Unlike your venture, Citadel is a sovereign nation, recognized as such by other nations, and it will not permit others to enter its system except on its terms. Citadel will determine when Shiloh is settled, not someone from Earth.

"From what you have stated publicly, you plan on sending a large number of colonists to Shiloh directly, without having confirmed that it is even habitable," Preacher said. "The Citadel Group wasn't that rash. We sent the earlier version of *Pathfinder*, with a small crew, to investigate Citadel and return with a report." His tone grew somber. "Several people didn't return from that trip. We used the information from that report to prepare for the trip with the main group of settlers. However, regardless of the status of Shiloh, you will not enter the system without Citadel's permission."

Lazarus didn't back down. "You're overlooking something. We don't need your permission to enter the system, since we can get through the radiation field on our own. The aliens got through and nearly destroyed Citadel itself," Lazarus reminded him.

"In fact, if it hadn't been for a stroke of luck that Austin survived exposure to the radiation long enough to destroy the alien ship, there wouldn't be anyone on Citadel to worry about," Pandora noted with a slightly malicious tone.

Preacher studied her face for a moment before replying, "You sound disappointed it worked out that way."

Again, Lazarus looked at Pandora before continuing, "Anyway, our point is that just as the aliens were an exception, so are we."

"Even if that were so, why would you want the utter chaos that would result if your colonists were to try to set up their colony and find out they aren't prepared for it?"

"We think that a group of risk-taking entrepreneurs will work things out and be stronger for it. Perhaps you're worried that your own settlements won't be up to the challenge of dealing with robust competition."

"Our settlements have faced and overcome far more daunting challenges, Lazarus, including ones that you should hope you never to have to experience," Preacher replied quietly.

"Anything's possible," Lazarus said. "One message you can send to Austin is that when we establish our colony on Shiloh, we won't accept second-class status. We expect to be an equal partner in any decisions involving the Citadel system, including its security and allocation of resources."

"You've never been to the Citadel star system, yet you're ready to claim a stake in its resources and an equal say in how it will be run, even though there is already a nation there with settlers going back ten years," Preacher noted skeptically. "If by some miracle you were to get there, you would do well to set aside any notion that you're entitled to make demands and instead be grateful to Citadel for the security that its presence provides. You haven't demonstrated that you have either the competence or the ability to make any meaningful contribution to the security of the place. Sam Austin takes his responsibilities to the people of Citadel seriously, and he isn't likely to undermine those responsibilities by weakening the security arrangements that have kept them alive. While I have my own thoughts about whether dropping a lot of people onto a planet that may not support them entitles you to any of the things you mentioned, the only way it will matter is if you reach Citadel. If that happens, you'll need to take it up with Sam directly," Preacher said without warmth. The display went blank.

Lazarus turned toward Pandora and said, "What the hell was that about?"

"I don't know what you mean, Lazarus," she replied in a tone that said otherwise. "I was just trying to rattle the old fox. I think it worked too."

"I don't care whether you think so. While it may bruise that ego of yours, you'd better remember that *I'm* the one who speaks for this group, not you, Diana, Heph, or Georgia." He stared at each of the others to emphasize his point.

"I don't see why the rest of us can't speak from time to time," she complained. "I can speak at least as well as you, probably better."

"Your mouth has gotten you into trouble before, or had you forgotten?" he warned. "Besides, you speak all the time within the group," he reminded her. "You all do. You just don't do it when we're speaking with outsiders. That's the way it's been decided, and that's the way we'll keep on doing it."

"For now," she said, "but things may change."

He glared at her coldly. "Is that so? Perhaps I should let our backers know that's how you feel."

The woman turned deathly pale and shook her head.

"I thought not," he concluded. He glanced at the others. "Nothing Preacher said changes anything, so get back to your assignments; we have a deadline to meet."

As they went their separate ways, Lazarus noticed that another woman had joined him, matching his stride. "What is it, Diana?" he asked.

"You know full well what it is," she replied. "How can you stand to be near her?"

He shrugged. "You know the answer as well as I do. Our marriage isn't something that makes me happy, but we're bound together. I can't go against those bonds any more than I can stop breathing."

"Have you really tried?" she demanded. "You have greater strength than you realize. If you were to get rid of her, then we could be together. It wouldn't have any impact on the project; in fact, it may run more smoothly this way."

"Do you really think our backers could be fooled that easily?" he asked. "It would probably mean our deaths even to try it. Or they could even make our punishment worse than death," he said with a shudder.

She blocked his path, barely inches away. "Whose body would you rather touch—hers or mine?"

The look in his silent gaze as it lingered over her was her answer. She turned and walked away.

Later, as he entered the quarters he shared with Pandora, she stepped out of the shower, wrapping a towel around herself as he closed the door.

"I see from your expression that that bitch has been at you again," she said without preamble. "I suppose she's been trying to convince you to get rid of me so the two of you can be together. When will she learn that you belong to me, not her?"

He frowned. "This is pointless, Pandora. We all know how things stand. You and I are bound to each other, and that won't change. No one is going anywhere. Not you, and not Diana either," he warned.

"One other thing that won't change is the benefits that come with being bound together," she said as she dropped her towel to the floor. "Remember the first time you saw me like this?" she asked.

"Of course I do."

"It wasn't my best moment, but we've improved upon it a lot since then." She walked over to him with a gleam in her eye. He sighed, but soon other things began to drop to the floor.

CHAPTER TEN

The general interest in becoming a colonist with Phoenix remained feverishly high, helped in part by the near-constant publicity the upstart group generated. As Lazarus had promised, the solar system had been inundated with new beacons as Phoenix set up its own network. The Phoenix leadership pointed out that they would be setting up their own beacons while in route to Citadel, creating an alternate means of communication that would enable them to keep in touch with Earth, Mars, and elsewhere even if Citadel didn't cooperate by sharing its own network.

It seemed like practically every other day a new Phoenix ship was undergoing tests to confirm that its warp-field generators and propulsion systems were fully functional. People were treated to the sight of Phoenix vessels traveling to all corners of the solar system. The trips took place so frequently that they soon became unremarkable.

During one of those unremarkable trips, Diana was in charge of a ship as it passed near Jupiter. She was on her link with Heph as she watched a display with a countdown underway. Once the magic number was reached, she instructed him to jettison toward the giant planet a nondescript container that had no beacons or other identifying signals. She watched as the container with the body of Jeff Coffey secured inside vanished rapidly into the distance, on a collision course with what passed for a surface thousands of miles below. There was a satisfied expression on her face as one of their problems was eliminated forever.

———

Preacher felt revulsion as he watched the spectacle of prospective colonists offering to pay outrageous amounts of money to get in on the ground floor of what Phoenix hinted would be a resource-rich paradise. He talked about it with Henkel.

"I'm reminded of the lessons that history teaches us about the inherently delusional nature of this type of venture. Sam's home in California is in the so-called gold country that was the focus of the California Gold Rush. Although a few people got rich directly from the gold they mined, the vast majority of the people who traveled there lived a lousy existence and went broke doing so. Most of the people who got rich were the ones who provided goods and services to the prospectors or who were shrewd enough to make money from speculation in land or other resources before it all crashed. Does that remind you of anyone?" he asked pointedly.

Henkel nodded. "What's even worse is that at least there really was gold waiting to be dug up in California. In this case, nothing in the way of riches has even been confirmed as being on Shiloh itself. Phoenix keeps glossing over that fact by suggesting that if Citadel itself has riches, so will Shiloh."

"They've also stated that they will have a right to some of the other resources within the star system even though Citadel has already established significant claims throughout the mining belt," Preacher noted. "Sadly, none of that seems to matter, and because Phoenix has been careful to operate outside of the jurisdiction of any planet bound nation, there isn't much anyone can do about it. I've protested to the AN," he said, using the common acronym for the Allied Nations, "and gone public more than once to try to set the record straight, but greed often makes people blind to the truth."

"It's strange to think that Sam may end up being the final arbiter of these issues with people in this solar system even though he doesn't live here and has never met any of them," Henkel said.

———

Once again, Phoenix had defied expectations by getting its fleet ready just a few months after the first ship had completed its trial. Twenty ships were arranged like a wagon train ready to cross the prairie, much as the first group of ships had been for the first migration to Citadel over ten years ago. With a thousand people in stasis aboard each ship, Phoenix was sending twenty thousand colonists across the vast stretch of space to take on an untamed planet.

Such was the Phoenix leaders' confidence that they didn't bother to stagger their starts by thirty-minute intervals. Instead, each ship departed just two minutes after the previous one, all those aboard trusting that they'd arrive precisely where they expected to arrive.

CHAPTER ELEVEN

The first humans to set foot on Shiloh had been on the planet for several weeks, taking in the new environment with delight. They'd set up their own quarters and lab on the planet, with everything isolated from the surrounding environment. They'd always worn isolation suits whenever they'd ventured outside their quarters. Their findings had been consistent with the data Citadel had collected. They hadn't just confirmed the data, however, but had gone beyond it. They'd taken many biological samples and run extensive tests. The tests had included exposing groups of human cells to the biological samples. Even after repeated exposure of the human cells to the local biology, there had been no signs of danger.

Finally, after consulting with Dr. Hall, they'd decided it was time to venture into the environment without the isolation suits. At first, just one volunteer moved around without her suit. After she was cleared medically, more of her colleagues joined her, happy to be done with wearing the uncomfortable gear. Finally, everyone had set aside the suits.

Several days later, two of the scouts were out a short distance from their base, collecting samples and taking additional readings. "I could really get used to the place," Rick Syn said. "I feel like I'm getting an energy boost just from walking around."

"That's not surprising, considering that the oxygen content in the atmosphere is slightly higher than on Citadel, and the gravity is slightly lower," Sheri Thwaite replied. She turned and waved her arms to take in the scenery. "It's amazing how much this place reminds me of Citadel, even though there are plants here that don't look like anything from Citadel or Earth."

"Even better, we haven't seen any signs of cheaters," Syn said. "I wouldn't mind never having to worry about those devils again."

"We've only covered a tiny fraction of Shiloh," Thwaite reminded him. "There could be a whole colony of cheaters or something worse twenty miles away, and we wouldn't know about it. We're still learning about Citadel, and we've been there ten years. It'll take more than one of these excursions to learn enough about it to decide whether we can even set up shop here."

"That's fine with me. As far as I'm concerned, what we've seen so far has more than covered the price we'll pay in the form of medical isolation before we can return to Citadel. Considering that we haven't had any problems from exposure to the Shiloh environment, it hardly seems necessary, but better safe than sorry." He looked at his chronometer. "That reminds me: it's time we got back to the others."

They got into their ground transport and began the trip to their base. The ride was anything but smooth, as there were no roads, and the terrain had no hints of trails from animals passing through. They frowned as they approached their base, wondering where their colleagues were. They scrambled out of the vehicle as they heard what sounded like a moan coming from inside one of the two shelters they'd set up. They halted in shock at the hatchway as they looked upon a man who had been the picture of robust health that morning but who was now unable to rise from the floor without help. He managed to summon the strength to reach out toward them with one arm. "Help me," he said in a weak voice. His strength failed, and his arm fell back to his side.

Thwaite looked at Syn. "So much for the notion that there's nothing here that's harmful to humans. I don't know if it will do any good at this point, but we need to get into our isolation suits right away. We may not have been infected by what's going around, and I don't want to find out what they're going through if that's the case. The others are probably in the other shelter or the lab or somewhere nearby. After I get into my suit, I'll use my link to track them and make sure."

She nodded toward the prostrate form. "Get into your suit and do what you can for him. I'll call our friends in orbit and let them know we have a medical emergency." Syn nodded, and Thwaite darted out toward the other shelter. After telling the stricken man that he'd be right back, Syn darted out after Thwaite.

Syn felt he was moving far too slowly as he sought to seal himself within his isolation suit. His mind created a tingly feeling in anticipation of a real infection that might already be racing through his body. Everyone in the scouting party understood the protocols for infectious diseases, so Syn knew that Thwaite's message with her link would bring the shuttle online and prepare it for isolation even before he had returned to the man in the shelter. All of their links now stayed open automatically, both to allow people to keep their hands free and in case people could no longer respond to an inquiry.

Thwaite had human cargo of her own to bring on board the shuttle as Syn arrived with the man they'd discovered. They managed to bring their limp colleagues within the craft before leaving to get the other two members of their party. Thwaite had already located them, and soon everyone was onboard. They placed their unconscious colleagues in a separate compartment.

As the shuttle lifted off, Syn kept access to the controls open in case it was necessary for the isolation module that waited to receive them to take over. While the shuttle raced toward its destination, Syn and Thwaite used the decontamination procedure to eliminate any unwanted microbes hiding on their suits or elsewhere within the shuttle. Once the procedure had been completed, they got out of the uncomfortable clothing. By the time the suits had been discarded, Syn noticed that both their shirts were drenched in sweat. He could feel his strength fading as he saw Thwaite's face take on an unhealthy pallor, her gaze unfocused. In view of how he felt, he assumed that his face didn't look any better. She didn't say anything as she crumpled to the deck. He was barely able to croak out a warning to the isolation module before he fell nearby.

———•———

Dr. Lynn Hall studied the displays as each of the six members of the Shiloh scouting party was placed into a sterile isolation unit. In anticipation of such a situation, the orbiting module had been outfitted extensively with diagnostic and treatment technology. The process had been completely automated, taking advantage of the ability to use remote-controlled attachments in an environment without artificial gravity to shift, prepare, monitor, and treat unconscious patients who were highly contagious, without exposing health-care providers to the danger. Even the process of setting up arrays that would take biological samples as needed, or would otherwise take care of a patient's physical needs, was automated. Once the patients had been secured within the isolation unit, artificial gravity was restored.

Hall and the rest of her team were in a part of the module that was sealed off from the patients. If necessary, further equipment and supplies would be supplied remotely via shuttle, and Hall and her team would be able to consult with outsiders via their links.

She watched two displays with special sadness as remote attachments drew sheets up to cover the faces of the two patients monitored by those units, an acknowledgment of the fact that those unfortunate souls would never have any more thoughts of Shiloh, Citadel, or anywhere else. The vital signs for the other patients weren't good, and she had flashbacks from the attack by another disease against one of the settler families on Citadel ten years earlier. She'd lost patients then too.

CHAPTER TWELVE

Austin had convened a new council to hear the latest message from Preacher and to consider the recent news from Shiloh. People from throughout the Citadel system were linked in to his display. He started with the situation on Shiloh.

"As we know, all six members of the scouting party on Shiloh have been stricken with an unknown microorganism. I have asked Dr. Hall to provide us with an update on their condition."

The image of a woman appeared on a display. "I wish I could be the bearer of good news, but I can't. Two of the members of the scouting party are dead, and all of the rest have been infected as well." She brought up an image of a module in space. "As you know, we planned for this possibility by setting up an isolation module in orbit about Shiloh. Fortunately, two of the scouts managed to load the others into a shuttle and launch it. However, if we hadn't been able to take control of the shuttle remotely, none of them would have reached their destination, as the two who had been in the best shape collapsed during the trip.

"While we'd hoped that we'd only need to use the isolation facility as a precaution to ensure that the scouts wouldn't transmit anything back to Citadel, it is now the place where our medical staff are doing everything they can to save the lives of these brave people."

"I'm sure no one wants to think back on the bug that killed the namesake of our transports, Doctor, but is what afflicted our scouts in any way similar to what afflicted Keith Thomas?"

"We thought about that too, Sam. We think that life evolved on the two worlds under somewhat similar circumstances, which has led to what we believe may be some similarities in the two bugs. However, they are sufficiently different that the one from Shiloh is highly resistant to the standard treatment we use for the Citadel bug. Our efforts are focused on modifying the treatment to address the areas where the dissimilarities prevail."

"This is never easy, but what are their prospects?"

"The other two who had already collapsed before they were brought on board the shuttle continue to fade physically and mentally, despite our best efforts at sustaining them. Unless something changes, I don't expect either one to last through the night. However, Sheri Thwaite and Rick Syn, the two who were affected last, appear to have the best chances for survival. You will remember that it took days for Keith Thomas to die. We once said that if he could hold out for another day, we thought we could save him. He didn't have that extra day in him, but fortunately, his wife Karen did, so we were able to save her.

She's continued to thrive in the ten years since then, and we used what we learned to develop an effective vaccine, so we know that the outcome of these situations may be a positive one. There's enough of a similarity between the two bugs that we believe a vaccine may be possible in this case as well. However, the first thing is to figure out how to kill it. We hope that Thwaite and Syn have the extra days in them so we can come up with that answer."

"Regardless of whether our people recover, would you recommend sending other people to Shiloh based on what we know at this point?"

Dr. Hall blanched slightly. "If you are referring to people visiting the planet surface without isolation suits, doing so would be extraordinarily foolish. While there may be areas on the surface of Shiloh where the disease does not thrive, we have no way yet of knowing where those areas may be. Also, until we've developed an effective vaccine, anyone visiting the place would need to be quarantined, at least until an effective treatment is available to kill the bug after infection has taken hold. Otherwise, we may find ourselves with a plague on our hands. There's a reason why everyone, patients and doctors, are all in a completely self-contained module. If, heaven forbid, something were to happen and the disease were to make its way over to us, you can take this module and launch it into the Citadel sun to ensure the safety of the Citadel population."

"Thank you, Doctor. You and your staff, along with your patients, are in our prayers."

Hall's image disappeared from the display. Sara spoke what was on the minds of everyone: "Did we push too quickly to allow people to be exposed to the surface environment, without having done a full vetting of the place?"

Liz shook her head. "Dr. Hall and her people did a broad range of biological scans, including atmospheric, water, and soil analysis. They also obtained specimens of the local flora and fauna and found nothing that would be cause for concern. They even exposed samples of human tissues to everything they found from the planet, without incident. The scouts did likewise while still in their isolation suits on the surface of Shiloh. All of the test results were negative."

Austin spoke. "The people who were affected were volunteers from the Citadel Group, with expertise in making these assessments. No one pressured them in any way into approving trials involving humans. They reviewed everything before making the decision to proceed, and they were the ones we would have asked for a recommendation anyway. What's happened is tragic, but not an indictment of our judgment." He looked back at the display. An image of Preacher appeared. "Let's hear from J. W. I have queued up his message past the introductory remarks," he said.

Some new lines seemed to have appeared in Preacher's face since his last message. "Astonishing as it is to report, Phoenix has done everything that its leaders said they'd do. They've demonstrated a fully functional warp-field generator, with the ability to establish a communications network that uses the same type of mini-warp-bubble approach to sending messages over long distances as we do, and they also have artificial gravity aboard their ships."

He nodded toward Henkel as he continued. "Astrid will talk some more about the technical side of things before we get back to what it means for Citadel."

Henkel approached a display, and images of *Firebird* and *KT-12* were placed side by side. "These images are scaled properly, meaning that they've actually gone a step farther than us and improved the technology to support a warp-field bubble for an even larger ship than our Keith Thomas transports. I've attached a file to this message with all of the technical data we've collected, by the way."

Her hands framed the image of the larger ship, to emphasize the size. "While it's hard to be precise about the potential capacity of these ships, Phoenix has claimed that each vessel is able to transport over a thousand colonists, mostly through the use of stasis chambers for passenger storage. We've been unable to confirm whether any passengers will actually be out of stasis during the voyage.

"You may be wondering how we've been able to confirm at least some of our findings. In the end, it was due to money," she said with a humorless laugh. "More precisely, it was due to the money that would be paid out by the insurance companies in the event the colonists are injured or killed, which forced the hand of Phoenix. The insurance companies insisted on being allowed to inspect the Firebird ships to confirm that they actually do what Phoenix has claimed they can do.

"Considering that this demand was repeated thousands of time, Phoenix decided to make a show of giving controlled tours of their ships. We've had reliable reports that there is, in fact, artificial gravity aboard these ships, as well as functioning stasis equipment for the vast majority of the colonists who would make the three-month voyage. Of course, no access to the underlying equipment was allowed, so we still don't know for sure how any of it works."

Bacas stepped up to the display. "They've already completed at least twenty-five of these ships, with more on the way. While they plan on keeping some of them in this system to compete with us in shipping items that require artificial gravity, they've made it clear that a huge wave of humanity will be heading toward you very shortly."

Preacher stepped up to the display and pushed all the images away, as if to eliminate distractions. "I'm sure you want to know what kind of colonists Phoenix is recruiting for this venture. I'm alarmed to say that they aren't interested in anything like what we want for Citadel. Phoenix doesn't seem to be doing any of the screening we have done to ensure that only the people who are best suited for the venture and who are interested in the long-term success of Citadel are selected. I've received multiple reports of people being accepted by Phoenix who were rejected out of hand by the Citadel Group, including some who thought they could buy their way into a spot on one of our transports. You absolutely would not want some of these people for neighbors anywhere, let alone on a nearby planet.

"Lazarus and the rest of them seem most interested in people who are willing to pay for the privilege of striking it rich quickly. They've pointed out the valuable resources available on Citadel and throughout the asteroid region and suggested that the same could hold true for Shiloh. The problem is it may even be true.

"However, even if the primary motivation is money, that doesn't justify the lack of training that might make the difference between life and death on a frontier world. From what we've been able to tell, many of these prospective colonists lack the basic skills needed to survive, let alone prosper. While Lazarus has argued that the risk-taking entrepreneurs who will serve as their colonists will be able to sort things out and prosper, it seems like Phoenix is just dumping these people on the planet after having taken their money."

Preacher brought up images of Citadel and Shiloh. "This brings us back to an issue I mentioned in my previous message. As you know, when we proclaimed that we had become a state, we made that claim with respect to the planet Citadel specifically. We've also maintained that our claim extends well out to the outer boundaries of the solar system, as we are responsible for the overall security of the entire solar system.

"While we've long acted as if we have sole authority to decide what happens in the Citadel system, we never made a formal claim with respect to any of the other planets in the system, because we hadn't tried to colonize them. We had a hell of a time as it was getting recognition that was specific to planet Citadel, and laying official claim to Shiloh or New Harbor wasn't worth the distraction it would have caused.

"Besides, it didn't seem necessary anyway in view of our total control over entry into the inner part of the system. The only non-Citadel ship to have ever made it to that part of the system was the alien scout ship, and there are sufficient defenses in place now to prevent a repeat of that situation."

He paused for a moment as another memory came to mind. "Of course, we shouldn't overlook the fact that Harrington and her ilk also made it into the system, but that was by stowing aboard one of our own transports, not because of a vessel they designed and built.

"Anyway, Citadel would appear to be on solid ground as far as simply refusing to give the safe path through the radiation field to other ships is concerned. However, Phoenix has claimed that its ships can navigate safely through the radiation field surrounding the inner part of the system. If true, this could have huge repercussions for Citadel.

"I've made some discreet inquiries, and it isn't at all clear that the international community would support an effort by Citadel to actively block a venture from trying to colonize another planet in that system. It probably wouldn't matter that Phoenix is trying to make a lot of money, since that was one of Citadel's objectives too. It also wouldn't matter that Phoenix seems to want to make things as difficult for Citadel as possible; it is inherent in colonization that people sometimes have neighbors, and they need to find a way to get along with each other.

"Ultimately, while the international community probably wouldn't stand in our way, they won't intervene on our behalf either. We've long made the point that no one in our neck of the woods has any say over what happens in your neck of the woods, and it appears the community, including our friends on Mars, is taking us at our word. They've suggested that they'd leave the matter to be resolved by Citadel and Phoenix."

More lines seemed to appear on Preacher's face. "Our best assessment at this point is that some twenty thousand colonists will be heading your way shortly, with more waves to follow as their ships are able to return. They don't seem to be well prepared for lives as colonists and appear to have been lured with suggestions that they are owed a living by that system.

"If even one of those waves settles on Shiloh, the very character of the Citadel system will likely be altered permanently, to the detriment of all. If very many more waves follow, you may find yourselves outnumbered by people who not only don't share your values, but may not even like you very much. Lazarus has served notice that they will expect their colony to be coequal with Citadel in your system, including how to deal with security matters and the allocation of resources. He didn't seem interested in hearing that Citadel wouldn't agree with his demands. In short, your biggest threats may come from within the system instead of from without, and you wouldn't be able to look to Earth for any assistance."

Preacher brought up the image of the five leaders of Phoenix. "This image was taken of the five leaders just before they started their original mining venture.

When I spoke directly with the five of them, the woman on the left, Pandora, was the only other person to speak, and Lazarus didn't seem too thrilled about it. My main impression of her is that she isn't just interested in a competitive rivalry with us, she truly doesn't seem to like Citadel very much.

"Anyway, who knew that this group of people would end up causing so much trouble? You may need to make a tough choice, even if it wouldn't sit well with the people back here, if you don't want these people as your new neighbors. I'm not sure what your next step may be, Sam, but you'd better make it soon!" Preacher's image disappeared.

"I'll be damned before we let others come here and try to take away everything we've built," Yabuno said with heat. "We control the entrance to this system, and we should deny entry to anyone who wants to screw with us."

"Agreed, Bret," Turner said, "but what if they don't need our permission to get in? They've already done things no one would have thought possible, like coming up with warp-field generators and artificial gravity within a few months after striking it rich. Who's to say they won't be able to navigate through the radiation field with the same ease?"

Turner shrugged. "Maybe we should accept the possibility that we've been eclipsed technologically and learn to live with it."

"Say that again, Alan," Austin said while staring at the image intently.

"What?" he said with a puzzled expression. "Maybe our egos are just keeping us from accepting that we've been passed by technologically."

"No," Austin replied, shaking his head. "You said that they developed warp-field generators and artificial gravity within a few months after striking it rich."

"Yes, that's what J. W. told us."

A grim expression played out across Austin's face as he said, "It isn't J. W.'s fault. That's the story everyone heard. It's bullshit, of course."

"You were looking at that image," Liz said. "What do you see?"

"Someone tell me what's wrong with it," he replied.

"Beats me," Yabuno said.

"Where was it taken?"

"Who knows? Somewhere in space, probably, considering the type of layout in the room. We already know they came from there. Maybe Mars."

"No, not Mars. Take a closer look."

"I see asteroids in the background, through that window," Liz said, "so they couldn't have been on Mars. In fact, they must have been among the asteroids themselves, perhaps near where they did their mining."

"That makes sense," Austin nodded. "Now, what *don't* you see?"

The answer flashed through her mind. "All mining operations, except Citadel's, lack artificial gravity and possess precious little of the real thing. I don't see anyone floating around."

"They're all standing by a rail," Yabuno said.

"It's a full shot, without anyone cropped out," Austin countered. "Is anyone touching that rail or using any other restraints to stay in place?"

"No!" Yabuno said excitedly. "They're standing around, just like they're in front of someone's house planetside. They already had artificial gravity before they even started!" He looked at Austin. "You don't think they came up with it, do you? You don't think they invented any of this technology?"

"No, I think they found it."

"Where?" The color drained from Yabuno's face as the answer arrived. "The aliens have warp-field generators. It stands to reason that they have those other kinds of technology as well. How the hell did these people get it?"

It was Austin's turn to shrug. "One of the tough things about tracking down the files relating to Harrington's efforts to contact the aliens is that you can never be certain you've recovered everything. For all we know, one of her people hid enough information to make it possible for someone else to duplicate their efforts."

"What good would that have done them?" Yabuno asked. "We've shut down all outside access to our communications network, including the alternative beacon they compromised. There's no way for someone else to send the aliens a message even if he or she found the files."

"What about when we took out the alien ship that was guarding the outer entrance to this system?" Turner asked. "We found messages that we assumed were between that ship and the complex we destroyed. We never figured out what they meant."

"Yes, but we deleted them," Liz said.

Turner looked skeptical. "Did we? Looking back, are we certain the aliens didn't pull a fast one on us and insert a back door into our own network that would allow them to communicate with someone like Harrington? What do you think, Bret?"

Yabuno was deep in thought for a moment. "It's possible," he admitted. "I can run some diagnostics to determine whether any communications traffic ended up in any unusual places." He groaned. "If that's what happened, we may have to rebuild the network from the ground up unless we can figure out how to sterilize their stuff." He glanced toward a display. "It looks like Melody and I will need to work on this one together."

Melody Lambert, one of the first settlers, who was also responsible for the communications networks throughout the system, grinned. "It won't be the first time we've had challenges.

Joe Albretti spoke. "Even if this all checks out, it doesn't explain why someone would be stupid enough to do another deal with the aliens," he objected. "It's been pretty clear that doing so would be signing your own death warrant."

"True," Liz mused, "but what if the aliens have learned more about humans? What if they simply dangled the technology in front of some greedy people without telling them where it came from? What few details there were about their warp-field generator were never released to the public. Also, nothing was ever said about communications networks or artificial gravity."

"It's possible it worked out that way," Austin acknowledged, "but there seem to be a lot of things these people know how to do all by themselves, such as build a first-class yard and design a ship to house the technology. Could the aliens know humans well enough to have conveyed all that information in a form that could be understood?"

"The design of their ships isn't as complicated as one might think, if we consider the warp-field generators, artificial gravity, and communications technology as separate items to be incorporated into the design later," Yabuno said.

"Back when we destroyed the aliens' complex, Harrington's technicians we interviewed seemed to think the alien files themselves may have created some of the warp-field generator components, strange as that may sound," Turner noted. "Perhaps what they provided this time did more of it."

"That's a good theory," Albretti said, "but we need to think about some facts. What are we going to do about twenty thousand colonists? They probably have no idea that their ships are poisonous."

"We now have a basis for denying them entry into this system," Austin said, "even if they can get through the radiation field, which we should assume they can, courtesy of their unknown benefactors. As far as we're concerned, alien technology is toxic to human existence, and we won't allow them in until we've confirmed that nothing toxic is on board their ships."

"What will we do if they refuse to allow us to inspect their ships? There are a lot of human lives that will serve as hostages."

Austin moved to a display. As the images of the defense system at the entrance to the safe path appeared, he said, "We will disable their ships, if possible, but we will stop them even if it means destroying them."

"That may be pretty difficult with twenty ships all at once."

"True," Austin replied, frowning. "They're probably counting on using that against us."

"The other question is: What we do if they allow us to inspect their ships, and we disable the alien technology? What do we do with the colonists? We're still not going to bring them through to Shiloh. Until we can solve the problem with the Shiloh bug, setting foot on the planet may be the same thing as cutting their throats. With the alien technology disabled, their ships won't be able to return to Earth."

"Curly?" Austin called out.

A woman brushed a long, wavy lock of red hair out of her face as she answered, "I'm here, Sam."

"We have some time before they get here, so I want you to take charge of a couple of projects. The first is to work with Joe to identify additional locations where we can position defensive weapons, and get them in place and online right away." Austin grinned. "He knows the best places to put any nasty surprises, and which ones to place where."

"Got it. What else?"

"What's the status of the mothball fleet?"

"The mothball fleet's still filled with ships that have had the hell pounded out of them by our encounters with the aliens, as well as other ships that are at the end of their useful lives," she said. "Each Keith Thomas transport is a hell of an important investment, and we don't just abandon them, not even the ones from as far away as the alien complex we destroyed. The only exception has been the transport that was infected with alien technology; considering what the aliens were able to do with it remotely, there's no way we'd ever allow that one back into this system." She stopped. "You already know this."

"Yes. Right now, we need more of our transports since we're probably going to have to return the colonists to Earth. We may also need to defend two solar systems at the same time."

"What do you want me to do?"

"I want you to bring back online every transport you possibly can and get them all fully armed and upgraded with the new warp-field generators."

Curly gasped. "Holy shit, Sam! That'll be a hell of a fleet!"

"We don't have enough crews for those ships," Albretti reminded him.

"We won't need full crews for every ship," Austin said as he walked to a display. He brought up images of key systems and gestured at them as he continued. "We'll just need combat crews for any ship that isn't carrying colonists back to Earth. The ships carrying colonists will be outfitted as stasis carriers, to reduce a lot of the environmental support needed and the crew size. It'll still be tight as far as manning each transport, but we should be able to do it."

"What about Earth?" Liz asked. "Phoenix has left some Firebird ships behind to carry things that need artificial gravity."

Austin's expression was once again grim. "I'm going to send a message to J. W. right away, warning him about the danger. I'll send messages to Pete Lee and Amelia Gordon as well. Hopefully, they'll be able to defend themselves against any mischief before things get out of hand."

———

The Phoenix ships appeared in a lonely stretch of space that contained nothing to indicate that intelligent life had ever passed that way. Lazarus took in the view on a display and nodded at Diana.

"Right on the money, Diana, although I wouldn't have expected anything else. Open a link to all of our ships."

"We're ready, Lazarus," she replied.

"Greetings, everyone," he began. "Now that we're clear of any prying eyes, it's time to make some room for our new cargo. Check back in once you've finished this step." He opened an internal link. "Heph, be sure to deploy a beacon once you've taken care of our cargo."

"We're on it," he replied.

The Phoenix leader enjoyed the scene, as what looked like a fleet of massive cargo containers drifted into view. They were only in motion through the momentum of being jettisoned; each one moved without any rhyme or reason along its own path and faded gradually into the background of deep space.

"So long, suckers," he muttered.

"It looks like a waste dump, like what ocean fleets used to do," Diana said without emotion.

"Not a bad analogy," he said with a slightly amused expression. "That's about all the importance they have for us at this point."

"The ships have reported in, and everything has been jettisoned," she confirmed. "Your link is still live, so you can go ahead."

"Good." He pointed to a spot on a display and said, "Prepare to make a jump to this location, to take on new cargo." His grin wasn't quite friendly. "We'll have something to trade with Citadel, after all."

CHAPTER THIRTEEN

Dan Bacas was getting ready to link in to a conversation with Astrid Henkel when he received a message from Gus Kramer, his deputy at the yard.

"What's on your mind, Gus?" he asked.

"You remember how we've been keeping track of anyone we know with yard experience who hasn't been seen or heard from for a while?"

"Sure. Who's missing?"

"Jeff Coffey. No one's seen him for months."

Bacas felt a shot to the gut upon hearing Coffey's name. They went back a lot of years together, having gotten their training under some of the same mentors. "How do we know Jeff's missing, and why would it take months to hear about it?"

"Remember, his wife died a while back, and they didn't have any kids, so there isn't any family to check in on him. He's been taking freelance assignments where he doesn't always stay in touch with everyone regularly. No one really thought about the absence until recently.

I talked with one of his other buddies and found out he was working for Phoenix in its yard."

Bacas couldn't believe it. "*Coffey* was helping them build their ships? Is he still working for them?"

Kramer shook his head. "They said he quit months ago, and they don't know where he is either." His expression was troubled as he said, "Something isn't right, Dan. Coffey *never* quits an assignment. He might not renew a contract if he doesn't like the job, but he doesn't quit. If he isn't there, it's because something happened to him. The question is whether it happened there or somewhere else."

Bacas remembered something. "Coffey kept a log of his assignments, didn't he? Sometimes he even included some interesting information about them."

Kramer shrugged. "Did he? I guess you know him better than I do."

"He began doing it soon after we started together. He refused to give it up, even though some of his employers might have chewed him out if they'd known. He used an old trick to transmit his images without being caught. He took a space farer's good-luck charm, the kind that's a chunk of an asteroid, and used special components that don't read as anything except 'dead' rock, with streaks of minerals and other materials. Check around to see if we can get a hold of it or the file with the information that it transmitted. If you need to spend some money, do it."

Bacas broke the connection and contacted Henkel and Preacher.

Preacher was already speaking with Henkel. "I'm glad I sent our message to Sam; at least he'll know that a fleet of colonists is on the way. It's too bad the most recent message from him arrived after the Phoenix ships departed. He has some pretty serious news about Shiloh. It seems there's a deadly bug there, somewhat like the one that killed Keith Thomas on Citadel back in the day. Several people are already dead, and the others are fighting for their lives. We could have warned the Phoenix people about the problem; maybe it would have slowed down their desire to charge ahead to a world they know nothing about. I'll make sure the people in this solar system know about it, though."

"I wouldn't take bets on Lazarus holding back from the trip, even with that news, J. W.," Henkel said. "He seems to be under a compulsion to prove himself that we just don't understand."

"He may be under some compulsion, but I doubt everyone who wants to come along for the ride feels the same way. People get cold feet pretty quickly about certain things when there's the chance they may be infected by something and go through a rather nasty death."

"That's assuming they believe the message," she replied. "I wouldn't put it past Lazarus to claim that Sam's making the whole thing up to maintain the status quo, and so on."

"Pardon me for interrupting," Bacas said, "but I may have a lead on someone who used to work for Phoenix at its yard. He went missing months ago, and Phoenix claims he quit, only this guy *never* quits. He hasn't shown up anywhere else either."

"While the connection with Phoenix is interesting, I don't see the reason for bringing it up," Henkel said.

"I know this guy, and he often keeps a log of what he's working on. Gus is trying to get a hold of that log in case there's something in it we should know about."

"You need to be careful not to make it look like the Citadel Group is engaged in industrial espionage," Henkel warned.

Preacher's expression was lighter. "Citadel itself is a different matter, however, being a sovereign nation. If you find anything, send it to me, and I'll have my son check it out and let us know if there is any cause for concern. If the question is one of protecting our security or taking a hands-off approach to their technology, our security concerns win."

Preacher looked worried again. "As we were saying, Dan, I sent a message to Sam about the fact Phoenix sent an entire fleet of ill-prepared and ill-equipped colonists to the Citadel system. While it appears that Phoenix has extracted very handsome fees from these people, the nature of its approach leads me to wonder whether money or disruption is the primary motivation behind the group's actions."

"Disruption, especially the way they've gone about it, would be an obscenely expensive objective," Bacas noted.

"Agreed," Henkel said. She faced a display and brought up several images. "We've made some estimates of what they would have taken in from their mining activities, plus what they've received from their colonists, and we've offset the estimated expenses from their shipbuilding, communication, and exploration efforts."

She pointed at an alarming figure. "There's no possible way they can sustain their activities for much longer, even by extracting huge sums from their colonists. It isn't an exaggeration to state that they've passed the point of no return. The only way they can sustain themselves now is to wipe out Citadel economically and step into Citadel's place. In other words, disruption and money are part of the same objective, which is to destroy Citadel."

"Did it have to be this way?" Preacher asked somberly. "Is that the only way a new venture in space can be successful?"

Henkel shook her head. "No, J. W., it isn't. If they hadn't poured their resources into building a huge fleet, but instead had focused on building a few smaller ships at a time, they could have tried to start a small colony somewhere and expanded gradually. While nothing about space exploration is ever guaranteed, that approach has worked in this solar system. It's logical, and people would have understood it."

She slashed the letter *X* across an image of Citadel. "These people want to destroy us. They want to have bragging rights over having the largest population in the Citadel system, and they probably want Citadel itself to be destabilized by what happens on Shiloh. We should assume they want to do much the same to us in this solar system." She gave Preacher a hard look. "The question is, what are we going to do about it?"

Preacher's expression back was just as hard. "We'll do whatever we need to do to survive, Astrid. We should upgrade our security around all of our operations, both on Earth and elsewhere. Dan, that means making sure there's no chance of any mischief taking place against our yard. Under no circumstances are any 'accidents'—either internal or external—going to happen so that our operations are damaged. I'd rather apologize later than explain to Sam why we relaxed and let someone get close enough to hurt us."

"What about the traffic in this system?" she asked. "Phoenix has been trying to pick up some of our cargo business."

"That's where *I* come in," he said slyly. "Many of these relationships go back years, and I intend to use every trick available to keep them. We have a great record when it comes to reliability, which Phoenix can only hope to match. The only weapon they really have is to try to undercut us on pricing; although we know from Astrid's calculations that can't last indefinitely, they are probably willing to take the losses in order to ruin Citadel. Some customers may be willing to overlook that objective in order to obtain a temporary benefit. However, a lot of the same customers who use our services in this system also use our services for shipments between the two solar systems. The ones who want to abandon us in this system may find themselves with a lower priority for cargo space than those who stick with us. Fortunately, there aren't many like that, at least not yet."

"Isn't that self-defeating, in the long run?" Bacas said. "If Phoenix survives, then it's inevitable that the group will pick up cargo assignments between the two systems anyway."

"Not anytime soon," Preacher scoffed. "The only cargo they could carry to the Citadel system would be their own, and there isn't any money to be made there for now. Besides, they're stuffing their ships with so many passengers that there isn't room for any cargo other than what they need for their colony. Even if there was any cargo, no one on Citadel would take it. Also, they won't get any business from the return trip, since we'll only ship our goods on our transports, and they aren't likely to have any of their own goods ready for a while."

"We'd better remind our transport captains to be on the alert for any mischief as well," Henkel said. "Any deviations from protocols that may expose them to danger from third parties should be avoided."

"It's more than that," Preacher said, his features darkening. "As of now, all communications are to be encrypted. We won't trust any traffic over any network, not even ours, that hasn't been scrubbed to be sure we're safe. Until we hear otherwise from Sam, we have to be prepared to defend ourselves against attack. While we don't know whether they have weapons aboard their new ships, we'd better assume the answer is yes. Our lives may depend on it."

———

Preacher met again with Henkel and Bacas. He took one look at their expressions and was shrewd enough to know the news would not be good. "Which of you wants to give me the bad news first?" he asked.

Bacas spoke. "I can't imagine anything worse than what I have, J. W., so I'd better go first. Remember that we've been searching for Coffey's log?"

"Of course. You've found it?" he asked with interest. "That must mean Phoenix is mentioned. What dark secrets does he have to say about them?"

Without a word, Bacas brought the log online, and they watched the images on a display.

Preacher grew pale. "This is truly terrible news." He turned to Henkel. "I doubt anything you'd have to share could be this bad."

"I'll let you be the judge," she replied, which Preacher found ominous.

Once again, they watched a display in silence. At the video's conclusion, Preacher's features showed grave alarm. "This is much worse than I thought. We've been wrong in some key aspects about this situation. I need to talk with Pete Lee and Amelia Gordon immediately. We're no longer talking just about our safety, but the security of the entire solar system."

He looked anxiously at an image of Citadel. "It's sometimes startling to be reminded that while we can send and receive messages within this system virtually instantaneously, it takes a month for any message to travel to or from Citadel. I just wish there were a way to let Sam know in time."

CHAPTER FOURTEEN

The Phoenix fleet materialized in another lonely stretch of space, having performed this move many times over the past three months. Lazarus watched what had become a routine task as a beacon was deployed and activated.

"This is the last one, Lazarus," Diana confirmed. "Our next stop will be in the Citadel system."

"Any sign that they are aware of our approach?"

She shook her head. "We've been careful to appear where they won't detect us."

He grinned. "That's about to change. Let's not keep them waiting."

———

"We have visitors, Sam," Yabuno called out, pointing at a display. Moments earlier, nothing had been visible beyond the entrance to the safe path except the usual endless darkness, speckled with countless stars, along with the six Citadel transports arranged defensively. They watched as a second ship appeared a couple of minutes after the first one, and then a third one a couple of minutes later. The entire fleet of twenty ships had assembled less than an hour later, ready for colonization. Austin didn't comment on the arrogance, bordering on insanity, of stacking so many vessels so closely together from such a long trip.

"They're hailing us," Yabuno said.

Austin nodded toward a display. "Let's hear what they have to say."

"Don't bother introducing yourself, Lazarus," Austin began. "I already know who you are."

"Do you? You may be surprised," he replied. "Should I introduce my colleagues, or do you already know them too?"

"Pandora, Heph, Diana, and Georgia," Austin replied. "From what I've heard, Pandora in particular doesn't seem to like us very much."

"You should get to know her first before making any judgments," Lazarus replied lightly. His tone grew more serious. "You know why we're here, of course. Ambassador Preacher would have given you his version of recent events."

"I've found him to be pretty astute when it comes to assessments of people and events. Why don't you tell me anyway why you are here?"

"We haven't made any secret of our intentions, Austin. We plan on entering this system and colonizing the planet Shiloh."

"Your plans will have to change. You will not enter this system," Austin said flatly.

"We don't need your permission," the leader of the wagon train replied smugly. "We can get through the radiation field by ourselves. Unless you plan on interfering with our ships physically and possibly harming thousands of innocent people, that means we're entering this system."

"You're not listening. When I say you will not enter this system, I mean it. If that means we have to damage some or all of your ships, we will do it." Austin's gaze turned cold. "If that means we have to blow any of your ships out of space, we will do it."

The Phoenix leader looked shocked. "I never took you for someone who would commit murder, Austin, but you're going to have to prove it. I doubt anyone back on Earth or Mars will be very forgiving when they hear about the atrocities you've threatened to carry out."

"I don't think they'll be very forgiving of your recklessness in exposing your people to something on Shiloh that may kill them all. We've learned that the planet you want to call home contains a highly contagious, lethal microorganism that has already killed four of our people who visited the planet recently. Two others are barely clinging to life. Going there would mean your deaths."

Lazarus's expression became dismissive. "How convenient to claim that the place is dangerous, when the subject has never come up until we showed an interest in colonizing it."

"There's nothing convenient about it, Lazarus. We decided to take a closer look at the place, and it's a good thing we did, for your sakes. We haven't yet come up with a treatment, let alone a vaccine. That's something you should have considered before bringing twenty thousand of your closest friends with you. It's no secret that it can happen. We dealt with it ten years ago on Citadel."

"I recall that you didn't abandon Citadel either," Lazarus replied. "You stayed there while your people worked on finding a cure, which they did in due course. There's no reason why our people can't do likewise."

"So far, one hundred percent of the people who have set foot on Shiloh have become infected with a lethal bug. The percentage on Citadel was vastly lower, so it was possible to treat it in due course."

"For all we know, your people just happened to visit a dangerous spot on the surface. We'll visit somewhere else. You'll have to do better than that if you want to stop us from entering this system."

"We can do much better than that, which means it's time for you to drop the act," Austin said. "We know where your technology really comes from, and we know how poisonous it is as far as humans are concerned. How much do you know about the ones that provided it to you? Do you know or care that they aren't even human?"

"Is that how you want to play it?" Lazarus replied sarcastically. "Any time you want something, you try to justify it by mentioning aliens to scare everyone."

He gestured around his bridge. "Does anyone here look like an alien, Austin?"

"What does your warp-field generator look like, Lazarus?" Austin countered. "For that matter, how are you generating your artificial gravity? Our experts will know in ten seconds whether you are bluffing, so think carefully before answering," he warned.

The people on the bridge reacted with disdain to Austin's demands. "This is outrageous, Austin," Lazarus said. "You can't compete with us fairly, so now you want to know how our technology works. Would *you* answer that question?"

Austin chuckled grimly. "Your acting is creative, even if your outrage is manufactured. We don't give a damn about the technology, if it is of human origin—we already have stuff that can do the same thing, so it isn't of any value to us. If you really claim that you created that technology by yourselves, then you will have to allow my people aboard your lead vessel to inspect your engine room along with anywhere else they want to go."

Austin stared at the display with a hard look. "There won't be any further negotiations. Well?"

The Phoenix leader looked at the people on his bridge, noting the subdued looks on the faces around him. His shoulders slumped. "You win," he said. "Send your people over." The image went dark.

"Something's wrong with this picture," Austin said. "His actions don't match with what we've learned about them."

"For all his bravado, he may not be in a position to jeopardize the lives of his colonists, if the dispute can be resolved peacefully," Liz said. "He couldn't have known about the situation on Shiloh, for one thing. He'd still have to answer to them if something goes wrong."

"We'll soon know," he replied. At a signal from Austin, one of the Citadel ships launched a shuttle toward Phoenix's lead vessel. Just as the shuttle closed on its destination, the larger ship moved toward the entrance to the safe path. With the shuttle in the way, no one had a clear shot at the challenger. At the same time, the remainder of the twenty ships broke formation and launched attacks against the Citadel defenses.

Notwithstanding the sudden nature of the ship movements, these attacks would normally have resulted in the destruction of all twenty vessels. However, everyone throughout Citadel was stunned to find that all communications throughout their system ceased. With no messages getting through to anyone, there was no way to coordinate the defense against the sudden attack. The defense network was also offline, which rendered harmless what had been a formidable array of rail guns. While *Firebird* and the next nine ships made their way through the safe path quickly, the rest of the enemy vessels wasted no time in attacking those weapons, along with the outnumbered Citadel transports.

To the shock of the transport crews, the larger vessels began to deploy EMP weapons of their own along with rail guns, even though the Phoenix ships hadn't been loaded with any rocks when they'd departed Earth's solar system. In short order, massive boulders hurtled through space toward the beleaguered Citadel vessels. Most of the transports were barely able to vanish into warp bubbles to escape the onslaught, although one was unable to escape in time and was out of commission without having fired a shot.

While certain visual channels and navigation beacons were still functioning, they only made it possible for the settlers to watch some of the destruction.

Yabuno cursed loudly as his fears about the alien presence within their network came true. While he'd come up with what he hoped was a solution, it required that he reboot the network, which would leave them even more vulnerable until it could be brought back online. He was aboard *Pathfinder* as it awaited *Firebird* and the other vessels from the other end of the safe path.

Austin had one advantage that the rest of Citadel lacked, which was that he was at his home, using the only network that hadn't been compromised by the alien messages. For over a century, he'd dedicated himself to maintaining security and encryption within his personal network that couldn't be broken, even by contact with a trusted network. While he watched in horrified fascination the nightmare that was unfolding in the outer part of the system, he managed to open a link to Yabuno.

"Sam, where the hell did they get those rocks?" Yabuno demanded. "We know they didn't have any when they left for Citadel three months ago. We know their holds were crammed full with passengers in stasis when they departed, because our people saw them being loaded. Now, with all of that ammunition, there isn't any room for anything else. Where in God's name are the people?" he asked in horror.

"That's something important that we'll have to deal with some other time," Austin said. "Right now, with what they're doing to us, you know what happens if they can keep our communications down like this."

"I know. I've been working on a way to sterilize the alien messages. The problem is that Melody and I will need to reboot the network and then do some follow-up tweaking to be sure it worked."

"How long will it take?" Austin asked impatiently. "I'm stuck here on Citadel, with the planetary defenses just as dead as everywhere else."

"We can't get the network back online before the Phoenix ships can reach you. Too bad about Shiloh. If we were able to solve the problem with that bug, we could at least try to evacuate some people. It's an inner planet to Citadel, so ships could get there without having to cross paths with *Firebird* or their other ships. No such luck with New Harbor; it's further away from the star than Citadel, with a location that would place ships right in Lazarus's crosshairs as they headed out. Also, we don't know as much about the place as we do Shiloh, so who knows what additional problems we may be buying by sending people there? Face it, you'd better prepare for something nasty. Staying at your current location may not be a good idea."

"Maybe not, but I'm going to try to get through to as many settlers as possible to consider evacuating to evacuate to Shiloh anyway. Unless they can reach one of the regional shelters, staying in their current locations means either being blasted to pieces by those bastards or heading out into the wilderness to be prey for cheaters. With luck, they can try to hide behind Shiloh without touching down, and hope to return once Phoenix is done with Citadel. It isn't a good alternative, but there aren't any good ones available anyway."

"Are you going to lead them there?"

Austin was silent for a moment. "No, I'm staying here."

"Why the hell would you do that, considering the choices for anyone who stays behind?" Yabuno demanded.

"Someone has to stay here, to make it seem like the population hasn't bugged out. Otherwise, it wouldn't be hard for Lazarus to figure out where everyone is hiding. He'd be able to wipe them out pretty easily in space, and there isn't any other place they can go. Besides, my absence would be noted."

Yabuno gave a sigh of frustration. "For all they know, you're on a transport and trying to kick their sorry asses, but there isn't time to argue about it now. I hope you know what you're doing, Sam."

"So do I."

Yabuno signed off, and Austin opened a link to the rest of the planet. "This is Sam Austin. I don't know how many of you can receive this message, but we are facing a dire emergency that requires making some hard choices without any time to ponder them. I have received confirmation that Phoenix ships are heading this way, with no guarantees about whether our transports can stop any of them. There isn't any question about their real intentions; they mean to destroy Citadel. Since our planetary defenses are down, the only options are to remain on your lands and face destruction by Phoenix or cheaters, or evacuate to a safe orbit around Shiloh.

"I urge you to make your way to Shiloh while you still can. I will stay behind and do what I can to make them believe the population is still here, and make things as complicated for them as possible. I hope we'll meet again after this is over. Good luck."

Austin kept his link open. Moments later, he received a message from Mark Albretti. "Sam, there's no way we're leaving our homes. We have emergency shelters that may help; they've been hardened against EMP attacks, and we're willing to take the chance that Phoenix doesn't have enough rocks to blast all of us to rubble. However, you will be a prime target for them. Knowing you, you won't leave your place, so send Liz and your kids over here."

"I doubt Liz will agree to leave, but she may be willing to send the kids to someplace less dangerous." His eyes misted. "Thank you for offering them a better chance of survival than they'd have staying here, Mark."

Other messages poured in, with the people of Citadel declaring their determination to stay put to defend their homes. There would be no evacuation to Shiloh.

———

Yabuno had taken the network offline and worked frantically to bring it back to life. He didn't even have time to watch any of the action on the displays nearby.

The deadly dance continued in the outer system, as only four transports were still operational. The other two simply drifted aimlessly, with no way to know if there was any life onboard. Eight of the Phoenix ships were still in action and maintaining an offense against the outnumbered defenders.

Captain McKinley, aboard *KT-5*, was leading as best he could without the ability to communicate directly with the other three ships. Fortunately, shipboard communications were still working, and he'd used this to his advantage to take out one of the enemy ships. He had a moment of satisfaction from noting that not all of the drifting ships were from Citadel. That brief moment was all he allowed himself before getting back to dealing with the ships that were still trying to destroy them.

He pointed to a display as he spoke to his navigator, Amy Soren, and his chief engineer. "Thread us between those two ships, Amy, after we go into a warp bubble. Position us to face the one on the port side. Chief, do you see where you need to launch another rock?"

"I see it, Captain. God, those things can take some punishment! I guess when you don't give a damn about the lives of your passengers, you can take insane risks."

"Follow up the rock with a couple of torpedoes. Once we have a good-sized hole ripped into that hull, we should be able to blast the ship apart. Let's move out, Amy."

A moment later, the images had transformed into eerie versions of their normal counterparts, as Soren guided the transport toward its objective. To their dismay, the ships moved away, leaving *KT-5* without a target.

McKinley nearly exploded with frustration. "Damn! We've been playing this stupid cat-and-mouse game for hours. They're still anticipating our moves and shifting each time we move out of normal space-time." With weary eyes, he scanned the display and sought another target they could approach before being outmaneuvered again.

True to the boast by the Phoenix leader, *Firebird* and its sister ships had passed through the safe path without incident. All pretense at being colonists had long been dropped, and they headed toward Citadel at extreme speed. Hours later, they saw *Pathfinder* blocking their path. Lazarus was vaguely amused as he watched the scout ship on a display.

"Daring us to cross that line, are you?" he muttered. "Get ready to be swatted out of the way."

Joe Albretti was acting as the captain aboard the scout ship, since Alicia Shaw had been pressed into service as the captain of a transport. Albretti watched the approach of the ten Phoenix ships on a display. One of the hard things about the fact the network was down was he couldn't send any messages to his wife, Sara, or their girl, Gina.

He got on his link to his chief engineer. "Chief, we're going to have to do some things other than how I'd do them normally. Do you have the special torpedoes ready?"

"They're ready to go, Captain."

"Good. I've noted the coordinates on the display. We're at too far a distance to be sure of our aim, but we need to do something to keep them off balance. I want you to launch a special torpedo and follow up immediately with a conventional one. When I give the word, we'll go into a warp bubble and cause some more trouble."

Albretti watched as the enemy ships closed the distance, and he knew his crew couldn't wait any longer. "Now, Chief," he said.

It wasn't possible to watch the special torpedo, of course. It raced toward its target in a mini–warp bubble of its own, which also made it impossible to track and target.

Albretti swore in frustration as the erupting distortions made it clear that the projectile had missed. However, the conventional torpedo had been launched as well. A terrible explosion rocked the ship just as they sought to form a warp bubble for their escape.

He got to his link. "Chief, what the hell happened? Are we still in one piece?"

There was a brief pause, either because the chief needed to clear his head or consult some displays. "They pulled a page from our playbook, Captain. An instant after we launched our special torpedo, they must have done the same with several conventional ones. One of those torpedoes must have reached us and detonated just as we were shifting out of normal space-time. Our warp bubble has collapsed, and several systems are offline, including weapons. We also can't maneuver."

———

Aboard *Firebird*, the Phoenix leaders reached much the same conclusions about *Pathfinder*. Pandora watched with particular interest, saying, "Let's finish that ship off for good!"

"First things first," Lazarus said. "One of their torpedoes detonated near one of our ships. Diana, what's the status of that ship?

A moment later, Diana replied, "They've suffered some significant damage, and the warp-field generators are in need of repair, but their weapons and engines are still working." A predatory look appeared in her face. "They can still help us take out Citadel ships."

"Agreed," he replied. "I don't doubt the repairs have already begun on the generators. Now, let's get back to our target. I want to start by frying that ship's systems. That way, there won't be any life support once we start knocking holes in its hull and their air rushes out. Even their survival suits won't be much use once we're finished with them. Open a link to our other ships, and I'll explain what we're going to do."

The vessels began to move toward the helpless scout ship, intending to form a semicircular pattern to ravage it with EMP bursts from multiple directions while avoiding any crossfire that might place their own ships at risk. Albretti watched the images on a display as they faced multiple EMP weapons coming online.

The crews aboard the Phoenix ships were shocked to find themselves pounded by a near avalanche of rocks, as what they had taken for ruined hulks in the nearby mothball yard suddenly came to life and pounced on them. They also had to fend off attacks from mobile rail guns and torpedo launchers that were now manned individually to offset the loss of control through a network. They began to beat a hurried retreat in the face of the deadly onslaught.

All except *Firebird*. Lazarus didn't waste time trying to protect any of the other ships in his fleet. His vessel managed to break away from the worst of the attack before suffering major damage. His destination was Citadel, and he was determined to cause as much damage to the planet and its people as possible.

Sara Albretti was in charge of one of the revived transports. She focused on one of the ships that hadn't broken away and gestured at a display as she spoke to her chief engineer. "Chief, I need to put a hole in that ship. Launch a torpedo at this spot."

A moment later, a conventional torpedo raced toward the huge vessel. The ship had anticipated the launch, however, and shifted just in time to avoid the contact. The torpedo's explosion only caused minimal damage. The vessel raced toward Sara's transport, hoping to catch the crew off guard, but they vanished into a warp bubble without harm. As they watched the ghostly image on the display, Sara spoke again with her chief.

"Chief, they probably think they know just where we'll be when we reappear, so we're going to mess with them and show up where they won't be expecting us." She gestured to a spot on the display.

The chief whistled. "That's taking quite a risk, Captain. We'll be right in their crosshairs if we get it wrong."

"Even if we get it wrong, they'll be in *our* crosshairs too," she reminded him. "Bring our rail gun online and load it with a particularly large rock."

They moved into position, noting that the other ship hadn't yet committed itself to a position. Finally, it began to move, and Sara spoke. "Now, Chief."

The instant Sara's transport appeared, she said, "Launch that rock and get us out of here!"

By the time they were back in their warp bubble, they could make out what might be a new hole in the side of their target. It was hard to be sure, since the image was more of a silhouette than something solid.

"We have company coming up behind us," the chief warned. "If we try to finish off the ship with the hole, the other one can take us out from behind."

"Shift so we come up from their underside instead, and launch a rock at them."

A moment later they reappeared and blasted a hole in the hull of an unsuspecting enemy. The first ship tried to attack them but was devastated by a rock from another transport. Sara nodded appreciatively at a display, grateful for the sign of teamwork. Network or not, they were working out how to take down their enemy.

She brought up the second ship on a display and gestured toward the newly created hole on its underside. At a word from her, a special torpedo raced toward that hole. They watched with satisfaction as a warp bubble erupted from inside the vessel, distorting it grotesquely before the structure was consumed by major explosions bursting out from other parts of the ship. She sent a conventional torpedo into the inferno, and the destruction was complete.

As desperately as she wanted to turn to *Pathfinder* and make sure her husband was OK, there were still other Phoenix ships that needed to be destroyed. She prayed it wouldn't take long to finish off the last ship, as she knew Citadel also needed her help. She worried about the damage *Firebird* might inflict on the planet that she called home and had to trust that its defenses would hold up until help could arrive.

Her trust was misplaced. The defense network was still down, so the formidable protective measures were useless against the huge vessel. Unlike the subterfuge of the mothball yard, there were no vessels on hand to spring out from behind innocent-looking cover to defend the planet.

———

Lazarus enjoyed watching the images on the display as the planet came into view. *Firebird* took position over the continent inhabited by the settlers. "I think we'll take the Town Square first," he said, relishing the thought. "That'll hurt them because what passes for a government is headquartered there. Then we'll take out anything constituting a vital function. After that, we'll take out Austin's place. That way, he may be able to watch the destruction of everything he's built and loved, before it happens to him."

"Austin is too dangerous to wait that long to kill," Pandora insisted. "Take him out first, and then deal with everything else."

The Phoenix leader glared at her before relaxing. "All right, Pandora. I'll overlook your attempt to give me orders this time. We'll take out Austin first." Before he could complete the thought, the ship rocked from an impact.

"Where the hell did that come from?" he practically screamed. "Their network is still down."

"There's a message on the display," Diana said in disbelief. "The sender claims to be Austin!"

Austin's face filled the display, his grim gaze proof that he was neither cowed nor despondent over the approach of the Phoenix vessel or the death it represented. "I guess you weren't interested in Shiloh, after all."

"No," Lazarus replied, regaining his composure, "that was just a means to an end. The end of you, that is." He looked away for a moment and said, "Launch a rock toward his complex."

He looked back at Austin and taunted, "Did you hear, Austin? You'll cease to exist in a few seconds!"

"Do you really think so?" Even in the moment, everyone on the bridge gasped at the words.

Further conversation was interrupted for a moment as the image broke up. Lazarus smirked and said, "Yes, I really think so, not that you can hear me anymore!"

His smirk faded as he heard Austin's voice again. "My hearing's fine. Is that the best you can do?"

Lazarus flinched at the taunt. "Launch another rock toward him. In fact, launch everything we have toward him!" he demanded.

Diana shook her head. "We can't do it."

Her leader was enraged. "Why the hell not? We need to do something before he launches another rock at us!"

"That's not the issue; we took out his weapons complex with our rock; that was what caused the interference."

"Then let's take him out while he's sitting there, completely helpless."

"When he launched his own rock at us, it took out all of our loaders and jammed everything up so it can't be moved around. If we hadn't already had a rock loaded, we wouldn't even have been able to use the rail gun. We sure as hell can't get anything out of the way to reload."

"Use the EMP weapon, then. Fry everything down there."

"We can only deploy the rail gun or the EMP weapon, but not both at the same time. With the rail gun jammed the way it is, we can't bring the EMP weapon into position to blast him."

"What the hell *can* we do?" he snarled.

She gazed at him with a feral look. "We can go down there with portable antipersonnel devices and take him out. He can't do anything to stop us, and if we're careful, he won't even know just where we'll be when we attack. He won't be any less dead when we're done, and it'll probably feel better to do it that way too."

CHAPTER FIFTEEN

As the shuttle descended to the surface of the planet near Austin's home, Lazarus discussed his plans with Diana. "Austin has made this even more interesting than it could have been, by making the layout of his main house a lot like his home in California. That gives us an opportunity to bring back some horrible memories for him before we kill him."

"So that's why you laid out the plan the way you did," Diana said. "We're going in much like the people who tried to kill him on Earth long ago. You want to torture him by bringing back whatever nightmares he has from the murder of his first wife."

Lazarus nodded. "The word is, she died in his arms. I wish we knew whether Liz Austin is there right now, so we could be sure of killing her in front of him as well."

"There's no way to be certain, but we'll make sure that if she's somewhere else, she'll be a widow shortly."

Austin walked around the great room in his house, although the place was dark. Earlier in the day, under other circumstances, he would have been enjoying the last vestiges of the sunset while he cradled a glass in his hand that held the delightful liquid that was a good Citadel wine. Although it had been a midautumn day, the weather was warm, so there was no need for a fire in the room's magnificent fireplace. Within a few weeks, the days would be a lot colder, and the fireplace would provide a wonderful warmth and ambience to the room. While technology could achieve much the same effect, some things were better when done the old way.

Even though he knew enough not to stand close to the large window, he could see a faint glow in the distance, a sign of the terrible destruction that *Firebird* had already unleashed on what had been an underground weapons complex near his home. Three men and a woman stood outside, watching over him. The team consisted of Lazarus, Diana, and two other men from their crew. Lazarus smiled to himself over the fact that they'd been able to approach to within a hundred meters of the main house in complete secrecy, shrouded in the total darkness. Under normal circumstances, it wouldn't have been enough, but the devastation to Austin's weapons complex had also compromised his security. He would have to rely on more traditional means of protecting himself.

One thing he'd done long ago made the intruders' task more difficult. The reason Lazarus had approached no further than a hundred meters was that that was the point where there were no countermeasures that could

prevent the intruders from being spotted visually. All veg-
etation of any kind had been removed, leaving a clear
field of fire from the house. While that countermeasure
was intended primarily to deal with any cheaters that
might have slipped past the outer wall, it served equally
well to deny cover to human invaders.

The general layout of the outside of Austin's home
was known, however, and the intruders were prepared
for the problem. Each of them carried something akin
to what had once been called an antitank weapon. It
was light, weighing less than fifteen pounds; simple to
use; and effective up to three hundred meters. It was
designed to be disposable after discharging one round.
The plan was for one round to be fired through the great
window, another to be fired into the front door, another
to go through the back door, and for the last to be fired
into the chimney where it emerged from the roof. They
would then storm the house and finish off Austin, if he
managed to survive the attack. The plan was strikingly
similar to the one that had devastated major portions of
Austin's home on Earth many decades earlier.

They were wearing headsets with visual displays that
were easy to read in the gloom. Lazarus sent a brief signal for his team to get ready to move in a few seconds.
The leader had activated a countdown program that dis-
played the time remaining until the attack was to begin.
He watched the display tick off the last few seconds.

Just before the display reached zero, he was startled
to see and hear a round already being fired at one of
the targets. He cursed as he heard the distinct sound
of the back door disintegrating. The man must have

been slightly jumpy and pulled the trigger a little early. Lazarus would pull a knife across the man's throat if his action cost them a successful mission. Lazarus fired at the great window. At almost the same time, he saw the window shatter. He had a good view of the chimney from his position, and he watched as it seemed to both burst outward as well as collapse downward. The front door blew inward, flinging deadly wooden missiles that blanketed the interior.

At virtually the same moment, every intruder started running toward the main house. They knew that all protection for Austin was gone. If he wasn't already removed from among the living due to the explosions, he would be dead within moments.

From multiple areas, angry flames shot up toward the dark sky, giving the place an illumination that it had never known before. Thick, dark smoke followed more slowly. Even from a distance, the scene looked hellish. The house that had been part of a picturesque setting for years was now partly in ruins. The great window was gone, with nothing but a ragged frame remaining, providing a path for flames to pour out wildly. The Phoenix leader was framed against the light from the flames. He slowed down to pick his way carefully through the remains of the wall, in order to avoid the fiery tendrils and find a path inside. One of his team headed straight toward the window, and the other one circled around to the other side of the house.

—⋅—

As Austin turned to look at a display, a terrible explosion rocked the room. Without thinking, he pulled out his pistol and started to get under cover. The back door disintegrated in a burst of flame. He had been standing on the other side of the fireplace and was knocked off his feet and away from it as a wave of air and fire rushed toward him. An instant later, the great window dissolved into thousands of fragments as another round from an antitank weapon detonated. The front door blew inward, sending deadly slivers the size of spikes hurling everywhere. Because the intruders had fired their other weapons early, Austin had been thrown out of the way of much of the blast from the window and the front door. With the great window gone, much of the force from the back door's destruction moved like an angry wave of air and launched debris out the hole from which Austin had often admired the views of the spectacular mountain in the distance.

The fireplace exploded, collapsing into a pile of large stones and wooden beams. The force hurled Austin across the room, slamming him hard into another wooden beam and leaving him partially stunned. He blinked as debris from the beam splashed into his face. For a moment, nightmares from long ago flooded into his mind, competing with the images from the present. Adrenaline surged through him, urging him to move even as the clouds in his head continued to swirl. His head cleared up enough to notice that someone was firing at him, and he shifted position as another round pierced the wall where he'd been kneeling a moment earlier. He realized that he'd lost his pistol and was now without a weapon.

Part of the ceiling had collapsed nearby, and he found cover behind a pile of debris. He turned and saw a dark figure outlined in the wreck of the archway that had led to the back door. Even partially stunned as he was, Austin knew the image was not that of a friend. He picked up a short log and threw it at the dark image. The man tried to bring his rifle up to fire back, but he too late by a fraction of a second. The log knocked aside the rifle, which buried itself within a pile of burning beams.

The intruder paused for only a moment before pulling out a knife and moving toward his target. Austin grabbed a handful of embers and threw them into the man's face. The killer stopped, swinging his knife blindly as he tried to scratch the hot fragments away and clear his vision. Austin stepped inside the man's swing and grabbed his arm. He heard the distinctive sound of the limb breaking as he twisted it and forced the knife through the man's chest and into his heart. After making sure that the wounds were lethal, Austin pulled the knife out, stepping away from the body as it collapsed.

He heard what sounded like gunfire coming from another part of the house, creating more anxiety as he fought for his life. *Where is Liz?* he thought. He felt a pang of regret over her decision to stay with him. She'd given him no choice, as he had expected, but she had agreed to send their kids over to the Albretti home. Austin had taken the time over the years to teach Liz how to take care of herself. Although she was at heart a kind, gentle soul, she'd do whatever it took to defend her loved ones.

She had been keeping an eye on a different part of the house, mainly the rear, in case any invaders decided to take the long way toward them. Austin tried to remember precisely where she had been at the time of the explosion, but he was having trouble focusing. He'd lost his link, which had kept him in touch with his wife and could have given him her location. There was a lot of smoke in the room, and visibility sucked, which distracted him further. The nightmares from earlier years kept crowding into his thoughts as well.

———

Liz got to her feet, unsteady for a moment as the house shuddered from the multiple impacts that had torn it half apart. She'd been upstairs, keeping an eye on the area behind the house, when she saw a figure push its way past a shattered door. Without thinking, she dove toward the person, realizing an instant later that the intruder was a woman. Her attack caught her opponent off guard. The intruder fired a couple of rounds from a pistol without being able to aim properly, causing no damage. As Liz kicked the woman's weapon away from her hand, she had to deflect a shot to her ribs from the assailant's foot. The shot hadn't caused any damage, but her own pistol went flying in the distance. She saw a blade flash briefly in the unearthly light, and she managed to grab the arm, seeking to bury the edge in the intruder's body.

Although the intruder had a wiry strength, Liz was extremely fit, and her training from Austin kicked in as she sought to stay alive. So long as she had control over the woman's knife hand, she didn't worry about bruised ribs. However, that wasn't her first objective, as she knew her husband probably needed help badly, considering the force and location of the explosions that had rocked the building. She kept a firm grip on her assailant as she pushed her into a wall with bruising force. The other woman grunted but didn't let go of the knife.

The woman's feet swept outward, and Liz found herself falling backward. Rather than letting go of the knife to steady herself, she pulled the woman with her, forcing them both to hit the floor painfully. They twisted around so that they were on their feet again, still fighting their holds on each other. Liz's strength flowed from the fact she was fighting for the sake of the man she loved. There was no hint of mercy in either set of eyes as each sought an opening to finish off the other.

———————

Suddenly, Austin heard two people crash into the room in the front of the ruined house, locked in a death grip and heedless of the dangers around them. They also seemed oblivious to the fact that they were getting torn up by the debris. Austin realized with mixed emotions that one of them was Liz. With a start, he realized that the other one was also a woman. He now knew for certain that this wasn't just a repeat of images from his past.

He turned and saw another dark figure outlined against the flames. The man wasn't anyone he recognized, so Austin assumed he was another enemy. He knew he couldn't cover the distance between them before being cut down by the man's rifle. The new intruder spotted the two figures who were still locked in their death struggles and moved toward them. He couldn't fire his weapon without hitting his colleague, so he slung the rifle over his shoulder and pulled out a knife.

With the rifle out of the way, Austin saw his opportunity. He charged at the man from behind, grabbed the weapon, and yanked it back hard. His adversary was pulled off his feet when the strap caught around his neck and arm. As Austin stabbed the intruder in the throat, the man kicked out with his feet. Austin tumbled backward and lost his grip on his knife. The man's wound was mortal, and he sank to his knees, but impending death didn't loosen his grip on his rifle.

As he swung his weapon back around toward Austin, several shots rang out, and red holes appeared in his head. His rifle flew from his lifeless hands as his body collapsed into a heap at Austin's feet. Austin looked back to see Liz, who'd apparently knocked out or killed her foe. She'd managed to find a pistol, probably from her adversary, and had used it to kill Austin's foe. Triumph turned to horror as a moment later a red hole appeared on her chest. As she slumped toward the floor, she tossed her pistol toward Austin.

The Phoenix leader had finally found a way into the hellish wreck of what had been Austin's house. He tried briefly to fan away the smoke in hopes of improving visibility, with little effect. He watched in the hazy gloom as one of his men tried to kill Austin, only to be stopped by someone whom they had somehow missed. It had been Lazarus who had aimed his weapon and cut down Austin's ally with a single round into the chest, not knowing the identity of his target.

He sneered at the gesture of the stricken person in tossing a pistol to Austin and at the image of some debris collapsing onto the now-prostrate form. He knew that only in ancient Hollywood would that pistol reach Austin before Lazarus was able to shoot the man full of holes. A moment later, however, the intruder found himself shifting targets as a knife embedded itself into a nearby timber. He'd allowed himself to be distracted over the gesture with the pistol and hadn't realized that Austin had yanked his knife from the corpse nearby.

Lazarus was furious. After their careful casing of the place, they had missed at least one person and still had no idea whether Austin's wife was nearby. He had seen one of his men die, there was no sign of the other one, and he had to assume that Diana was lying somewhere either dead or unconscious.

He laid down a line of covering fire with his rifle and advanced toward his enemy. Despite the horror of the moment, Austin had no choice but to duck. As he moved, he tried to shift to a different spot, but another burst of gunfire drove him back. He knew that if he stayed where he was, he'd be dead in a few moments. He reached out with his pistol and fired several rounds in the direction of the intruder.

As Lazarus flinched, Austin dove toward a large pile of debris with various layers that might offer more protection. Another burst of gunfire followed him. His arms were bloody from sliding into the jagged shards. He saw an opening through the debris that wouldn't be visible to his adversary and took aim. He waited until the intruder walked into view and then fired two rounds toward the man's leg. He knew he had scored a hit when he heard a scream.

Although the wound was painful, it didn't stop Lazarus from pursuing his quarry. While sprawled in the debris, he did a quick self-assessment and pulled himself up. He limped out of range and worked his way around to where he could get a good shot at his target. Austin saw a moment where he could get off a shot and pulled the trigger. The empty *click* was loud enough for both men to hear. His enemy smiled and kept moving into position. Austin had to shift again, and in doing so, he leaned against an unsteady part of the debris.

Suddenly, a beam fell across his legs, pinning him. Although he knew he wouldn't be able to get the beam off before his stalker got into position to shoot him, he never stopped struggling. Lazarus reached his position and brought his rifle to bear on Austin. He pulled the trigger and they both heard a *click*.

No! Lazarus thought with frustration. He had lost his extra clips at some point and knew that there was no time to look for them. Fortune was on his side, though—he still had a knife and saw that Austin had no weapon.

As he approached Austin deliberately, he saw his prey continue to push deep into the debris to lever himself up. Although there was a little movement, it wouldn't be enough. *His hands are probably cut to shreds by now*, Lazarus thought to himself. For the first time, he spoke. "Look around, Austin, at the ruin I've made of everything you hold dear. Does it bring back any nightmares for you? Have any images of your dead first wife come back to haunt you? How about any touching moments when she died in your arms? Speaking of wives, know that if your wife is around here, she'll die. If she isn't, then she'll be a widow, since I promised my backers that you would die, and I'm about to keep that promise."

Austin realized that Lazarus didn't know he'd shot Liz. His cold, blue eyes bored into his enemy's face as he said, "Do you really think so? Who are your backers?"

Lazarus smiled and said, "My backers don't have a name that would mean anything to you, but I can give you an idea, anyway."

"Don't bother," Austin replied. "From the smell, I'd say your name used to be Flynn. You and your ilk are creatures of the aliens now."

Lazarus seemed slightly crestfallen by Austin's anticipation of his news. "Don't try to tell me that you've known all along, Austin. If you had, you'd never have let us line up outside the door to your system. We've spent many months setting up our elaborate smokescreen around Shiloh, and no one ever saw it for what it really was. Like everyone else, you focused on your ridiculous concerns about whether we'd take away your business interests or go into competition with you or be bad neighbors and disrupt your existence here. It was so easy to distract you while we set our trap. Thanks for falling into it."

Austin shrugged. "I always knew you and your people were twisted, and I knew there was more to it than what we surmised after figuring out that there was a connection with the aliens' technology. I've never been comfortable with the notion that you and your people were just greedy savages who happened to be duped into using the alien technology.

"I was damned-near certain when I watched your ships begin their attack. There's no way colonists would have fought in a highly coordinated way, with no prior training, just to establish a base on a sister world. You also had to know that, even with the advantage of the alien technology and the element of surprise, you would have lost the battle but for the help you received from the attack by the alien code on our communications network."

Austin sized the man up with a shrewd glance. "Your names are interesting. The meaning behind yours is obvious. I take it Pandora is Harrington. Considering the evil that she's unleashed on the world, she was well named. I'll bet the name Diana comes from the huntress of Roman mythology, which would make her Powers. I don't know the others' names; they're probably some of the lowlifes that you used as operatives, or maybe some of the scientists you hired."

"You once told me that we would have a most unpleasant conversation, Austin," Lazarus recalled. "This is the last one you'll ever have, and I'm actually enjoying it," he taunted.

Austin's cold gaze held its own challenge. "We're not done yet. All I can say is, it won't turn out well for you."

Lazarus's composure slipped, and he decided that it was time for Austin to die. As his razor-sharp blade moved toward Austin, a bloody hand reached out from the debris and grabbed the intruder's wrist. Austin jerked backward with his shoulders, throwing his adversary off balance. Austin's other hand came out of the debris, equally bloody but holding a jagged piece of glass. The predator's hand grabbed Austin's wrist, and a deadly game commenced. Austin never took his eyes off the face of his opponent. Although Austin was still pinned by the beam, the other man was off balance and couldn't shift his position. The wound in his leg made it even more difficult to get any traction.

Lazarus couldn't believe the power of the hand that clamped onto the wrist of his knife hand. He felt the first signs of true panic as he realized that his hand was starting to go numb from the force of Austin's grip. He also realized that the bloody hand that was holding the glass shard was moving slowly toward his throat. He looked back at the man he had thought was his prey and saw that the coldness of Austin's eyes had extended to his face, creating a grim look that held no hint of mercy. He was looking into the face of death itself.

Lazarus realized that although Austin was the one who was pinned, *he* was the one who was really trapped. He tried desperately to halt the movement of the glass shard, but he could only stare at it with helpless fear. He fought to wrench his other hand away from Austin's death grip, without success. He no longer knew whether he was even holding his knife. Suddenly, Austin channeled his fury into a great surge and thrust his own makeshift blade through the intruder's throat, severing the artery.

"The only thing you got right was that this would be our last conversation," Austin said with contempt. "You should have paid more attention when I said it wouldn't end well for you. You were so intent on re-creating what happened long ago that you didn't even realize I did the same thing to you that I did to the piece of shit who tried to kill me on Earth." Lazarus tried to gurgle a reply but collapsed. Austin shoved the dying man away. He was finally able to shift the beam enough to get his legs free.

The fury of the moment passed, and his head cleared enough for him to remember Liz. He cried with anguish as he saw the debris covering the place where he had last seen her. He sprang over and started hurling boulders and large beams out of the way with frantic speed, heedless of the impact on his lacerated arms and hands. Finally, he saw a hand—ashen instead of a healthy color. In what seemed far too many moments, he had cleared enough rubble out of the way to pull his wife's body out. He prayed that Liz had managed to avoid any significant internal injuries. At least she was still breathing. He fought to control the urge to sob as he held her in his arms amid the ruins, as he had done with another woman he'd loved long ago. Her eyes fluttered open weakly, and then she spoke.

"Did we stop the bastard, Sam?"

"Yes, Liz, we did," he replied tenderly. Upon hearing the news, Liz fell silent.

A moment later, Austin was sprawled senseless on the floor nearby, as Diana stood over him. "He was *my* bastard, Austin. You have no idea how much you're going to pay for stopping him."

She took no satisfaction from the fact they'd brought down Austin's wife. Diana dropped the log she'd used to clobber him and dragged him toward the shuttle that was parked just outside the perimeter fence, making no effort to be gentle with her unconscious burden. She ignored the fires that were still burning as she made her way to her ticket to escape. She didn't worry about whether there were any cheaters roaming around nearby; she was prepared to give a lethal reminder to any of the dangerous animals that this was not the night to tangle with her.

CHAPTER SIXTEEN

As Diana's shuttle approached the huge ship still in orbit, she opened her link to *Firebird*'s bridge. She heard the familiar voice of Pandora. "Tell me you have good news, Diana. Is Austin finally dead?"

"No, but his wife is, and I have Austin with me. He's the worse for the wear and out cold. After I get through with him, he'll wish he were dead."

"What's wrong?" Pandora asked in alarm. "Where's Lazarus?"

"Lazarus is dead," Diana said tersely. "Austin cut his throat."

Pandora's only answer was a terrible shriek.

"Get a hold of yourself!" Diana said sharply. "We need to get out of here, and we don't have much time before their transports show up and surround us. I want you to check to see if any transport is heading this way."

"Yes, I see one on the display."

"Just the one?"

"Yes," Pandora replied, somewhat mechanically.

"We still have a chance, then. Fortunately, Austin's home is on the opposite side of the planet right now, so this infernal rock is blocking their view of us."

"What good will that do? The Citadel moon is out of position to shield us from them. The moment we try to leave, they'll see us."

Diana hit the console in frustration. "You're no use to me right now! Georgia! Can you hear me?"

A new face appeared. "I hear you, Diana. What do you need?"

"That's better. Get everything ready to move the moment that transport enters into orbit. With any luck, we'll keep moving with them and leave once they halt over Austin's home." She looked at a display. "I'll be there within sixty seconds, and I'll take care of the rest. Have we cleared out the logjam around the loaders?

Georgia shook her head. "We don't have the people to do it."

A malicious look came over Diana's face. "I think I know how to solve that problem. Tell Heph I want to talk to him."

By the time Diana entered the bridge, Pandora had regained some of her composure. "Tell me what happened down there, and why you're alive when Lazarus is dead," she began.

Diana was in no mood for conversation at the moment, and stood inches in front of the other woman. "I don't have time to talk things over with you. You don't know anything about running this ship, even with the help of our backers' technology, so shut up while I try to get us out of here."

Pandora fumed but stayed quiet.

Diana moved to the navigator's chair. She glanced at a display and turned to Georgia. "What's the word on our other ships?"

Georgia gestured at another display and replied, "There are only two of them left among the inner group that came with us, and they've each suffered heavy damage."

"What about the Citadel ships?" she demanded. "Tell me we've taken most of them out in the bargain."

She pointed at a display for her answer. "They've taken some damage, but their ships are still functional. Just as we were on the offensive initially due to the element of surprise, they've returned the favor this time. While we were distracted by what we thought would be an easy kill with *Pathfinder*, they pounced on us after hiding within that mothball-fleet junkyard of theirs. They also seem to be coordinating their maneuvers more effectively this time."

Diana stifled any further comments, as a display reminded them a ship was approaching. "Is everything secure for maneuvering?"

"Yes," Georgia nodded. "We can move anytime."

"Good. We'll move in twenty seconds."

As the countdown ran down to zero, *Firebird* began to accelerate, matching the movements of the Citadel transport precisely. Finally, as the transport hovered in orbit directly over what was left of Austin's home, the way was clear for escape.

As they raced away from Citadel, Diana saw from a display that the battle had moved far away from the crippled scout ship. "Heph," she called on her link, "is everything ready?"

"Yes, Diana," he replied. "The cargo holds have been prepared as you wanted."

"Good. The moment we get in range, put some lines on that ship and haul it inside."

———

The shuttles touched down near the ruins of the main house, some coming from the transport and some coming from other settlers. The only illumination came from the fingers of flames that flickered from a few places within the house. Some of the searchers moved around the compound, checking to see if there was anyone in need of help. Others made their way to the shattered pieces of what had once been a beautiful house, not knowing if anyone was even alive. A few checked out the crater where the weapons complex had once been buried.

As Sara looked inside, she saw Mark's wife, Karen, kneeling in the debris, holding Liz. Several of the rescuers broke down and cried as the medical team moved in, detecting faint signs of life and working feverishly to prevent the loss of another brave soul.

The sight of Liz stunned Sara, and she wandered through the wreckage, desperate for any sign of Austin. She whirled as a voice called out, "We've found a body; it looks like a man." Just as she reached the grisly find, the rescuer shook his head. "It isn't Sam."

Sara flinched at the emotions racing through her mind when she realized that her friend might be the dead person in the rubble.

Another voice called out, "We've found another body; it looks like a man." The rescuer whistled. "Someone cut his throat," he said, before someone else stifled him for forgetting about Liz lying nearby. Once again, Sara raced over toward the body, only to find that it wasn't Austin either.

The compound was large, and it would take some time to check out every place where a man could have crawled while his life ebbed away from a lethal wound. Sara went over to Karen, and they held each other in silence for a while. The searchers continued with their grim task, but no one had yet located Sam or anyone else.

"I found a blood trail," a voice called out. "Wait, there may be two trails." The searcher pointed toward the perimeter wall. "The trails lead that way." Several people followed the trails as the search throughout the compound continued. Reluctantly, Sara had to pull away from her friend and her sister-in-law and head back to her shuttle. There was still work to do.

CHAPTER SEVENTEEN

Albretti was the only one aboard *Pathfinder* who watched the approach of *Firebird,* wondering what it meant for Citadel. Yabuno was still too busy trying to bring the network back online to watch any other displays, while Albretti's crews were equally occupied trying to restore their own systems.

"How are you doing, Bret?" he asked. "*Firebird* is coming back, and it's slowing down for an approach. If we can't do anything, it's probably a rock or an EMP burst in a moment."

"I wish I could say we're almost there, but I still need more time."

"We've run out of time. They're so close they could practically touch us, so I guess they want to be sure they don't miss." He turned to his friend. "It's been an honor to know you."

"Save the honors," he snapped. "We aren't done until there's nothing left but outer space."

Even as Albretti admired his friend's spirit, he frowned. "Something's wrong. I see a rail gun deployed, but there isn't a rock in it." He manipulated a display. "Wow! Something pounded the hell out of their load-ers. Looks like everything is jammed tight." He grinned. "That must have been courtesy of Sam's rail gun on Citadel. I guess you're right; we aren't done yet."

His grin faded as he watched the hatch to the main cargo hold opening and lines being deployed in their direction. "We may not be done, but I sure as hell don't like where this is going next. Looks like they want to haul us inside their monster."

———•—

With *Pathfinder* secured within *Firebird*'s hold, the huge vessel once again raced toward the safe path, and escape. A check with a display confirmed that although there was a transport in pursuit, there were no vessels near enough to stop the Phoenix ship.

For the first time in many hours, Austin, Yabuno and Albretti were in the same room together. At three differ-ent places in the compartment, each man was tied to the legs of a desk that was fastened securely to the deck. The desks were too far apart for them to reach each other. No one had tended to the wounds on Austin's arms from the fight in the wreck of his home, and they were caked with dried blood.

In spite of the moment, Yabuno said, "Pardon the cliché, but I'm sure glad to see you, Sam. There wasn't much reason to hope you'd come away from their visit in one piece."

Austin chuckled lightly in thanks. "Same here, both of you." The warmth faded from his gaze. "I have some bad news about Liz."

The color drained from Albretti's face as he asked, "What happened?"

"They attacked my home, although 'attacked' doesn't begin to describe what they did. The main house has been pretty much blasted to rubble. Liz insisted on being there with me, while the kids stayed with Karen. I think four people came after us, including Lazarus and Diana. At one point, Liz knocked out Diana, then took out one of the others, and then I took out the other one. The guy she shot was about to shoot me, so she saved my life."

Austin's gaze darkened with pain. "Lazarus showed up and shot her in the chest. I don't know if she's alive or dead. She was still breathing when I saw her last. Before I could do anything further, someone clobbered me from behind. I know it wasn't Lazarus," his said grimly, "because I stabbed him through the throat before checking out Liz. I assume it was Diana." A look of revulsion washed across his face. "You aren't going to like hearing who these people really are."

A voice spoke up. "The feeling's mutual, Sam."

Their heads whirled to see Pandora and Diana standing in the hatchway. For a moment, malevolent glares were exchanged wordlessly. Austin noted that Diana had taken the time to clean and bandage her wounds from her fight with Liz.

Yabuno stared hard at Pandora before he spoke. "There's only one bitch I've known like you, and her name is Courtney Harrington."

Albretti looked at Diana and said, "That must make you Mara Powers. You've changed your appearance several times now, and I can't say I like any version of you."

As both women bristled over the insults, Austin spoke. "The last time we saw you, you were on your way to being taken apart by the aliens. What happened; did they get the same feeling I have every time I see you and decide they didn't want to be anywhere near you?"

Pandora slapped Austin's face. "Don't talk about things you don't understand. What we went through makes hell seem tame by comparison." She shuddered slightly as she continued. "They did what they said they'd do and took us apart. They did it in both a physical as well as a mental sense.

"Of course, if people are just taken apart, they don't last very long," she said with a shrug. "At some point, after they'd learned about us from having taken some of us apart and watching those people die, they decided to put some people back together."

"At first, those people died pretty quickly too, because the aliens still didn't know enough about how we worked," Diana said. "Others were put back together, but weren't really human anymore. Sometimes the bodies worked but not the minds, and sometimes it was the other way around.

"They didn't take us in any particular order; some of us just happened to be luckier in being among the later ones they took apart, if it's possible to be lucky when being taken apart. They had gotten better at putting us back together by then."

"Why don't you look anything like you did originally?" Austin asked.

"That type of physical appearance didn't mean anything to them, so although they learned about the distinctions between males and females, they didn't worry about matching things like hair color, facial features, size, and so forth, with what we'd been like before they took us apart. The calendar age still matched, but not much else, except by accident. Believe me, if you survived what we survived, the last thing you worried about was how your features had changed." She gestured at the front of her body. "If you still had the same physical equipment, then you were doing OK."

"Where did all this happen?" Austin asked. "The aliens couldn't have had another base nearby like the one we destroyed. Did you go back to their home world?"

"We were taken back to another base, which we believe is closer to their home world but still a vast distance from it. We don't know how close it is, because we don't know how long we were traveling. Our backers haven't shared everything with us."

"You were obviously transported back to our original solar system at some point," Austin said. "We know no alien ships actually entered the system. How did you get back in?"

Diana shook her head. "You don't need to know the details. Just know that space is vast, even when talking about the edge to a solar system. We just had to find a place that was sufficiently far from any monitoring devices and enter the system."

"You couldn't have reentered the system in the shuttles you'd been using when you were captured. If you had, those shuttles would have shown up somewhere," Austin countered. "They still belong to Citadel, and they'd be too hot for anyone to handle, even among the more dubious elements based out in space. The Citadel Group is very good at keeping tabs on such things, and Citadel has been clear about what will happen to anyone hiding that kind of information. Also, people would figure out the connection with you and start to talk. There hasn't been even a hint of anything about you."

"That will just have to be our secret, Austin," Diana said coldly.

"Why didn't you just try to hide and start new lives? You were already dead to us; with the changes to your features, we probably never would have discovered you. I'll bet you even had access to some of Courtney's money."

The women managed to stifle most of what sounded like a harsh bark at Austin's question. "You can't really understand everything that happened to us," Pandora said. "When they put us back together, they made some changes to what makes us who we are. Although we know what we were before, we are compelled to obey them now. Even if we were to hear nothing from them for decades and set up new lives for ourselves, the moment they were to give us an order, we would obey it, even at the cost of our own lives."

"That's one reason for the new names," Diana said. "We never use our former ones, even among ourselves."

"Who came up with them? Some of them seem to be more revealing than you may intend," Austin noted.

"They came from the mind of Lazarus," Pandora said. "He obviously had some notions about several of us, and the aliens lacked enough of a reference to be able to select anything on their own." Her features showed her displeasure. "Evidently, he decided that I was akin to Pandora, with the cliché about her having loosed all the evils into the world." Her expression was thoughtful for a moment. "I'll agree that I stirred things up, but I didn't have any choice."

"Still in self-pitying denial, I see," Austin said pointedly. He looked at Diana. "You were the assassin, and I know you once hunted Sara Albretti, so I understand your name. Lazarus rose from the dead, so his name is understandable. Why Georgia and Heph for the others in your inner circle?"

"Georgia was once Dr. Farmer," Diana replied. "The name George means 'farmer,' among other things, in Greek."

"I see," Austin said, "Other than his own name, which came from the Bible, Lazarus stayed with Greek origins or sometimes their Roman counterparts for names." A flash of understanding appeared in his face. "I'd guess that Heph is a nickname for the Greek god Hephaestus, who was the god of metalworking and crafts. I'll bet he was the one in charge of your space yard."

Even Pandora had to acknowledge the sharpness of Austin's mind. "You win, Sam. Fortunately, you never had a clue when it mattered. You were so distracted by the prospect of having an unwelcome neighbor, you never considered whether we had anything else in mind."

"One thing I understand is that you and Lazarus were an item," Austin asked. "Is that something the aliens did to you?"

Pandora nodded. "When the aliens understood the concept of marriage, they decided to bond some of us together. They didn't quite understand that marriage is supposed to be something that two people choose for themselves, though. However, it's a moot point; once we were bonded, we may as well have been married. In fact, we often use the word 'marriage' to describe the bond."

"Why did they bond the two of you together?"

"They learned that I had once had great power among humans and was, in fact, the person making the decisions relating to the deal we struck with them." Her eyes narrowed. "That was the deal you ruined, of course."

"How sad for them," Austin said without sympathy.

"They decided that while I was a leader, I did not always have proper control of myself, so they bonded me to someone that they believed to be strong in his own right. They assumed that the combination of the two of us would make for a stronger leader."

Diana spoke. "It didn't work out that way, though. In fact, they decided that Lazarus would be the better leader after all and demoted Pandora. She still has problems with it," she concluded gloatingly.

Pandora glared at the other woman. "One thing I wish they'd dealt with was the fact that this one never gave up her desire for Lazarus, even after he had been bonded with me. She tried more than once to give herself to him and to turn him against me."

Austin looked at her, waiting for the answer.

"That's part of the bonding. We don't cheat on each other, even if we have physical desires for others," she gloated back at Diana. "It drove her insane every time she tried and failed to seduce him, especially since they'd once been lovers."

"You deserved each other, Courtney," Austin said. He noted that she seemed ill at ease with the mention of her former name. "I see that hearing your real name bothers you, but you'll need a better name than Pandora if you want to be called something else."

"What about Her Majesty?" Yabuno said. "It always worked for me."

Before Yabuno ended up on the receiving end of something harsh, Austin intervened. "Why do you call the aliens your 'backers'?" he asked. "From what you've said, they're more like your masters."

"They *are* our masters," Pandora said simply. "Originally, when we were sent to Earth's solar system to set up our operations, we were instructed never to refer to them as anything other than our backers, even among ourselves. That way, we would never make a mistake in public. People understand that commercial ventures often have backers, but are confused and leery about having masters." She looked at Austin with cold amusement. "Even though we're long past worrying about maintaining our subterfuge, the habit has stayed in place."

"One thing I don't understand is how you became sufficiently advanced to be able to design and build your ships. While I get it that the aliens supplied the really advanced technology, building your own yard was pretty damned impressive."

"Several of us were given special knowledge for specific tasks," Pandora explained. "Heph was given what he needed to design the ships and the yard needed to build them. He was originally a scientist, so it made sense to build upon what he already knew."

"I was given special knowledge to operate those ships," Diana added. "As impressive as it may sound, they really only gave us knowledge that they obtained from the traffic over your network." She looked at Yabuno. "You never understood what our backers had done, until it was too late."

"If you can't be good, I guess it helps to be lucky," Yabuno muttered.

"Who received the knowledge needed to find the minerals that financed everything in the first place?" Austin asked.

"Georgia did," Diana replied, "although it was more like they just told us where to look."

"What special knowledge did Her Majesty receive?" Yabuno asked sarcastically.

Pandora fumed as Diana couldn't resist answering the question. "She didn't receive any special knowledge. She's just as ignorant now as she was before we ever met our backers."

"What happened to the colonists you brought with you?" Austin asked. "We know they left with you, in stasis, yet you showed up here with a hold full of rocks, and no passengers." He didn't bother to hide his revulsion. "Where did you dump them?"

"Far away, where their bodies will drift in space forever," she replied dismissively. "Once we left Earth's system, we appeared somewhere else, dumped the bodies, and collected the rocks we'd need for our attack. We then got back on course and appeared in your system on schedule."

"They didn't deserve to die like that. Don't you feel *anything* for humanity?" Austin asked sadly.

"We aren't part of humanity anymore."

"If you're their creatures now, what are they like?"

"We really don't know; we've never met them directly. Even when we were taken apart, it was done remotely, although not with conventional tools."

"We just know that we do what they tell us to do," Diana said.

"What are they telling you to do now?"

"I know you're pumping us for information, Sam," Pandora said, "but it won't matter anyway. What little remains of Citadel will be destroyed, and we will take back to our backers the ancient derelict that you've been holding in the Citadel system for safekeeping. As you know, they've wanted that ship since long before even you were born."

"You're on the run," Austin scoffed, "and you fell short this time, with all the advantages you had."

"Most of your fleet here has already been destroyed," Albretti said. "We'll get to the rest soon enough."

"You forget about our fleet in the other solar system, which will have already moved to destroy all major human habitations on Earth, Mars, the Moon, and elsewhere," Pandora said. "Thanks to weaklings like President Lee, the places back there aren't nearly as well defended as here, so they'll fall easily. Our ships will then head here and join our fleet from the outer part of this system, and we'll complete our task."

"By that time, we will have rebuilt everything, and you'll still have lost."

Pandora looked at all three prisoners the way a cat eyes a helpless mouse. "We have Sam Austin, the leader of Citadel, plus Bret Yabuno, the technical genius of the place, and Joe Albretti, the famed captain of *Pathfinder*, all under our control. You represent much of the heart of Citadel. Without you, the rest will be lost.

"We have a few hours to go before we reach the safe path, and we need some assistance in clearing away the items that have blocked the loader. Although there's little gravity to worry about, everything is jammed together so tightly that plenty of muscle will be needed to loosen it enough to clear away. Since most of the functions are automated through their technology, we need almost no crew for these ships. In this case, that means the people on board *Pathfinder* will do the work for us."

"I think the aliens have left you delusional, Courtney, if you believe our people will help you," Austin replied.

"No delusions are involved." She turned toward Diana, who approached a display.

"Fortunately, one of the things about our relationship with our backers is that sometimes we have a certain amount of leeway in how to go about doing their bidding," Diana began.

"What do you mean?"

Hatred rippled over her face. "In different ways, Lazarus meant a lot to both of us, so neither of us has any love lost for you, Austin. That means we can make an example of you that will also motivate the *Pathfinder* crew to obey us." She brought up an image of the prisoners. "This is now being broadcast to the crew."

She looked straight at the display as she spoke. "You can see we have Sam Austin, Captain Joe Albretti, and Bret Yabuno restrained. Just so you understand we mean business, Austin is about to die. If you still refuse to help us, another one will die. If you make it necessary, all three will die, and then we'll start with other members of your crew, to provide additional motivation."

She moved toward Austin with her knife. "While I'd like to cut your throat the way you did to Lazarus, I don't want to interfere with your ability to beg for help as you bleed out, so I'll cut an artery in your wrist." Austin was unable to resist as she grabbed a wrist and made a deep cut, as promised.

Austin summoned vast reserves of energy to break free and avoid the fate the Phoenix women had planned for him. The effort was in vain, and his strength faded as blood gushed from his wound. Yabuno and Albretti fought with inhuman strength against their bonds as Austin's blood drained into a shocking red pool around him. Their bonds held, and they watched in helpless fury as their friend's face became a pale mask of what it had been.

"Keep your eyes focused on me," Yabuno pleaded, as Albretti snarled a curse at the humans who were no longer human. Austin willed his eyes to stay locked on Yabuno's for longer than seemed possible, before he finally lost his struggle and his gaze became unfocused. The man who had led Citadel against the evil launched against them by both humans and aliens slumped to one side, and the bleeding stopped. Diana stepped over the motionless body and confirmed there was no pulse. She dropped the knife at his feet and turned back toward the display.

"There are still two more people here I can kill if you don't do as we say. By the time I reach you, you'd better have made the right decision, or I'll just walk back here and kill another one of your leaders while you watch." She turned the display off, and the women walked out of the compartment without another word.

CHAPTER EIGHTEEN

The two men had no idea how much time had passed, but it had been enough that the fact they were still alive meant that the crew must be helping the Phoenix people. They couldn't bear to look at the body or the pool of blood that reached out from it. Austin had always appeared indestructible to them, so it seemed impossible that he could be dead. He was supposed to be immortal!

"It wasn't supposed to end like this," Yabuno said. "He was supposed to outlive us all, telling tall tales about us to our great-great-grandchildren. Hell, even extreme radiation couldn't kill him." He smiled sadly as a thought came to mind. "He recovered fully and used to joke that the fact that he could still father children with no health problems or signs of genetic damage was proof he hadn't been sterilized. How can he be gone?"

"I don't know how I'll do it, but I will find a way to kill Harrington and Powers, with my own hands if necessary," Albretti said in a low voice that was thick with emotion. "I still owe them for kidnapping Sara back when they were supposedly still human, and for trying their best to inflict on her what they stepped into instead. Also, they've continued to inflict misery everywhere they turn." Albretti's emotions ebbed as the time of their captivity wore on.

"I wonder how long it will take to clear the logjam?" Yabuno said, with nothing else to talk about.

"What I saw looked pretty bad," Albretti replied. "It's funny that they have all that amazing technology, but they still need people to do some things for them."

"I'd like to do some things for them," Yabuno muttered.

The response was muffled. "What did you say?" Yabuno asked.

"I didn't say anything."

The response was muffled again.

"Now *you're* doing it," Albretti said.

"No, I'm pretty sure *I'm* doing it," a voice called out weakly.

The men stared in the direction of Austin's body and saw that it was moving. "Sam!" they said together. They wanted to rush to his aid, but they were still restrained.

"How is it you're still alive?" Yabuno asked.

Austin managed to raise his head to reply. His face still showed the strain from his ordeal, but it was no longer a pale death mask. "You remember a conversation we had several years before we even left for Citadel for the first time, about how things have been changing for me very gradually?" he asked, his voice still weak.

"Sure, I remember." Yabuno thought back. "You said you'd been getting stronger over the years and that you were healing more quickly than before from injuries. You didn't say anything about coming back from the dead, though!"

"It was news to me too. Anyway, you saw some more of the healing when I recovered from the massive radiation poisoning from passing through the radiation field."

"Yes, I remember that, Sam," Albretti said quietly.

"I'm sorry, Joe. I wasn't downplaying the actions of the others, like Gina."

"It's OK. If you hadn't survived, none of us would be alive today. What's that have to do with why you're alive?"

"The process has been continuing. If Diana had shot me in the head, I'd probably be dead, but by cutting an artery, whatever internal strength I have developed has been working on healing it. I'm not quite sure how my blood supply has recovered so quickly, but my wound is healed enough that I'm OK. I'm also not sure why I haven't suffered brain death from the lack of oxygen, but I'll guess that some sort of stasis took place while the healing was underway, preserving my vital organs. Who knows? Thank God they took me for dead."

"We're still stuck here, though," Yabuno reminded them. "Even *you* are sitting right where she left you. If she sees you, still alive, she'll probably shoot you in the head or find something even nastier to do to you to make sure you're dead."

"I'm not sure what would be nastier than what I went through this time," Austin said. He looked down at the knife on the deck. "She made a mistake, though." His feet weren't tied, and he was able to manipulate the weapon so that his two feet, pressed together, were able to hold it. He leaned down and a moment later had the weapon clenched between his teeth, near the hilt. He tilted his head toward the same wrist that had bled out not long ago, and he began the tedious job of sawing through the cords with something that wasn't intended for the task.

While Austin might be immortal, it didn't stop his neck from feeling the strain from working in an awkward position for a long time. Soon, there were new wounds near the old one as the blade moved back and forth and sometimes missed its target.

Yabuno and Albretti alternated between watching the hatch or the display. The display had been turned off when Diana had left, and it wouldn't be a good sign for them if it came back on. They didn't bother watching Austin, trusting that they'd know soon enough when he had freed himself. The slightest noise set them on edge, since they knew it could mean that the assassin had returned to finish the others off.

They heard a different kind of noise and turned back to see that Austin had finally cut the rope binding one of his arms. He flexed his fingers for a moment as the circulation returned painfully. In spite of the need for speed, Austin stayed patient. If he acted before his hand was able to hold the knife properly, the weapon and their hopes might bounce away out of their reach. Once the strength had returned to his hand, he took the knife from his teeth and made quick work of the rope restraining his other wrist. He pushed himself up out of the pool of his blood as he waited for the circulation to return to his other hand.

"God, you're a mess," Albretti said, grinning as Austin moved to him and sliced through his bonds in a couple of seconds. Albretti endured the pain of returning circulation as Austin freed Yabuno. In less than a minute, they'd recovered from their captivity. There was new strength in Austin's voice, and his movements were no longer hesitant.

Yabuno walked to the display, and they watched the scene near the loader. A lot of large pieces of equipment were still jammed next to the rail gun. "Nice job, Sam," Albretti said. He pointed to a spot near the rail gun. "I don't even have to hear them to know there's an argument over whether they have to cut away part of the housing for the rail gun itself."

They saw *Pathfinder*'s chief engineer arguing with a man they assumed was Heph, with each man making increasingly frustrated gestures.

Yabuno chuckled. "I'll bet the chief is giving Heph a load of crap about needing to cut away over half of the housing and then removing some of the internal components as well. While it *is* a nasty problem, he can probably get away with yanking the housing for the secondary unit and then sliding a couple of the interior mechanisms to one side. That should give them enough room to start moving stuff out of the way. It isn't a ten-minute job, but it shouldn't take a couple of hours either."

He shook his head. "Their man may have some special knowledge, but he doesn't have the practical experience that would tell him how to solve the problem that isn't in a technical manual."

Albretti spoke with a touch of humor in his voice. "Bret has a good point, and I think we should go help them with the problem." He looked at Austin with disapproval.

"We have to do something about your appearance, Sam. With all that blood, you'd stand out long before we could get close to the guards."

Austin shook his head. "There's no time, and we'll just have to take a chance that we won't meet any guards. It's a reasonable risk; Harrington said they don't have much of a crew anyway." He motioned toward the display. "What can you do about any alarms or the rest of their security?"

Yabuno was dubious. "This isn't our system, and I don't know their protocols. I may cause more harm than good, including letting them know we've gotten loose. I think we should take a chance that they wouldn't need many alarms relating to basic operations of the ship, considering how everything is automated. One thing I should be able to do without causing problems is to check out the path to get to our crew. The last thing we want to do is wander around this maze."

"OK, that makes sense," Austin nodded. He moved to pass through the hatch but found it was locked. He grinned sourly. "I guess it was too much to hope that she'd make two mistakes in the same room." He looked around the compartment and noticed an air vent in the ceiling. He stepped back and then took a quick leap up to it. He managed to cave in the cover and keep his grip on the edge, hanging there for a moment as he shifted around.

"You do realize that you can't fit through that opening," Yabuno said.

"I don't need to fit through it yet," Austin answered. The opening was only a couple of feet away from the hatch, and Austin jammed his legs into the hatchway and pushed back on the edge of the vent. The room wasn't designed as a prison, and the synthetic material began to give under the strain. Austin kept pushing until he'd crumpled the edge back far enough to fit through sideways. He held on tightly as he rotated ninety degrees and worked on forcing the other sides apart. In moments he had ripped apart enough of the false ceiling to be able to get up past it.

Austin wedged himself up, feet first, so that his legs were next to the hatch, above the false ceiling. He began to kick hard at the ceiling material, and a section broke away slightly from the bulkhead. He jumped back down and moved to Albretti. While standing on his shoulders, he levered himself up and grabbed hold of the ceiling that had pulled away, and then he braced his legs against the bulkhead. The process was a simple one; he just needed to hold on while straightening his legs out. It only took a moment for the entire section of the ceiling to tear away, exposing the bulkhead above the hatchway. The other two caught him as he fell to the deck.

"What does that do for us?" Albretti asked.

Yabuno grinned as he held the knife. "It exposes that housing up there, which should give us access to the mechanism for opening the hatch manually. I see a lip along the edge, which may give you something to grab. I'd better hold on to this thing until you've done your part; you've already been stabbed once today!"

Austin nodded, and they gave him another boost, carrying his weight on their shoulders. He grabbed the lip Yabuno had pointed out. This time, the muscles in his arms bulged with the force needed to fight against the material. He managed to lever himself up and brace his legs against the bulkhead once more. Finally, the housing tore away from the unit with a horrible shriek. Austin knocked the others to the ground from the force of his fall, but they suffered no injuries. Now it was Yabuno's turn to stand on his friends' shoulders and work the mechanism to open the hatch, using the knife as a tool. He had barely reached it when the hatch popped open.

He chuckled. "You just need to know what to look for!" He walked back to the display to call up the path and then joined his friends. The three men stole through the hatchway silently.

———

Diana was becoming frustrated at the pace of the work to clear out the jammed materials. She was also becoming suspicious of the efforts by *Pathfinder*'s chief to help them. She decided it was time to give them another incentive to step up the pace. She walked toward the compartment where she'd already left one dead body. When she was done, there'd be a second corpse inside.

———

The three men made rapid progress through the huge ship. As they went along, Yabuno gave them a verbal diagram of their path, in case they were separated. As Austin had speculated, they encountered no one. It was possible that no one was present anywhere except the bridge, engineering, and near the loaders. The possibility of such a large vessel being so fully automated was hard to comprehend.

Finally, they reached their destination. As they gazed upon their colleagues while under cover, they saw three armed guards nearby. Austin measured the open distance they'd need to cover before reaching the guards and thought it would be possible, with luck, to reach them before they could raise an alarm.

As if someone had been reading his mind, a display came to life with an image of Diana coming from the compartment that had been their prison, alerting everyone that the prisoners had escaped. All eyes turned to watch the message, and Austin knew that it was time to move. They raced toward the guards with frantic haste, worried that something would trip them up, but the guards were oblivious to their approach.

They were within a few feet of their targets when rifle rounds splattered the deck in front of them. As they skidded to a halt, they were shocked to see Diana standing nearby, holding a rifle steady on them. Her expression was a combination of shock and admiration as she stared at her former prisoners.

"I thought sending out that message would lull you into doing what you did, but I only expected to see two pigeons." She stared hard at Austin. "I know I killed you, Austin! I watched you bleed out, and I even checked your pulse; you were a corpse. How did you survive?"

Austin didn't bother with an answer.

"Maybe you really can't be killed," she mused out loud. "I guess the only way to be sure is to send you on a one-way ticket out an air lock. Even if you don't need to breathe, you'll just drift in space forever." Her gaze shifted for a moment to the other two. "On the other hand, you two are just as mortal as I am."

She raised her rifle as she aimed at Albretti. "I'll make that bitch of a wife of yours a widow, Captain Albretti."

Before she finished her sentence, Austin threw his knife. Through instinct or just dumb luck, she raised her arm to block the weapon. She screamed from the unexpected pain as the blade buried itself in her forearm. As her rifle clattered loudly onto the deck and she moved back to cover, Austin, Albretti, and Yabuno closed the distance to the shocked guards and put them down with ruthless blows.

Heph tried to escape, but Albretti's military training kicked in. In an instant, he had a guard's rifle up and aimed, and put a round through the former scientist's head. The man was dead before his body crumpled to the deck. A glance through an empty hatchway showed them where Diana had escaped. While Albretti would have been willing to make good on his threat and pursue the wounded assassin, Austin was in no mood to waste time playing cat and mouse with her.

With some difficulty he sought to herd everyone back toward *Pathfinder*, which was stored in the main cargo hold nearby. He couldn't be heard over the sheer volume of joyous noise, as people wanted to reassure themselves that he was really alive. Finally, their captain got them to quiet down, and they made their way along the path that Yabuno had memorized.

As they approached the scout ship, several displays came to life with Pandora's image taunting them. "Did you really think we couldn't figure out where you'd try to run and hide, Sam? Even now, the safety protocols have been disabled and the cargo hold is being depressurized, so thanks for making it so easy to kill all of you at once. You'll never get the hatch opened before you all suffocate.

"I hear you're a hard man to kill, so we'll follow Diana's suggestion and just vent all of your bodies out to space once you're all dead. Even if you don't need to breathe, you'll never bother anyone again; we won't even be able to hear you. Have fun as you watch the bodies of your friends while you and they drift forever."

Although Austin knew Pandora's taunt about getting the hatch opened was true, he never stopped running toward the ship, and neither did anyone else. They began to feel the effects of oxygen deprivation, with each step seeming to take longer than the last and the distance to the hatch barely seeming to shrink. As the downward cycle continued, Austin was surprised to see the hatch open, seemingly on its own. He didn't question their good fortune as they stumbled up the ramp, however. Albretti was the last one aboard as he and Austin grabbed a few stragglers who had trouble finding the edge of the ramp. *Pathfinder*'s captain was desperate to push everyone fully inside before the scout ship decompressed along with the rest of the hangar. At last, he was able to punch the button to close the hatch behind them. The huge blasts of air rushing out past them finally ceased.

He kept running as he shouted, "Everyone to your stations!" The sudden influx of oxygen was like a stimulant, and their legs felt light as they raced away from the hatch. Austin followed the captain, while Yabuno headed to engineering. As they burst onto the bridge, everyone moved to his or her station without a word. Austin stood at the main rail, as he had done many times, and faced the displays. Albretti sat in his chair, turned toward Austin and grinned. "Welcome aboard, Sam."

"You are a clever bastard, Joe," he said admiringly. "You hid some of your crew on this ship and then put the chief and some of his people out there where everyone could see, figuring they'd never think to look for the rest of his people, didn't you?"

"It's a good thing I did, or we'd never have gotten back on board in time," he said.

"Tell me they've been working on this ship's systems," Austin said eagerly.

"Consider yourself told. I'm waiting for a status report."

Austin frowned. "Too bad Bret wasn't on board, or you might have the network back up by now."

Albretti's expression took on a sly look. "Bret may not have been on board, but Melody was. Now that Bret's back, I hope they'll be able to wrap it up, if she hasn't already done so. I guess you weren't the only miracle worker around!"

"Captain, this is the chief. I have a status report."

"What's the word, Chief?"

"We have weapons and propulsion back up and running. The warp-field generators will be back online shortly."

The captain turned to Austin. "Anything you'd like to do, Sam?"

"Getting the hell out of here comes to mind," Austin said with some heat.

Albretti pointed at a display. "We don't have access to their systems, and that main hatch is still closed."

Austin replied, "We have torpedoes, don't we?"

Albretti's eyes widened at the thought. "From inside a ship? If we can't blow out that hatch, what kind of backlash will we get?"

Austin gestured outside. "Not much, since they depressurized the hold. There won't be the same pressure recoils that you'd have with an atmosphere, and no gasses to ignite. It may be different in a smaller ship, but they outfoxed themselves by building one so big, and with a cargo hold to match. That hatch is far enough away that it's worth the risk."

Albretti nodded. "Chief, bring our engines online, so we can hover for a moment. Get some torpedoes ready; we're going to have to make our own key for that hatch."

The ship had a different feel as the engines came to life. *Pathfinder* was facing away from the cargo-hold hatch, and Albretti looked wistfully at the image on the display. "It's tempting to try to blast them from inside the ship."

Austin shook his head. "Tempting, yes, but we don't know what's on the other side of that bulkhead. We've come too far now to screw things up by making a bad decision."

Albretti nodded and gestured toward a display for the position for his navigator. The image began to move, looking like a pan of the hold's interior. As the exterior hatch came into view, Albretti got on his link.

"Chief, do we have a couple of torpedoes loaded and locked?"

"They're ready to go," he replied with an edge to his voice.

"Launch one and take out that damned hatch!"

"My pleasure, Captain."

They had an unusual vantage point, since normally torpedoes were launched at targets much farther away. Being this close to this type of weapon seemed surreal, as the projectile raced toward the huge hatch. It was just an instant before a blinding light flashed in their faces. As the glare faded, they could see stars in the distance. An ugly hole had been ripped in the hatch, but there wasn't enough room for the scout ship to get through without being gouged by twisted shards.

Albretti went back to the display. "Launch another one, targeting this spot, and set up a third one for in case we need it."

The chief acknowledged the order, and they watched another projectile, identical to the first one, streak toward an especially ugly forest of jagged shards. Once again, the flash was blinding. As the glare faded, they were able to confirm that much of the danger had been blasted out to space.

Albretti decided to take a chance on a third torpedo and gave the launch order to the chief. Moments later, there was no doubt they had room to escape safely, as much of the main hatch no longer existed. *Pathfinder* moved forward and was free of its former prison a few seconds later. As the enemy vessel raced away in the distance, the scout ship rotated to face the other ship. It powered up its own main propulsion to get to maximum speed as quickly as possible to give chase. Once again, *Pathfinder* was the hunter.

CHAPTER NINETEEN

A larms blared from several locations on *Firebird*'s bridge, none of them with good news. As they tried to make sense of everything, Diana brought up an aft view on a display. They were shocked to see they had a new pursuer, one that they'd assumed was out of action.

"Our cargo hold was supposed to be filled with dead bodies from Citadel. Instead, they got aboard their obnoxious little ship, which should have been useless to them. How did *Pathfinder* get back online, and how did it get off this ship?" Pandora demanded.

"I don't know how they got it back online," Diana said, "but we don't have a main cargo hatch anymore, thanks to the torpedoes they used to blast it."

"You were responsible for our security, and you failed."

"Don't stand there in judgment of me, Pandora," Diana warned. "That isn't your role, much as you'd like it to be." She gestured at another display. "Besides, we have other problems."

"What now?" she asked sourly.

"With the cargo hatch gone, even if we could form a warp bubble, which I'm not sure we can, we couldn't maintain it; it would collapse in spectacular fashion."

"Can we get through the radiation field?"

Diana nodded. "Yes, we can still do it, without frying everyone aboard."

"That means we have to get through before their ship can catch us and start launching torpedoes," Pandora said. "We'll then need to meet up with our ships that are still active in the outer region of their system, and transfer to one of them. Can we do it?"

"It'll be close," Diana said with a shrug. "Fortunately, we already were at top speed when *Pathfinder* broke free. It took a while for its engines to get up to maximum speed, even after it positioned itself to give chase. The other good news is that our technology allows us to get through the radiation field faster than they can, so we should be able to put more distance between us, even though we'll have slowed down hugely."

"What about our weapons? Can we use them?"

"No," Diana replied, shaking her head. "I'm convinced their chief engineer was doing his best to hamper our efforts. I was about to give them another incentive to get moving when we discovered that Austin and his people were missing. Everything back there is a mess now, with Heph dead and the added problem of a shattered cargo-hold hatch. We don't have the people to deal with it."

Pandora glared at her colleague. "Our plan should have worked. I see repeated instances where your failure to do your job led to our plan not being successful."

Diana glared back at her rival. "I've already warned you about standing in judgment of me. Besides, I've at least done something, including destroying Austin's home, capturing him, and getting us away from Citadel in one piece. No one knew he could come back from the dead; otherwise, we'd have already dealt Citadel a hard, perhaps fatal, blow. All you do is sit back and carp about everything. For now, just shut up, unless you have something useful to offer. We'll get to the other things at the right time." She looked over at a display. "We'll be entering the radiation field in about ten minutes. Once we're through, we'll be able to link up with our other ships and get a status report."

———

Austin gazed at a display with intense interest. "Can we catch them before they get into the safe path?" he asked.

Albretti checked another display and shook his head. "They'll have just enough time to sneak in before we can catch up. Besides, they can get through the safe path faster than we can."

"What about the hole where their hatch used to be? Won't that slow them down?"

"It's in the rear, with the rest of the ship helping to shield their sorry asses as they move along."

"They won't be able to form a warp bubble, with that damage," Austin noted. "That means they'll have to transfer to another one of their ships." He grinned as he continued. "That also means we have something better to do than to try to follow them through the safe path."

Albretti chuckled at the thought as he got on his link. "Chief, get ready to prove just how good a job your people did in fixing this ship."

———

After a tactical pause, Captain McKinley and his crew were ready to try some more maneuvers against the dwindling Phoenix fleet. Even though the enemy ships had the advantage of being networked together, often acting as a single unit, the Citadel ships had, gradually and painstakingly, managed to recover much of the initiative they'd surrendered in the early hours of the engagement. The numbers were once again nearly even, with three Citadel transports facing four Phoenix ships.

McKinley continued to be frustrated over their lack of ability to communicate with each other effectively. With the communications network down, makeshift efforts to broadcast directly with other ships were almost always hampered by the interference generated by repeated bursts from EMP weapons. Neither McKinley nor the rest of the crew dared dwell on the fact that they were desperate for information on the fate of Citadel.

He pointed to a display and spoke to Soren. "Let's try it again, Amy. When we reach this point, we'll go into a warp bubble and move to this point. How are we doing for weapons?"

Soren checked a display and reported, "We're down to a half dozen conventional torpedoes, five special torpedoes, and seven rocks. We still have our EMP weapon, of course, but we need to be fairly close to make it effective.

We're going to have to make this run count, Captain, if we're going to put them away," she said, the concern plain on her face.

As *KT-5* approached its target point and went into a warp bubble, the nearest two Phoenix vessels shifted position, knowing that the smaller ship wouldn't be able to stay in its bubble indefinitely. They moved toward where they expected their adversary to reappear, and they waited.

To their shock, a familiar ship appeared in an unexpected location and opened fire with a conventional torpedo, ripping a hole in the larger ship's hull. A moment later, a special torpedo followed the first one straight through the hole, and an ugly wave of distortion burst out from inside the ship. A small explosion followed the wave, joined by a much larger one. While the other ship turned to face *Pathfinder*, *KT-5* appeared and launched a conventional torpedo. With a hole torn in the hull of the other ship, *Pathfinder* made fast work of it by launching another special torpedo. For a moment, Citadel had a numerical advantage.

However, *Firebird* itself was bearing down on them rapidly, having navigated the safe path successfully. *KT-5* was preparing to break off the attack when Soren spoke. "Captain, the communications network is back up, and we're receiving a message from *Pathfinder*."

A moment later, familiar images showed up on a display. Albretti brushed off the glad tidings, saying, "There isn't time for saying what we all feel right now. What you need to know is that *Firebird* doesn't have any weapons, so you don't need to run from it. It's just a bluff, while its crew tries to transfer to another one of their ships. Let's keep the pressure on them."

However, at the same time they were hemming in *Firebird*, the two remaining Phoenix ships were racing back toward it, to offer support. *Pathfinder* and *KT-5* vanished into warp bubbles as rocks flashed by them. By the time the Citadel ships reappeared, the three remaining enemy vessels were streaking toward deep space.

Austin's sharp eyes caught a glimpse of movement far ahead, and a display confirmed that the few members of *Firebird*'s crew were taking shuttles to one of the other ships. The moment the transfer was complete, all three ships reversed course and went on the offensive against the Citadel transports. Since *Firebird* was networked in with its other ships, it responded just as quickly as the others to maneuvering instructions, even without a bridge crew.

This time, however, the Phoenix ships were facing three transports, plus the scout ship. They also didn't know that the network was back online and that Austin was laying out for them the role each of them had to play.

"Remember," he reminded his forces, "*Firebird* doesn't have weapons, can't form a stable warp bubble, and doesn't appear to have any crew anymore either. Therefore, they'll probably use it for blocking maneuvers and possibly even to ram one or more of our ships."

He pointed to a display. "*KT-5*, I want you to stay on this course, but not go into a warp bubble right away. So long as they see you, you'll serve to herd them where we want them. When you reach this point, if they start to flinch, then you can dive into a warp bubble and then get ready for an attack. *KT-4*, I want you to take this position. Once again, don't go into a warp bubble right away; let's mess with their heads. *KT-19*, same task, on this path."

Austin's expression darkened. "While you're keeping them off guard by staying in their faces, *Pathfinder* will be shifting around in a warp bubble. We won't have the same time constraints you have as far as maintaining your bubbles, and they'll be nervous over the fact that they won't know where one of the chess pieces is hiding. Any questions?" With silence for his answer, he said, "Let's go."

The crews aboard the Phoenix vessels were slightly confused by the new formation of Citadel vessels facing them. In the hours since the attack had begun, they'd become used to a series of maneuvers that had been repeated enough to enable them to anticipate next moves, although the transports had come up with enough wrinkles in their maneuvers that they'd been able to take out more of the enemy vessels than they had lost. What the Phoenix ships faced now was more than some wrinkles. With this formation, there wasn't anything for the alien network to anticipate, and their response was less aggressive than in previous attacks.

"Why are they using that formation?" Pandora demanded to know. "We've never seen it."

"That's likely the reason," Diana said. "It probably also confirms that their communications network is back online. This has the look of something Austin would orchestrate."

They sought to converge rapidly on *KT-4*, hoping to startle the crew into an early retreat into a warp bubble.

However, *KT-4* continued on its path, as did *KT-5* and *KT-19*. Instead, at the last moment *Pathfinder* appeared from underneath them and launched a conventional torpedo at the farther enemy ship, scoring a direct hit. The scout ship was already gone from view before the other ship could react.

While *Pathfinder* was causing distractions, *KT-5* and *KT-4* reached their spots and vanished. *KT-19* continued to approach the three ships and launched a torpedo at the nearest one. As the Phoenix vessel sought to maneuver out of the projectile's path, *KT-4* appeared and launched a rock. The transport vanished a moment later. The rock blasted a massive hole in the ship's exterior.

KT-5 appeared off to one side and launched another torpedo. The Phoenix ship now had two holes in its hull without having fired a single shot in its defense, and was vulnerable to a shot from multiple directions. *Firebird* moved to provide cover for the side with the most damage.

Too late, they realized that using *Firebird* as a shield could prove to be a liability, as it hampered the enemy fleet's ability to engage in certain maneuvers. Just as *Firebird* provided cover for much of the exposed flank of the heavily damaged ship, it also blocked that ship from being able to act against two of the transports as they appeared nearby.

The transports used *Firebird* as cover for their own maneuvers, launching two rocks against the first Phoenix ship the moment they came in range, with no way for the other enemy ships to retaliate. The projectiles raced toward their target, smashing *Firebird*'s engines into

CHAPTER TWENTY

S even Phoenix ships had stayed behind in Earth's solar system, ready to strike without warning and wreak havoc on human communities on Earth, Mars, and elsewhere. With the pretext of undertaking cargo runs, the vessels would be able to approach their targets without being taken for enemy ships. By the time any defenses could be mustered, it would be too late for humanity.

Two ships approached Mars, moving past its defenses without a challenge. A Citadel transport was already in orbit, but without any weapons deployed. The ship was probably on a commercial run, transferring cargo to Earth that needed to be in a gravity environment. A Mars patrol ship was also in the area. Once again, the patrol was routine, with no weapons deployed.

The Firebird ships approached on an orbital path that blocked any view of their forward areas, while one deployed its rail gun and the other deployed its EMP weapon. In a moment, the one ship would swing around and take out the Citadel vessel with a single, well-placed projectile. A second one would be directed toward the

EMP installation on the surface, obliterating it and leaving much of the planet defenseless. While the place was reeling from the attacks, the other ship would wipe out all orbiting infrastructure with several focused bursts from the vessel's EMP weapon. They would then coordinate their attacks on the surface installations of Mars, until there was no life remaining on the Red Planet. They assumed that the Mars ship wouldn't be any real challenge to destroy.

A countdown appeared on a display on each of the enemy bridges. As the seconds reached zero, the vessels went into action. The first one swung around, ready to obliterate the oblivious transport, and the other moved toward the orbiting infrastructure. The Citadel transport finally began to move, although it was much too late to save itself.

———

Amelia Gordon watched the action on a display, preparing to order that the planet's defense systems take out the threat. Suddenly, all communications failed, as did any control over their defenses. "Frank, what just happened?" she demanded of her defense minister.

"We've lost control over everything, Amelia," Francis Castillo replied in a shocked tone.

"What about the EMP weapon? Can we target them with it?" she asked desperately.

He shook his head. "That communications network they deployed must have done something to *our* network, although I don't know how. While we thought we were springing a trap for them, they've done the same for us." Castillo looked at a display. "We can't even talk to the ships out there to let them know what's happened. For all we know, they can't talk to each other or even use their own weapons. Unless they can turn things around pretty damned quickly, we're a sitting duck, much like we were when the aliens attacked." They didn't need to talk about what that would mean for Mars.

———

Suddenly, the larger ship found itself reeling from the impact with a rock from an unsuspected direction. Directly below them, a Keith Thomas transport materialized out of a warp bubble, while moving slowly toward the enemy ship. It was using the older approach of shifting in and out of warp bubbles. The transports sacrificed a certain degree of freedom of movement and engaged in maneuvers that the aliens sometimes considered more predictable. On the other hand, the transports didn't have the same time constraints while staying in a warp bubble. This allowed them to keep the Phoenix ships off balance, setting up opportunities to take out the enemy.

The disadvantage of this approach was plain, as the transport seemed to take a long time to get back into a warp bubble, time that the Firebird-class ship spent bringing its rail gun to bear on the new target. However, the ship reeled from another attack, this time by the transport that it had planned on targeting originally.

With its EMP weapon already deployed, the second enemy ship headed back toward the two transports at high speed. Both transports vanished into warp bubbles, and the two larger ships planned on waiting for the one they knew would have to reappear all too soon.

They ignored the Mars ship; they assumed that Mars had somehow figured out their plans and was setting them up for a blast from the planet's EMP weapon. The ship would stay out of range, to avoid being caught in the waves of destruction that would have been engulfing the intruders. Since Phoenix had already launched its surprise attack on the planet's communications and defense capabilities, the ships wouldn't know that there would be no help from the planet.

While in their warp bubbles, there was no way for the transport captains to tell if the EMP weapon had been deployed or had inflicted any damage upon the intruding vessels. They therefore watched the countdowns on their display, to know when to reappear. However, as a precaution, they moved to different positions to place themselves outside the range of any planetary EMP weapons.

They reappeared, expecting to find their foe crippled, only to find themselves scrambling to avoid contact with a rock hurtling toward them, as well as a blast from an EMP weapon.

Captain Charles Stewart, aboard *KT-26*, was not amused. After designating the next maneuver on a display, he demanded, "What the hell happened to our support from Mars?"

His navigator replied, "We've lost all contact with Mars, Captain. We also can't raise the Mars ship. It looks like their entire network is down."

"That's no coincidence," Stewart replied. "Phoenix must have done something to screw up their network. What about ours?"

"Everything is up and running, and we have communication with *KT-21*." The color drained from his face. "The Citadel Group is reporting an attack on Earth, and another one on our yard. Every major network in this solar system except ours is down."

"Thank God for Preacher's orders about encryption," Stewart said. "Astrid was clever enough to take it a step further and seal our network off from the rest of the traffic in the system." He looked back at the display. "No more time to worry about it now. Get *KT-21* online; we have more work to do. See what we can do to establish communications with the Mars ship."

He spoke with the captain of *KT-21*. "We can't raise the Mars ship, so we'll have to make our plans accordingly." He pointed to a display. "If *KT-26* attacks from above, right here, then your ship can attack from below, in this location, and they won't be able to support each other. If we play this out the right way, we can each launch torpedoes and then duck out of sight before they can react. We can then follow up either with special torpedoes or rocks, depending on the damage from the first torpedoes."

"We'd have a better chance of getting off those second torpedoes if we could arrange for a slight distraction, Chuck," the other captain noted. "It takes a while to get into and out of warp bubbles."

"Captain, the Mars vessel is making an approach toward the Phoenix ships," Stewart's navigator reported.

Stewart grinned. "I guess they figured out we need a diversion too. Let's move."

The intruders were out of position to launch a rock at their new foe and lacked the range for their EMP weapon to be effective, so they had to abandon their plans to stalk the transports. Although the vessel didn't have a rail gun or EMP weapon, it had torpedoes ready for launch.

They shifted so that one Firebird vessel faced the oncoming ship and the other guarded the back door. While they were in motion, a torpedo from the Mars ship streaked toward them, only to be destroyed by a laser burst from the intended target. The smaller ship veered off course just as the rail gun launched its payload. The rock smashed into the side of the ship, crushing one of the engines, but failed to destroy any vital systems.

While the enemy ships were focused on the threat in front, the transports reappeared on either side—one on the high side and the other on the low side, as Stewart had planned. Each launched two torpedoes, all of which found their targets, although the Phoenix EMP weapon managed to disrupt the efforts of *KT-21* to return to a warp bubble. As the transport fought to escape, the other Phoenix vessel swung around with its rail gun deployed. A moment later, a large rock smashed into the struggling vessel, damaging its weapons.

As the enemy vessels prepared to pummel *KT-21* into oblivion, the other transport reappeared with a special torpedo ready to launch; no one could follow the projectile as it streaked through one of the holes blasted in the hull earlier. Moments later, the interior of the ship was visible as it distorted outward, followed by a massive explosion. The rail gun was blasted free of the dying ship. *KT-26* vanished again.

The other enemy vessel kept on with its EMP attack, hoping to finish off *KT-21* before the other transport was ready with a new weapon. The gamble was that it would take several passes with another weapon to cause enough damage to force the larger ship to break off its attack.

The Phoenix crew was shocked when *KT-26* appeared just off its bow, directly in the path of the EMP weapon with its rail gun deployed. They hadn't expected the transport to save time by not moving back to a safer distance or by serving as a shield for the other transport. The ship shrugged off the impact from the weapon and launched a rock at nearly point-blank range. The damage was immediate and devastating, and ensured the Phoenix EMP weapon would never function again.

Stewart didn't bother changing over to another weapon. Moments later, another rock crashed through the larger vessel, colliding with numerous rocks in the vessel's hold and bursting out near the rear. The action of so many rocks crashing around nearly gutted the ship.

The captain of *KT-26* made a point of letting the crew of the intruder vessel see the transport switch over to a standard torpedo. The last thing they saw was the slight hint of the projectile's path toward them before it entered the ruined hulk and detonated, bursting the ship apart from within as the rocks inside took off in many directions. The transport was safe within a warp bubble as it moved away from the scene of the vessel's disintegration. *KT-21*, freed from the onslaught of the EMP weapon, also made its way into the safety of its own warp bubble and likewise moved to a safe distance away. Mars had survived.

CHAPTER TWENTY-ONE

Captain Hull, in command of *KT-12*, had no time to react to the shock he felt over the news that Earth's communications and defense networks were down, as were everyone else's, except for the Citadel Group. He was preoccupied over the fact that three transports—his, *KT-18*, and *KT-22*—were the only ones available to defend Earth against attack from four Phoenix vessels. Although the Space Command would normally have helped provide security around the Blue Planet, the service's vessels were spread throughout the system in anticipation of attacks.

Hull shook his head. Even though Preacher had warned both the United States and Mars about the danger from Phoenix, Mars had been better prepared than Earth to meet the threat, thanks to President Gordon being a better leader than President Lee. In spite of warnings from Preacher and the Citadel Group, Lee had decided to trust the security of his planet to the mighty, largely automated defenses that ringed the place.

That decision led to Earth being placed in a potentially disastrous situation with the loss of the communications and defense networks that now plagued Earth. The death toll would already be high if not for Preacher's decision to order the three transports to remain nearby. With no way to recall any Space Command vessels or even to let them know they were needed desperately, the burden of defending the planet was now entirely with Hull and the other transport commanders.

———

Earlier, Hull had watched a display as four Phoenix ships had approached Earth. He had been placed in charge of the group, and he had had the transports take up defensive positions inside the orbit of Earth's space-based defense platforms.

He'd spoken to his navigator. "Can you identify the specific ships and where they last picked up any cargo?"

After consulting a display, his navigator had replied, "Their markings show them to be *FB-4, FB-7, FB-15,* and *FB-13.* Although a couple of them have carried cargo in the past, none of them has an active cargo manifest from any place in this solar system. We're also pretty sure they aren't carrying any cargo from Citadel," he'd added wryly.

Hull had nodded and opened a link to the other transports. "They're probably going to try to bluff their way past the defense platforms or get past them in a sneak attack, so be alert. We've already discussed initial tactics, although we'll likely need to adjust them. If they somehow manage to approach Earth, be ready to get out of the way of the planetside EMP cannons."

Once the visitors were just outside the range of the defenses, Hull had ordered the transports to deploy their weapons. The other ships had balked at answering to the Citadel Group vessels when challenged. Hull hadn't backed off.

"*FB-7*, there is no record of your having taken on any cargo with the Earth as the destination," he'd said. "You and your fellow ships are ordered to leave this space immediately, or you will be fired upon."

"You have no right to face us like a warship, with weapons deployed, Captain Hull," the captain of *FB-7* had complained. "Yours are Citadel Group vessels, and you have no jurisdiction here." He'd gestured vaguely toward space. "Only Space Command ships can do that, and there aren't any nearby, so we have just as much right to approach as you do. This is one time where you don't get to act like bullies, so stay out of our way," he'd said dismissively.

"We aren't going to argue the point. If you come within range of Earth's defenses, you will be fired upon and destroyed."

"I doubt it," the captain had replied. He'd nodded to his navigator, and the ships had moved toward the planet. They'd come within range of the platforms and proceeded past them without incident, to Hull's astonishment.

The captain of the Phoenix vessel had spoken again. "It seems that you are mistaken, Captain Hull. You should try to get your threats straight before using them on others. Acting like a warship in Earth jurisdiction is a serious offense. Stay out of our way, or you'll find yourself answering to charges before the AN for your criminal actions."

As the ships had raced toward Earth at high speed, Hull's navigator called out, "We can't raise anyone on Earth, Captain; their networks are down! We can't raise Mars either. Only the Citadel Group network is up."

So much for their claim that Earth doesn't view these assholes as a threat, Hull'd thought to himself as he'd ordered the transports into action.

———

The only reason the transports had survived the initial onslaught was they already had their weapons deployed. The Phoenix ships had to preserve the fiction of being friendly, so they had to wait to deploy their weapons until after getting past the defense platforms. Hull hadn't wasted any time. He pointed to a display as he spoke with his chief engineer. "Chief, launch a rock at that ship."

Moments after the chief responded, they saw a giant projectile race toward *FB-4*, making direct contact. While the larger vessel sustained damage, it didn't stop, and Hull knew they'd have to maneuver to get another shot. Other rocks hurled through space at the intruder ships, inflicting serious but not fatal damage.

Hull's greatest worry was that Phoenix would be able to keep the transports engaged in a way that would leave at least one of their own ships free to devastate Earth. The Citadel Group vessels were hampered further by the fact that even a miss from a rock could be deadly, regardless of which side launched it, when they were fighting so close to Earth. An impact on the surface below would resemble a planetside nuclear detonation, which hadn't been seen in over a century and a half.

The situation therefore forced Hull to adopt unorthodox tactics. He spoke with the other captains as he pointed at a display. "*KT-18*, this is where I want you to be when you disappear into a warp bubble. *KT-12* will be on a parallel course in a warp bubble, just a few seconds behind. Reappear here, where they can't fire at you without hitting each other, and take out whichever one has a rail gun deployed."

He pointed to another position. "*KT-22*, come out of a warp bubble here, and launch a rock at *FB-15*. It's already taken a nasty hit and may not withstand another. Don't go back into a bubble before taking a shot at *FB-13* with another rock."

He held up his hand to cut off the protests that were coming. "I *want* you to be a target for just a moment, because they won't be looking for *KT-12* to be right where a transport has just disappeared. I also know how risky it is to appear so close to another ship in a separate warp bubble, but we need to take some chances if we're going to take them out while we're outnumbered."

KT-18 launched a torpedo, which was destroyed before it could reach the enemy vessel. The Phoenix ships turned away from the transport as it began to shift into a warp bubble. Hull had anticipated the direction in selecting the spot where *KT-22* would appear. To guard against surprises, two of the Firebird ships kept their weapons trained away from *KT-22*, even as the transport launched a rock that devastated its target. *KT-18* pressed its luck by launching another rock at *FB-4*.

Despite precautions, none of the Firebird crews noticed that *KT-12* had appeared directly under *FB-7* as it sent a torpedo hurtling toward *KT-22* in retaliation for the launch by the transport. Stewart returned the favor with a quick torpedo that ripped through *FB-7*'s hull, followed by a special one that blew it apart as it distorted from the inside. As *KT-12* disappeared into a warp bubble, *KT-18* appeared between *FB-4* and *FB-15* and devastated the latter vessel with another rock.

As *KT-18* prepared to launch a special torpedo to complete the destruction, *FB-4* made the ruthless assessment that *FB-15* was of no further use; *FB-4* took aim and blasted *KT-18* with its EMP weapon, regardless of the impact on its sister ship. The torpedo was damaged, and the *KT-18* crew jettisoned it with frantic haste before it detonated. By the time the distortions faded back to normal, the enemy ship had its torpedo launcher deployed and blasted the transport, taking out its engines.

KT-12 appeared, unaware of the EMP attack on *FB-15*, and finished it off with a special torpedo. Hull took quick stock of the situation. He didn't need to talk with the chief engineer aboard *KT-22* to know that the transport's weapons had suffered heavy damage. He could also see that *KT-18*'s engines were nearly useless at the moment. Two of the huge enemy vessels were still functional, and they slipped past *KT-18* and headed straight for Earth. The only reason Earth hadn't yet suffered the equivalent of a nuclear catastrophe was that the ships needed to deploy their rail guns. The captain of the transport with the crippled engines didn't dare try to launch a rock; any damage to their weapons might lead to a miss that would devastate a population on the planet below.

He realized that there was only one option available. "Chief! We need to get into a warp bubble and slip past those bastards before they can finish deploying their rail guns." Hull pointed to a display. "This is where we need to end up, and we have to do it now, before they've deployed their rail guns."

"This close to a planet?" the chief asked skeptically. "We'll do it, even though we'll be gambling with whether Earth's gravity will let us go where we want, and whether it'll be in one piece."

The image on the display shifted, leaving virtually nothing visible while the transport practically raced toward Earth. The ship seemed to be tossed around violently as it came out of its warp bubble, still facing in the direction of Earth.

Hull realized that the buffeting was real, as the smaller vessel had presented an ideal target for the weapons from two ships to destroy, before attacking Earth directly. "We're taking a hell of a beating, Captain!" the chief called out over his link. "They've even stopped for a moment while they decide what part of us to smash next.

Hull knew that he couldn't allow any rocks to get past his ship. He noted that the enemy ships were alternating their shots, and he waited to swing his ship around at the precise moment needed to get off a shot of his own, while he still had a ship left. The transport shuddered again, and the chief reported that most of their cargo of rocks was lost, with partial engine damage added to the list. At Hull's orders, his ship lurched around and managed to launch a huge projectile from its rail gun at close to point-blank range.

While the target's weapons were destroyed, the other enemy vessel launched another rock, this time without really aiming. *KT-12*'s rail gun was struck at an angle, knocking it out of action but leaving the rest of the weapons bay still intact. Fortunately, the rock was deflected away from Earth. Hull ordered the wreck of their weapon to be jettisoned and for the torpedo launcher to be deployed.

He knew they'd never be able to bring the transport around in time to fire at the enemy with the functioning rail gun, so he took the shot at the other ship while it was still possible. An instant later, the interior of the vessel distorted, and then it detonated. The lives of perhaps millions of people on Earth depended on what happened next. The fates were kind, and the distortions pushed the rocks in the stricken vessel's hold away from Earth.

The transport shuddered from another impact, and the chief reported that they could no longer deploy their weapons. As Hull faced the enemy ship and pondered the lousy options remaining, he was shocked to see *KT-22* move directly between them. The transport made a turn and rammed an engine into the weapons bay of the larger ship, crushing it.

Hull knew that the ship could still accomplish widespread destruction by crashing deliberately into Earth with a cargo hold still partly filled with asteroids. The ship began to move forward, confirming that the enemy had thought of the same thing. Hull had a desperate inspiration. "*KT-18!* Can you target that ship?"

"You know what happens if we miss, Captain?" the captain warned.

"I know what happens if we don't try," he replied. "Take the shot, if you can."

They sensed the giant projectile more than they actually saw it as it raced toward what was now a suicide ship. Moments later, they watched as the rock smashed into a massive engine, ripping it loose from its moorings and sending it hurling at an angle that rammed it into the ship. The rock itself deflected enough that it didn't head down to the unprotected planet.

"That was a hell of a bank shot. Is their cargo hold still intact?" Hull asked.

"Still intact," the navigator confirmed.

"Good," he said, pleased that they hadn't created another problem with rogue asteroids. "*KT-22*, we'll need your help."

"I know," the captain replied, grinning. "You want to go nose to nose with them, to push those bastards away from Earth. Between the two of us, we may have the engine power to do it."

"Let's line up for the approach," Stewart said.

The last Phoenix ship was worked frantically to bring its remaining engine back online, after the other engine had crashed through the vessel, followed by the rock itself. Just as it began to move again, the two transports made contact, gently at first, then with increasing power. The one engine was larger than the engines aboard the Citadel ships, and both of those ships had suffered engine damage. For the moment, the remaining power to the transports' engines was enough to cancel the enemy ship's forward momentum.

Sections of the hulls of all three ships began to buckle under the stress. However, Phoenix had had to accept compromises when making such large vessels, especially within the short time frame its backers had adopted. One of those compromises was to have less structural reinforcement in certain areas. Austin had long insisted that the transports be prepared to serve as warships if needed, so the Citadel Group hadn't made that compromise. The chief reported that the forward structure was now holding firm, and *KT-22* reported likewise.

Hull ordered the thrust increased, and at first they stayed where they were as other forward sections of the enemy ship continued to buckle. Finally, the buckling ceased as the transports reached reinforced sections of the other vessel. Gradually, they moved forward, and they began to notice the distance opening up between their original position and Earth. When Hull felt they'd gotten back to a safe distance, he ordered both transports to disengage from their enemy. As the Phoenix ship continued to move backward for a moment, the extensive damage to its forward section became clear. With the opposing thrust gone, the Phoenix ship's engine finally was able to cancel its reverse momentum and prepared to move forward again.

The downside to canceling momentum was that the virtually still ship presented the easiest target for a rail gun. The vessel seemed to be waiting for the giant rock that smashed into it, colliding with the other rocks in the cargo hold and ripping apart the ship's interior.

"Nice break shot, *KT-18*," Stewart said with a chuckle. The warmth faded from his expression as he said, "Now finish it off."

The special torpedo that raced toward the crippled vessel had no lack of openings through which to reach the devastated interior. An instant later, the last threat to Earth was nothing more than a fireball.

Hull gave a long sigh of relief before opening a link to the other transports. "That was a hell of a job, everybody," he said, "but we aren't quite done. *KT-22*, there are some stray rocks we'd better track down and collect, before they cause some problems. Then we're all due for a trip to the yard. Dan is going to have a fit when he sees what we've done to his ships!"

CHAPTER TWENTY-TWO

Dan Bacas watched a display as it showed the approach of a Phoenix ship. He'd already received word from the Citadel Group about the attacks on Mars and Earth and the fact that theirs was the only network still up in the solar system. He was worried about the damage that even a single ship might cause to his yard, since it couldn't maneuver and a ship could. He'd already heard reports about the rocks the Phoenix ships were carrying and was under no illusions about the shape his yard would be in after multiple encounters with those high-speed projectiles.

This wouldn't be the first time the yard had been under attack, unfortunately. He remembered all too well how the aliens had almost totally destroyed the place years earlier, as they had sought to wipe out all life in the solar system. Later, after they'd rebuilt the yard, Bacas had had to abandon the place to the destructive forces that Harrington had sent against it as part of Harrington's War. He still resented the fact that her ambitions and lack of any moral character had led to his having to order the destruction of six of their transports, rather than allow them to fall into the hands of her people and be used to harm Citadel.

The attacks on Earth and Mars had a purpose of destroying the main population centers within the solar system, since the settlements on the Moon would be easily destroyed once the Earth populations had been wiped out. The other locations in space, which were mostly mining operations, didn't have large populations, so they counted little toward the survival of the human presence in the solar system. Likewise, there wasn't any significant population within the yard, so the only reason for an attack would be to settle old scores.

If what Preacher had shared with him was true, then Harrington and the aliens were allied somehow. Bacas could only guess at the animosity that would lead to their enemies going after the yard at the same time that they attacked major targets such as Earth and Mars, but it probably was based in part on the fact that each had attacked the yard, only to see it rebuilt.

Regardless of the motivation, the yard was now in great danger. Because of the historic sensitivities relating to the use of rail guns and giant rocks in that solar system, they hadn't been able to set up mobile launchers near the yard for protection. They had, however, set up mobile torpedo launchers around the perimeter of the yard. Even better, Bacas could control them remotely, since their network was unaffected by whatever mischief their enemies had inflicted upon everyone else.

The problem was that the effective range of a torpedo was much less than that of a rock launched from a rail gun, and the speeds were nowhere near the same. Where projectiles were concerned, only a special torpedo could outrun a rock from one of those cannons. The effective range was no better than with regular torpedoes, however, due to the challenges of using a warp bubble to target something over a significant distance.

Bacas knew he needed to keep the pressure on the Phoenix ship and hope for help to arrive. He didn't bother with a challenge to the vessel to warn it away. Instead, he launched torpedoes from a couple of locations. Although they raced toward their target unerringly, the torpedoes were both destroyed by laser fire. He launched greater numbers of torpedoes, creating a cloud of projectiles. He was disappointed to note that even as the weapons raced toward the vessel at the same time, laser fire from the enemy vessel dispatched them all.

The vessel wasn't there just to serve as a target, however. Bacas saw the first rock heading toward the yard at extreme speed and winced as it took out a support structure as if it were made of matchsticks. He was glad he had ordered all of the ships tethered in the yard to face directly toward the enemy ship, as it meant they would present the narrowest profile for a projectile.

He saw another rock hurtling down its deadly path and launched a special torpedo to intercept it. Just before making contact, the projectile erupted with a distorted warp bubble. The rock was deflected around the bubble and around the yard, continuing harmlessly into space. Bacas sent a note to Kramer that the yard staff should track each of the asteroids as best they could, to report their paths to anyone who might need a warning. That would depend on their surviving long enough for other networks to come back online, however.

Again, a rock hurtled toward the yard, and again a special torpedo erupted in its path, deflecting the giant around the yard. As expected, the enemy ship began to approach the yard, to make a shot that the defenses couldn't intercept in time. As he watched the Phoenix ship increase in size on the display, Bacas sweated over the fact that notwithstanding the directive from Preacher to take steps to protect the yard, it wasn't a military outpost, and he didn't have an unlimited supply of special torpedoes. He hoped what he had would outlast the supply of giant projectiles aboard the enemy ship. He wasn't encouraged by what he'd heard about the capacity of the ship's cargo hold.

The vessel was noticeably closer as it launched another rock. Again, Bacas launched a special torpedo, but it failed to detonate in time, and the projectile raced toward the yard. Moments later, it missed one of the main hangars but smashed into a transport docked there for repairs, blasting a large hole in the unprotected hull.

Another dense giant hurled toward the complex, ready to wreak more destruction, but this time a special torpedo deflected it from its destination. Bacas had the measure of the task from this distance and managed to deflect another rock in time to avoid a collision.

To provide a distraction, Bacas launched three torpedoes toward the huge vessel. Again, lasers destroyed them quickly. The enemy craft moved even closer to the facility, still seeking that point where the defenses wouldn't be able to deflect a shot in time. Bacas cursed as another rock streaked toward the yard. The special torpedo just barely reached the rock before deflecting it away from its target. Another rock followed, and the next special torpedo was too late to be of any use. One of the main hangars was blasted completely away from the rest of the structure. It seemed to have nowhere to go as it drifted in space, along with the two transports inside.

At this distance, Bacas was barely able to deflect the giants that kept coming. He knew he wouldn't be able to keep it up for much longer, as he was running out of special torpedoes. He even had to resort to firing from other mobile platforms positioned around the complex. As one launched, he was amazed that it passed close by a support structure without incident as it met and deflected another rock.

It was possible that the Phoenix ship's supply of rocks was dwindling as well, since the vessel narrowed its distance from the yard, perhaps to make every shot count. This time, a rock seemed to brush by a special torpedo as it crashed into another support structure, tearing it apart from the transport that was tethered to it.

The ship seemed to edge even closer, as if to come in for the kill. Bacas looked at a display and noted the distance. There was no way for the rail gun to miss anything it targeted now. He sent a message to the rest of the complex.

The captain of the enemy ship had failed to notice another reason why the transports in the yard were all facing him, as they were in perfect position to use their weapons. Although the ships weren't fully functional, several of them had weapons that were. The prohibitions on mobile rail-gun platforms didn't extend to transports that carried their own rail guns.

He never saw the first rocks hurling toward his ship, but he felt the vessel shudder from the impacts. He tried desperately to use his lasers to destroy the swarm of incoming torpedoes, while seeking to target the transports that had rail guns. The downside to a shortened distance was that the wave of projectiles that seemed to surge toward his ship overwhelmed his lasers. Too late, he learned that there weren't enough lasers in his arsenal to prevent multiple torpedoes from blasting their way into his ship and tearing it apart. At last, Bacas had the privilege of launching one of his remaining special torpedoes toward a ragged opening in the hull of their would-be destroyer. He watched a display as the vessel's interior burst outward in a fiery death. The last of the attacks in the solar system had ended, and the yard was finally safe.

Bacas didn't worry about any damage to the yard from the destruction of the Phoenix ship. After all, he had the keys to the repair shop, and he planned on making the place presentable for when the rest of the transports showed up. He sent a note to his crew: "That was a hell of a job, everyone. Now we have another one ahead of us. Gus, get crews organized to collect the hangar and the transports that are drifting around, along with the other parts of the place they blasted apart. We're going to have plenty of visitors shortly, and I'll be damned if they're going to come here and think we don't know how to keep the place looking tidy!"

CHAPTER TWENTY-THREE

Two months later, the Citadel system no longer showed any signs of the devastation the Phoenix invaders had wreaked on its outer defenses. Most of the damage from the savage attack on Austin's home had been repaired as well. The casualties had been remarkably few, and most of the transports that had been taken out of commission had been restored to service.

To everyone's great joy, Liz was well on her way to a full recovery from her wound. In the smoky haze that had swirled through the wreck of Austin's home that day, Lazarus had been unable to get a good look at his target and had missed hitting any of Liz's vital organs by millimeters. In another bit of good news, Dr. Hall had reported that they had managed to save the lives of the last two afflicted members of the Shiloh scouting party, both of whom were expected to make full recoveries. The battle against the original bug they'd fought on Citadel years ago had given them critical insights into how life worked on Citadel at the genetic level, which helped them to combat other native diseases as they encountered them.

Hall felt that they had begun to gain similar insights into how life worked on Shiloh. While a vaccine wasn't yet available, Hall felt that the long-term prospects for settlers on Shiloh looked promising.

At Austin's request, Yabuno and Albretti put out the word that Diana had provided a faked image of Austin's death. He hadn't wanted to deal with a new dynamic where people might deal with him differently, for good and bad, if they thought he couldn't be killed. For now, only the three men knew what had happened, although he planned on telling Liz when the time was right. He again met with some of his closest advisers and friends to consider where things stood. He began by directing their attention to a display, where a familiar image appeared.

J. W. Preacher's warm gaze appeared in greeting as he began, "I'm very happy to be able to send these greetings, Sam. As you know, we've had our hands full here, what with having to handle an attempt by our old enemy to wipe us out. Sadly, from what you shared in your last message, that term now applies equally to the aliens *and* Harrington, as they are now the same enemy.

"As you advised, we've been on the lookout for Harrington's ship ever since she left your system, one step ahead of her destruction. Obviously, there's been no sign yet of her, Powers, or their ship, as they would have been two months out when we received your message and sent this one to you in reply. You can be assured that I will let you know if she shows up here; if she does, she'll definitely receive a cold welcome!

"As you know from other messages that were sent just before this one, the efforts of the aliens to obliterate our settlements and cities on multiple worlds have failed completely. Dan Bacas has performed miracles in getting his yard back in shape and repairing the transports that were damaged during multiple attacks. While everything isn't quite back to normal, by the time you receive this message, we should be in pretty good shape."

His expression turned crafty. "Part of the reason their attacks failed relates back to something that happened months ago. I've advised you about some of this already, but it bears repeating in order to bring everything up to date. Dan learned about the disappearance of an old friend who had actually worked on the construction of the Phoenix yard and the first ship, *Firebird.* The friend's name was Jeff Coffey, and he had a habit of keeping a log of the projects on which he worked, although his employers didn't know it.

"One day, Coffey decided to act on his curiosity about the new technology by entering the engineering section of *Firebird* and using a disguised recording device to record what was there." Preacher motioned to a display as he said, "This is what he saw."

Even though they knew what to expect, there were gasps as a horrifying image appeared—one that resembled the alien device that had taken over a Citadel transport several years ago. What could only be described as tentacles reached out from the main body and embedded themselves in various crevasses within the rest of the propulsion system. The item was much larger than the one aboard the transport, perhaps to support the greater size of the Phoenix vessels.

Yabuno pointed toward another alien device that was nearby, embedded within another system. "Since we saw these images originally, we've concluded that that other monster is the artificial-gravity system," he said. "Normally, the two systems wouldn't be so close together, but in their setup they may actually provide a certain amount of support for each other." He frowned. "They seem to be a much more extensive part of the ship's systems than we'd realized; there wasn't much of these systems left aboard any of their ships over here to evaluate."

The image shifted to back to Preacher. "I'm sure I don't have to tell you what that was, although I couldn't say whether Coffey understood the implications. We think he was intercepted and murdered to prevent him from telling anyone about what he'd seen. It was only because of the diligence of Bacas and Kramer that we received that vital piece of information. From that point forward, we knew that we needed to keep a closer watch on their activities, and never to assume that we could let our guard down."

His expression took on a look of deep concern. "I'd like to say having that information was enough to put an entire system on alert, but old habits sometimes die hard. It took one more piece of information to get even Earth to take us seriously and to stop brushing off our fears as simple jealousy or anxiety over the possible competition.

"I'd always felt that there was a huge, unanswered question concerning the identity of their original financial backer. In spite of their narrative to the effect that they got rich from hitting multiple jackpots while mining among the asteroids, someone had to have funded those

early efforts. While there certainly is a lot of money floating around out there, all of my inquiries kept confirming that no large sums had been provided by any of the
people who could have supported those activities.

"Finally, we located a trail of funding that didn't seem
to have a starting point, at least not one that made any
sense. It appeared to have come from an account that was
supposedly closed. We learned that the account hadn't
been closed, but was just inactive, and had been reacti-
vated recently. While the first impression was that we were
just looking at a bunch of opportunistic thieves, some further digging revealed the name of the person who controlled the account." Preacher's gaze turned cold. "It was
Harrington's account. I don't believe in those types of
coincidences, and the connection between Harrington
and the aliens was already known. While there was the
question of where Harrington herself was, it didn't take
long from that point to figure out she must have been
the woman who called herself Pandora. The physical age
was right, and there were aspects of her personality that
I noticed when I spoke with her that had bothered me
for reasons I couldn't quite explain. Harrington's hatred
for you and Citadel helped to unmask her. I concluded
that Lazarus was probably Flynn and Diana was probably
Powers.

"Unfortunately, we didn't figure out their identities
until after they'd departed for Citadel and were too
close for any message to get to you in time to be of use.
However, I was able to meet with Pete Lee and Amelia
Gordon and convince them to take action before it was
too late. When the Phoenix ships tried to confuse us by

attacking from multiple locations, we were ready and fought them hard from the start. They made things tough for us by managing to shut down every communications and defense network in our solar system, except for the Citadel Group's systems. In spite of that challenge, for the first time Citadel transports and a Space Command patrol ship actually cooperated in the defense of our solar system. One thing we agreed upon was there would be no prisoners taken; with the aliens in control of the ships and Harrington and her people helping them, they would take advantage of any sign of weakness and try to use it against us. As it happened, they were in no mood to surrender anyway and kept fighting for as long as their ships continued to function.

"Not much of their technology remained intact," he said, shaking his head. "Virtually every one of their ships ended up consumed by a fireball, with nothing left behind for any meaningful study. In one or two instances, the fireball erupted after the ship had been severely damaged and rendered unable to proceed further, so it's unclear whether the fireball was a consequence of the damage or something calculated to prevent us from learning anything more about them. In any event, I can't say I'm sorry about the loss of their technology. Nothing but evil has ever come from it." He chuckled. "I was glad to convey your thoughts on the matter to the Allied Nations. I'll summarize their response."

The image froze as Austin spoke. "Before you hear the rest of J. W.'s message, it may be useful to hear my message that he forwarded to the AN."

Austin's image appeared, his somber expression reflecting the strain of recent events. "To our friends at the Allied Nations, I have bittersweet news to report. As you have heard by now, Citadel was the subject of a brutal and unprovoked attack by the group known as Phoenix, as they pretended to head a great wave of so-called colonists. While we were, after some long and at times brutal efforts, able to prevail against our enemy and destroy them or drive them off, it was at the cost of several lives and the destruction of major portions of our outer-area defenses." Austin practically glared in outrage. "The reason any of this was even possible is that they were the creatures of the same aliens that sought to destroy us once again, not all that long ago. The aliens had left behind some unassuming messages that had stayed in our network, only to spring into life and disrupt our ability to communicate with each other at a critical moment.

"The worst part about the attack was that it was carried out in part by another of our enemies. As shocking as it may be to hear this news, we have proof that Courtney Harrington and several of her people did, in fact, survive their encounter with the aliens and became their servants and tools. They were the people who created and maintained Phoenix, even though their appearances had changed. Harrington was the one who called herself Pandora. While her name and appearance may have changed, her hatred for Citadel and the nations in your solar system, and her lack of respect for human rights and lives, has not."

A look of great sadness tinged his expression. "Not surprisingly, they were never interested in colonizing the planet Shiloh, but only wanted to use that issue as a smokescreen and distraction for seeking to destroy us. That meant they jettisoned into space all twenty thousand of the colonists they had tricked into coming on board their foul ships, and then they filled their cargo holds with rocks gleaned from space. They launched many of those rocks against our ships and other defenses, causing widespread destruction. Fortunately, although they were able to reach Citadel itself, they only managed to destroy one house, losing three of their people in the process, including Lazarus himself. I should know," he said in a cold tone, "because it was me, personally, they sought to kill and my house that was ruined.

"We have managed to destroy all vestiges of the communications network they sought to establish in this system, and we have instructed the Citadel Group to do likewise with respect to our enemy's activities in your system. We will also destroy the beacons they deployed to maintain communications between those systems."

Austin's expression hardened. "This brings us to a fundamental fact of political life, which is that we are on our own out here. No improvements in either travel or communications will ever change that fact. We've long asserted with justification that what happens out here is for us to address, in part because of the facts I just mentioned. One thing that is unfortunate is that some of our friends in your system took that to mean they would not provide any declaration of support for a related part of that reality, which is that Citadel controls all matters relating to this system. This led to Phoenix operating in your system to assemble a fleet that was used in an act of war against our nation.

"To address this situation and avoid any future uncertainty, Citadel hereby declares its sovereignty over the entire Citadel system. This includes deciding which planets are suitable for colonization and by whom. It also includes the right to decide when any of the planetary bodies within the system will become a direct part of the nation that is Citadel. I have asked Ambassador Preacher to appear before the Allied Nations to make this point and to work with all of our partners to confirm this reality publicly.

"As a sovereign nation, Citadel will never again tolerate similar actions by any entity to take hostile actions against us, even if those actions take place in another solar system. If need be, we will take whatever measures may be necessary to defend ourselves. That will include a right of inspection of any ship that declares an intention to travel to the Citadel system for any reason. Citadel has adopted a policy of preemptive defense when it comes to non-Citadel ships purporting to enter our system."

Austin's gaze turned colder. "Preemptive defense includes taking lethal measures to prevent unauthorized entry into our system, so human lives will not be accepted as bargaining chips to be used to place our security in jeopardy.

"As far as the fates of Courtney Harrington and her people are concerned, they are war criminals and fugitives, and a new warrant for their capture, dead or alive, has been issued by Citadel. We don't yet know where they will end up, but if it is in your solar system, the Citadel Group will hunt them down without mercy. Those who choose to give them any shelter or assistance will find themselves subject to a similar lack of mercy."

Austin's expression lightened. "Fortunately, our fleet of transports is largely intact, so we will be resuming shipments between our systems almost immediately. Ambassador Preacher will have more information for you on that subject."

The message ended, and Preacher's image reappeared. "The AN Security Council passed a strong resolution of support for Citadel's position and pledged cooperation in capturing Harrington and her people. Presidents Lee and Gordon have done likewise."

He chuckled. "In fact, Amelia made it clear that what she wanted to see was Citadel simply claiming its rights, so that the rest of the community of nations would know where Citadel stood and could ratify that position. She's right, and the community has been happy to ratify reality, especially since no one here believes any longer that they have any say over what happens out there. The only voice that counts is Citadel's voice."

The humor in his expression faded. "The Security Council also expressed support for the status of Harrington and her people as war criminals again, and restated its support for earlier resolutions calling for her capture by any means. That's about as close to 'dead or alive' as you can get.

"In the meantime, since Phoenix was careful to keep its activities in space and outside the jurisdiction of any planet government, Citadel is taking the position that it doesn't need anyone's permission to go after the operations of those monsters. While there will be financial claims against Phoenix by the families of the people who were murdered, there isn't actually any entity with jurisdiction over the matter.

"Under principles generally recognized by the space community, the waivers of claims the would-be colonists all signed are considered valid. They were also required to obtain insurance against any claims for loss of life. Since virtually all of them were well off, to be able to afford a place on a ship in the first place, their families will be taken care of financially. The only ones that will miss out on a nice payday will be the lawyers.

"I have therefore taken the liberty of asserting that since the primary objective of Phoenix was the destruction of Citadel, Citadel has the primary claim against the assets of Phoenix for war reparations and will therefore make all decisions relating to deciding the disposition of any Phoenix assets. I have also made it clear that any alien technology that is recovered will neither be given a valuation for claims purposes nor be shared with anyone. It will instead be treated as a public menace that needs to be eradicated.

"The Citadel Group has already made a public show of rounding up what little is left of the wrecks of the Phoenix ships and hauling them back to its yard. Everything is under heavy guard by Citadel transports, and no exceptions are being made for anyone who wants a closer look. Since our solar system would have been devastated without our transports repeatedly placing themselves in harm's way while defending Earth and Mars, no one is raising any objections.

"The reality is that there may be few useful assets available anyway, if our analysis about their financial affairs is accurate. We believe they put everything they had into building their fleet. We just want to be sure we have the ability to claim everything they had, in case there's any information that would be useful in dealing with the aliens. Astrid and her people are scouring and securing everything Phoenix left behind. Another benefit is that people once again won't have any alien technology around to tempt them into making a deal with the devil."

Preacher's expression took on a disappointed look. "One last thought is that I believe this will be the end of Lee's career, and deservedly so. Again, he failed to provide adequately for the security of Earth, even after we provided warnings about the danger. He placed too much trust in the security of Earth's admittedly formidable automated defense systems and not enough in the notion of having some Space Command ships nearby in case assistance was needed.

"In view of the ultimate failure of those systems when the aliens brought down Earth's communications and defense networks, I shudder to think about the devastation that would have rained down on our world if we hadn't placed several transports nearby. We owe a tremendous debt to all of the transport captains and crews, and especially to Captain Hull for his brilliant tactics that saved us all. Likewise, Amelia Gordon has acknowledged to me the new debt Mars owes to Citadel for the efforts of Captain Stewart and the crews aboard two transports to save their lives.

"That's all for now, except that I can guess at some tough decisions that are ahead of you. You know you'll always have my support. God bless all of you."

CHAPTER TWENTY-FOUR

"I hope Harrington is sufficiently stupid to show up just long enough to have her ass blasted to hell," Joe Albretti said.

"Harrington may be that stupid, by I doubt Powers is," Sara Albretti replied. She looked at Austin. "Since we know there's an operation of some sort within reach of our technology, the question is whether to do something about it, and if so, what it would be."

Austin nodded at Yabuno. "Bret, Alan and others have been checking out the alien technology. Bret, why don't you bring us up to date on your efforts?"

Yabuno walked to a display, and images of Citadel beacons appeared. "While it would have been nice to assess the wreck of *Firebird* right away, we had more pressing stuff to do. We went through every nook and cranny in our communications and defense networks to root out any contamination from the alien code." With a sigh he declared, "It's been a pain in the ass, but I don't believe there are any more surprises waiting for us."

He replaced the images of Citadel beacons with images of alien beacons. "We then tracked down and collected every alien beacon and device that littered our system, thanks to Harrington's people. We have a team taking a couple of transports back along the path to the other solar system, collecting those beacons as well."

Yabuno's expression darkened as an image of a Phoenix ship appeared. "We're well aware that Harrington could be hiding somewhere along that path, so our transports are heavily armed. They have instructions to shoot first, to avoid any surprises. That's also why the beacons are being destroyed as they are collected. We already have a few samples here for review, so having beacons out there only benefits Harrington. If we break up that network, we make it impossible for her to use it to make contact with her backers.

"Our network is intact, of course, so we can still communicate over vast distances. To be on the safe side, we'll replace every one of our own beacons as we collect theirs, to eliminate any possibility of further contamination. Ultimately, our efforts will extend to rooting out every beacon in the other solar system and destroying them all. We figure that when they set up their network, they were able to introduce something into the other networks back there that shut everything down at the wrong time, although it is possible that it originated from this end and made its way to the other solar system via beacons. In view of the encryption used at this end, it's probably the former."

Yabuno made another gesture, and *Firebird* appeared on a display, the physical damage to it obvious. "Recently, we've begun to pay more attention to the wreck of *Firebird*. Something's happened to the alien technology that was running things on board, because it doesn't function the way it did before. We don't know whether it's because their network has been destroyed or because there isn't another one of their ships close enough to contact, or just because of the extensive damage to the conventional side of the engines. J. W. reported in his message that all of the Phoenix ships that attacked them in Earth's solar system ended up being consumed by fireballs. It's possible that the damage to *Firebird* wasn't sufficient to trigger a similar response. To be on the safe side, we have disengaged the rest of the ship's systems from the alien technology so that nothing bad can happen to our people while aboard, like a life-support failure. We've built a control module that supplies power and instructions to the ship's systems."

"Why would there be anything important to find on the nonalien side?" Sara asked. "Wasn't it the alien technology that did everything?"

Yabuno shook his head. "That's what we thought at first, but we realized that the aliens still had to deal with the limitations inherent in humans. The humans had to have the ability to act at least semi-independently of the preprogrammed settings, which meant that the human side of the ship had to have certain information relating to the mission."

"Did that information include the location of the aliens' complex?" she asked.

Yabuno chuckled as a new image appeared. "Good question. As best as we can tell, this is an image of that complex. As you can see, it looks something like the one we destroyed, only bigger. Unlike the other one, it appears to be more than just a place for ships to dock. It looks like a small city and can probably handle more ships as well."

There was a hint of a shudder in his expression. "This is probably also the place where Harrington and the rest of her people were taken after they were captured. I'm not saying that what happened to them there wasn't something they brought on themselves by their flagrant disregard for what it means to be human, however. I just want us to know this is probably where people were taken apart and sometimes put back together, not always successfully." He looked carefully at Austin. "There's nothing to say that they wouldn't do the same to any other humans that showed up there."

"Point taken, Bret," Austin said, nodding. "How long would it take to reach this complex, using conventional means of propulsion?"

Yabuno shrugged. "It's probably safe to say that we'd spend an impossibly long time just trying to reach them via conventional propulsion. I can give you a better estimate of the time it would take using our warp-field generators. It would probably take around a month to reach them from here. After Alan and I have more time to review their files, we may be able to refine that estimate."

"What would be the purpose behind visiting them, Sam?" Turner asked. "They lost again and probably can't try that approach against us anymore."

Austin walked over to a display and brought up an image of the ruins of the other complex. "As we know, when we went back after the dust had settled and recovered our transports that had been damaged and abandoned during our mission to destroy the original complex, we left behind a series of beacons to keep tabs on anything that may happen out there. They're linked back to us here, so we have virtually real-time information on the situation. What do the data have to say about the status of the site?"

"That's just my point. The data tell us they've never returned, not even to recover what was left of the burned-out shells of their ships."

An image of the larger complex appeared next to the ruined complex. "That's also my point, Alan. Apparently, pushing them back from this point to their larger complex wasn't enough to stop them from trying to destroy us again, even though we warned them against it."

"Don't you think the fact they didn't face us directly, but used human proxies, shows they took us seriously?"

"They took us seriously," Austin acknowledged, "but that just means they used those proxies in an elaborate scheme against us. The result was that they tried to destroy us anyway. We have to consider whether pushing them back even further would finally put them in a situation where attacking us is untenable. It's possible that all of the resources they have used to act against us have come from these two facilities. If we remove this one from the table, there may not be enough resources available to maintain the conflict."

"That's a lot of speculation to base a decision on."

"We haven't always had the benefit of traditional facts at our disposal to make decisions. If we hadn't made some conclusions based on less-than-perfect information about Phoenix and hadn't prepared for their appearance here, we probably wouldn't be having this conversation; we'd be dead. I want to get us to the point where we don't have to keep making unconventional assessments in order to stay alive."

Yabuno spoke. "The good news is that they don't seem to have the desire to build ships similar to ours, without human help. So far, they've stayed with their own designs, which don't appear to use the same weapons we do, although we know how lethal they can be. The Phoenix ships have given us an idea of what it could be like if we had to face our own weapons; I'd hate to deal with the full-blown version of their technology, combined with our rail guns and ability to launch torpedoes."

Turner brought up another image, and the ancient derelict came into view. "Don't forget that the key reason why we succeeded in destroying the first complex is that the very prize they sought became the means of their destruction. We could never transport the derelict to this new location, and it would be madness to think that they'd put themselves in a similar position to be destroyed by a single burst of energy."

"Can you think of any other way the derelict may help us?"

"I'm continuing to work with the symbols that seem to deal with moving through a warp bubble. That's still a weakness with our transports; although they can achieve a stable environment within a warp bubble, we can't make it last very long. We watched as the alien technology began to take this fact into account and took out a number of our ships accordingly."

He glanced back at the image of the large complex. "If we visit them without having solved that problem, we stand a good chance of losing a lot of our transports, with plenty of humans available for more dissections by the aliens. The difference is that this time it would be our friends who would be our mortal enemies."

"I understand your concerns, Alan. I never take lightly any encounter with the aliens, and visiting this facility is no different."

He brought up an image of the beautiful landscape within his property, with the great mountain framed in the background, its frosty cap of snow gleaming brightly in the sunlight. "I'd much rather spend my time being thankful for and enjoying everything we've been blessed to have on Citadel, than worrying about an attack that may never show up. I'm sure everyone else feels the same way."

The image of the alien complex reappeared. "However, I'm concerned that the time we spend not trying to deal with them may be time that they're spending coming up with another plan for our destruction. In fact, so long as any humans remain their creatures, they have the possibility of infiltrating human society as a significant weapon, either here or back in the other solar system. Unless Harrington shows up in the Citadel Group's solar system, the only other place she could be would be this complex."

"That's assuming she hasn't been stranded somewhere, or worse, while trying to sustain a warp bubble."

Austin's expression grew darker. "Previous reports of her demise have proved to be exaggerated, and we don't have any information to suggest it's happened at this point." He sighed. "While waiting is not always the easiest course of action, we should wait until she's had enough time to reach the other solar system and for that feedback to have reached us before making final decisions on anything else. However, some planning would be a good idea."

———

Later, when Liz and Austin were alone, Austin was quiet in a way that told Liz something was on his mind. She asked him about it.

He waited a moment before speaking. "There's something I need to tell you, and I'm not really sure how to begin, so I'll just say it. Everyone has heard the story about how Powers faked an image of slicing open one of my arteries and watching me bleed to death in order to motivate the *Pathfinder* crew to do what the aliens wanted."

She locked her gaze on his. "Was it really a fake, or did she do it?"

He kept his gaze steady. "The image was real. She cut open an artery, and I bled out. She checked for a pulse, couldn't find one, and left. Somehow, the artery healed on its own, and I revived. I even had blood in me again."

"Why didn't you tell me sooner?" she asked, looking away for a moment. "We never keep secrets from each other."

"I've been meaning to tell you, but we haven't had a lot of time lately," Austin began uneasily. "The main reason is that I didn't really know how to talk about it. It isn't the easiest thing to bring up; I don't understand what happened myself, so I'm not sure what to tell you."

"Do you think you may have come back from the dead?"

Austin shook his head. "I don't believe I really died, but others may think so. Despite what it looked like, I probably didn't bleed out as much as people thought; I think that while I was lying in a pool of blood that looked more substantial than it really was, my body went into some kind of stasis before the wound would have been fatal. The stasis made it look like I was dead. Once my body healed the wound, I revived. It didn't take very long for me to return to full strength, and the blood I lost must have been replenished somehow. I can't explain how it happened, though it must be related to the same thing that enabled me to heal from the massive radiation exposure years ago." He frowned. "I'm not sure I like the implications if the answer to what happened is something else."

She pulled him close as he continued. "What I don't want to have happen is for people to start testing to see what they can do to me. Just because I revived doesn't mean I ever want to go through anything like it again. I sure as hell don't want people to stop thinking of me as being human, perhaps even being afraid of me. That's why we put out the story about the image being a fake."

His expression became slightly less serious, and he continued. "As you said, we don't keep secrets from each other, which is why I just told you about it. Within the entire population of Citadel, you are the only one, other than the three of us who were there, who knows what really happened."

"Outside the population of Citadel, Harrington and Powers know, if they're still alive. If they are, the aliens probably know as well."

Austin nodded. They held each other for a long time, without needing any words.

CHAPTER TWENTY-FIVE

J ust over three months after Harrington's escape from
Citadel, Preacher met with Henkel and Bacas to discuss the situation. After exchanging pleasantries, they
got down to business.

"I need to send another report to Sam," the ambassador said. "I assume there's been no word about
Harrington's ship?" he asked.

Henkel shook her head as she stood near a display.
An image of the fugitive vessel appeared. "Nothing, J. W.
There's been no sign of her ship anywhere near this system, and none of our beacons between here and Citadel
has reported any 'stops' by a ship along the way, other
than by Citadel transports. While we should maintain our
vigilance for now, it looks increasingly unlikely that she's
going to show up here."

Preacher's expression warmed at the news. He turned
toward Bacas. "What's been happening with the wrecks
of the Phoenix ships? Any trouble?"

"No, not really," Bacas replied. "We've completed
our inspection of all of the ruins of their ships. With one

exception, they were nothing more than burned-out shells, so we towed them to our sun and sent them to a fiery resting place. The one exception wasn't in much better shape, but we did a salvage operation on it."

Preacher had a puzzled look. "What do you mean by 'salvage?' I thought there wasn't anything useful from any of the wrecks."

"I'm using the word a little differently," Bacas explained, as he walked to a display and brought up an image of a ship that had clearly suffered massive damage. A close-up of a damaged component appeared nearby. "I mean that although the alien technology is so badly damaged that it is hardly even recognizable, we don't know the full extent of what it can do, so we removed it physically from the ruin and placed it in a controlled environment." He grinned. "It can't do anything creepy, like start to grow and take over a ship. Speaking of ships, we towed the remainder of that ship to our sun and sent it to its own fiery resting place, to join with the ashes from the rest of the wrecks."

Preacher nodded. "Very good, Dan. What about the rest of their technology?"

Henkel spoke. "The rest of their technology consists of the beacons they placed around the solar system. We've scoured the place and looked far beyond the system, to make sure we've collected them all."

"Are they based on alien or human technology?"

"Outwardly, they're based on human technology," she replied. "That was expected, since they would have known that Citadel and other groups would have inspected them. Everyone would have known the game was up if the beacons hadn't looked human."

"You used the word 'outwardly,'" Preacher noted. "What did you find when you delved into them further?"

"The human part of the technology can't transmit communications the way ours can. There are alien messages in them that probably are what make them work."

There was an eager look in his expression. "Have you been able to translate the messages?"

"No," she said, "it appears that new symbols were used, ones that we've never seen. I've already forwarded them to Alan Turner to take a turn with them. What's curious about the beacons is that they appear to be receiving signals from somewhere."

The warmth faded from Preacher's face. "Where?"

"We don't know, but we're sure it isn't from within this solar system. We're checking to see if there's anything still in this system that these beacons could be talking with, but our best guess at this point is that this is an external attempt at communication."

"What do you think it means?"

Henkel's tone was full of concern. "It means that the aliens are still interested in us, J. W. We should worry anytime that happens."

Preacher nodded. "I agree. Please give me a copy of your files for my report to Sam. One other area we haven't addressed is the rest of their files. What have you found?"

"We've found virtually nothing relating to their technology," Henkel said, her disappointment plain. "They made a conscious effort to wipe everything relating to their technology before they departed for Citadel, even though they also had ships remaining here. They probably already had everything they needed on board their ships. With plenty of ships and their own communications network, they wouldn't have had any trouble getting what they needed."

"What about the rest of their files?"

Henkel's expression brightened slightly. "We had a little more success. We've received more information relating to how they set up their operations, including how they got access to Harrington's funds to get started. Harrington seemed to know where to go to get what she wanted, and her money made things happen. There are probably going to be some prosecutions for corruption," she added. "Incidentally, her money is gone, although she may have other funds available that we don't know about. She was quite wealthy at one time."

"I doubt money means much to her anymore," Preacher noted dryly. "What about the Phoenix operation's money? Where is it?"

"That money is gone too, even the fees they collected from the colonists. It appears that everything went into building their fleet. As you said, they probably don't care much about money, except as a means to an end. Once they'd destroyed both solar systems, money wouldn't have had any meaning anyway. At that point, if they'd wanted resources, they would have simply taken them."

"How certain are we that we've eliminated any chance of their taking down the networks in this system again?"

She sighed. "There's no way to be absolutely certain. However, we've become pretty adept at recognizing alien symbols and code. Bret has been a huge help as well, as he's forwarded information they've gleaned on their end about how everything works. We've destroyed the alien network and provided a lot of help in sterilizing everyone's networks, without giving them access to our encryption protocols." Her gaze lost some warmth. "If we give them that access, then we weaken our own security with respect to both human and alien threats. In view of human nature, some day that weakness would be exploited by people without regard for the impact on us."

"I agree," Preacher said, nodding. "It was only because we have never shared that information with anyone else that we were able to avoid having our own network brought down. I hope this information will be of value to Sam."

———

Austin's refurbished study had no trouble accommodating the people he had asked to join him. They'd just finished listening to the latest report from Preacher. Austin looked around the room. "Thoughts?" he asked. "Bret, let's start with you."

Yabuno nodded. "One thing that comes to mind is that J. W.'s point about being worried anytime the aliens are interested in us is dead on. I'm worried about the fact that someone or something is trying to use those beacons to communicate with someone or something in that system. While I agree with Bacas's assessment that the alien technology they salvaged probably doesn't work, we can't be sure we know the scope of its capabilities. I'm very concerned that the alien beacons could cause problems there that they may not be able to handle, especially in view of the time delay in communications between the two systems. I think we're better off with Bacas destroying what they salvaged and continuing to keep a close watch on the beacons.

"Besides, that's something we'll have to keep in mind here, since we've noticed the same signals coming through the beacons we've captured. While I think the precautions we've taken are sound, now that we know the beacons are still active, we should reconsider whether those precautions are still the right ones."

"One question we should be asking is, to whom are these signals addressed?" Liz said. "It can't be a coincidence that signals are ending up in both places." She brought up a familiar image. "The aliens may be trying to locate Harrington or even sending her further instructions."

"It's also possible that not everyone from Phoenix was on board their ships," Sara noted. "There may be some people in that solar system who are receiving further instructions, along with instructions that are intended for Harrington. Face it; there could be more people back there from Phoenix, and we might never know it. We know that none of Harrington's people looks like he or she did before being disassembled and then reassembled.

"About the only things that remain the same are age and gender, and we're not even completely sure about gender. From what Sam, Bret, and Joe shared with us, Powers seemed a little vague on whether all of the survivors still had their original genders, or 'equipment,' as she put it, although she may have been referring to some of the earlier subjects, who weren't put back together properly. In short, there isn't much use in trying to track down Harrington's people who have since vanished."

"That reminds me," Austin said, "we never reviewed the postmortems on Lazarus and his colleagues. Liz has been consulting with the medical staff."

She walked over to a display, and images of Flynn and Lazarus appeared. "As we already know," she began, "these are images of the same man. We don't actually know his real name, since even Flynn was probably a fake. However, at least superficially, there's nothing similar about them, except for the apparent calendar age and gender. Apparently, the aliens can't make someone young just by taking the person apart and then putting him or her back together."

"What about the DNA? Did the aliens change it, or just shift around tissue?"

"The problem is we don't know how they did what they did, and there's no DNA sample available for comparison. All we know for certain is that the DNA is consistent with the physical appearance, which suggests that at the least, the DNA was altered."

"My impression from their comments was that they had been taken apart at the cellular level. What evidence did the doctors find to support the notion that they were taken apart at all, regardless of the level?"

"Strangely, there wasn't any evidence of that kind of cellular trauma at all." She looked at Austin quizzically. "What are you thinking?"

"I'm curious how much of what they think happened is what actually happened," he mused. "I don't doubt that something happened to them, both physically and mentally, that was excruciating to endure. I wonder if what they underwent was the physical agony from the body reacting to the changes imposed by having their DNA resequenced radically, perhaps multiple times, along with something that deconstructed their minds and put them back together." He shrugged. "That isn't the most important thing to consider right now, though."

"A key question is, where is Harrington hiding?" Melody Lambert asked. "We know she isn't anywhere near here; our network extends quite a distance out from this system, and nothing has shown up. We've also confirmed that she isn't hiding anywhere along the path between our two solar systems, unless she's staying far from the beacons. While we don't have the same flexibility to track things around Earth's solar system, we're still confident that she isn't hovering just outside that system, waiting for further instructions."

"That suggests that she returned to the aliens' complex, assuming her ship was still capable of generating a warp-field bubble," Albretti said. "Otherwise, she's probably dead or dying very slowly if her ship broke down trillions of miles away from anywhere."

Austin looked at Turner. "What can you tell us about the alien messages that Astrid forwarded?"

Turner stood in front of a display, and the alien symbols appeared. "Her files with the messages arrived a week ago, so that isn't a long time to do a fresh translation." He grinned. "However, you know I love a challenge, so I've continued to refine my translation protocols. I consider their symbols to be less advanced than the ones the builders of the derelict used." His grin faded. "As it happens, I completed my translation a short while ago."

The room was dead silent as he looked into each person's face before continuing, "The aliens aren't done with us yet. The first message is something like a demand for a status report from Lazarus. The second one acknowledges that Lazarus is dead and that they failed, and it orders the ship to return to their complex for briefing on a new plan for a full-scale invasion of Citadel, this time with every ship at their disposal. It includes capturing several Citadel transports and converting the crews over to their side. With some modifications to the transports, they'll finally be able to invade our system and finish what they tried to do the last time. They believe our weakness is that we won't be willing to destroy our friends, even as they try to kill us."

"Any other details, such as where they'll strike to get the transports?" Austin asked.

Turner shook his head. "Those are the kinds of details they would have gone over when the Phoenix operatives returned to the complex."

"We don't know how they knew about the failure of the mission? No indication that they'd heard from Harrington?" Austin asked hopefully.

"There's nothing about it in the message," Turner replied. "However, it isn't clear where else they could have obtained the information, if not from Harrington. The most plausible answer is that Harrington is alive and is either back with them already or is on her way."

"When was the message received? That may tell us when Harrington would have left for the complex."

"There's no way to be sure, but it was probably just before Astrid sent it. Perhaps it was just over a month ago."

"That means Harrington may not even be there yet," Albretti said eagerly. "If they're waiting for her before they start, then we could get there to deal with them before they could get anywhere near any Citadel transports."

"What if we're the ones that are bringing the transports?" Austin asked.

"What do you mean?" Albretti asked, slightly crestfallen by Austin's reaction. "You've been making the case for our doing something to get rid of them for good, and now you don't sound as sure of yourself."

"I haven't changed my mind about wanting to eliminate them as a threat," Austin said firmly. "I want to make sure that we're doing it on our terms, and that we're not being manipulated to serve someone else's motives."

"The threat about capturing our transports and turning our people into their creatures is real." Albretti looked at his wife. "I don't like having to think about what I'd do if Sara were one of them."

"If I were one of them, I wouldn't be me anymore, not really," she replied. "I wouldn't even look like me. I'd hope that you'd kill whatever I became, and remember what I was, rather than sacrifice everything here, including our children, for a person who no longer existed."

"You're both right," Austin said. "Regardless of whether they're planning on moving against our people or are just bluffing in order to manipulate us, we can't go on trying to live with that threat always hanging over our heads."

It was his turn to take in everyone around the room, a determined look in his gaze. "We're going to need to put together a plan that makes use of everything we've learned, whether it's about them or ourselves or anything else we can think of. We'd better get moving because we only have a few days before we're heading out."

CHAPTER TWENTY-SIX

Liz made use of her organizational skills to oversee the preparations for what might be the final battle for Citadel. Because of his leadership role as well as his wide range of practical skills, which he didn't always advertise, Austin met with many people, going over strategies and making sure everything worked together.

"You see the problems with the new approach," Yabuno explained, as he nodded at a display. "Alan's taken things just about as far as possible to maintain a stable warp bubble with the transports. One day, we'll be able to stay there the way we can with *Pathfinder*, but no one knows when that day will come.

"For now, we still have to measure the time in minutes, although we've stretched things out a bit from a few months ago. We've already seen that the maneuvers become somewhat predictable and the aliens learn to use that technology against us. We won't have the benefit of the derelict hovering nearby, giving us cover and serving as a weapon as well."

Albretti spoke. "One thing that hurt us the last time is the fact that the technology was so new, we hadn't had a chance to try anything with it. Another thing is that we had no ability to communicate with each other, thanks to their taking our network offline. Third, they were able to link everything together and have all of their ships operate as an integrated fighting force." He brought up a familiar image. "This time, they'll be using their own vessels. Although those vessels are a hell of a lot nastier and tougher than what Phoenix put together, they don't operate as a fully integrated fighting force. Individually, they're very clever, but it isn't the same. Also, they've never embraced rail guns, so we shouldn't have to worry about ducking from huge rocks hurling through space, unless they're ours!" he said, grinning.

"Your points are well taken," Austin said, "but the thing that often causes one side to lose a battle is complacency. We have to assume that they know our strengths and weaknesses very well by now, including anything that Harrington and Powers may have shared with them about us. About the only thing they haven't seen up close is a Citadel transport, other than *KT-20*, which their technology took over briefly before we destroyed it. That time, I doubt they bothered to try to learn anything about our technology because they assumed they'd destroy the ships we used to attack their complex anyway.

"However, we never expected that they'd be clever enough to plant technology within our communications system that would be as devastating as it was, either. That's a reminder that we can't afford to make any

turned to leave. "I hope you don't mind if I stop by and say something similar to your people."

She shook her head, but not in opposition to Austin. "In addition to the fact that they need to hear those words, what time we lose from the distraction of your visit will more than be made up by the increase in energy after they've heard you."

———

Austin met with Yabuno, Turner, and Lambert to discuss communications. Austin began, "You know better than anyone what a nasty surprise they left for us from the earlier encounter with them when they got the derelict. How certain are we that there won't be a repeat this time?"

Turner gestured at the symbols that appeared on a display. "I have a pretty good understanding of the symbols they used to sandbag us last time, and there's nothing like that around."

"What about the beacons?" he asked. "Why are they active? Is there still a link between those things and our network that they can exploit?"

Yabuno shook his head. "While we're not sure why the beacons are still active, there isn't any link between them and our network." He looked at Lambert without humor. "We went through a lot of trouble to make sure."

She nodded. "We went through an *excruciating* level of detail to make sure, Sam. We pretty much had to rebuild the network, which we've refined since then. In dealing with what they did, we learned a lot about their own capabilities, which helped us to develop new protocols to prevent something like that from happening again. I know we need to guard against complacency, but there's just no way they can compromise our network. It isn't complacency when you've done the hard work to be sure."

"All right," Austin nodded. "We'll head out tomorrow. Try to get some rest."

———

Joe and Sara were in bed, discussing the events to come.

"Hard to believe we're going to be on another assignment that will keep us apart for a month out and, hopefully, a month back," she said, sighing. "We belong together in the same bed, and not on two separate ships."

"With all the transports that have been recommissioned from the mothball fleet, we need transport captains. You're a valuable commodity, being a former captain of a transport with combat experience," he reminded her. "So is Alicia Shaw, which is why she's commanding a transport instead of occupying the chair aboard *Pathfinder*."

"You have lots of combat experience," she pointed out.

"Aboard *Pathfinder*, yes," he acknowledged, "and even in training exercises aboard Space Command ships before I joined Citadel, but not aboard Citadel transports."

"I think that's more because of Sam's confidence in you as the best captain for handling *Pathfinder* when there's a crisis. He put you there in the first place because of all that field experience you just mentioned, which included more than one type of ship."

"He also put me there because I needed something different after Gina died," he said quietly. She reached over to stroke his face. He took her hand gently and said, "I never could have imagined that that assignment would lead to our finding each other."

"Neither could I, or that I'd be lucky enough to have two babies with you." A gleam appeared in her gaze. "In fact, it's time for you to put another one in me."

"Now, with everything that's been happening?"

"Especially now, my love. If we hold off, we let them win by giving them power over our living our lives. Besides, we won't have another chance for a couple of months, and there's no way I'm waiting that long to get started." She pulled his hands down to her breasts, laughing gently. "I've said many times I *want* you to look at me, and you've always admired my rack."

He looked over her naked body with a similar gleam in his gaze as he said, "You're not wrong, but as superb as it is, that's not the only part of you I've always admired."

She giggled, saying, "We have all night to check out everything you've admired, and I want to check out some things about you I've admired as well, but I want to get started with making that baby *now*."

CHAPTER TWENTY-SEVEN

They'd been underway for a week, and Austin and Liz were in their stateroom aboard *Pathfinder*. Yabuno and Turner were along as well, and the three of them had continued to discuss technological refinements.

"I wish Melody were here," Yabuno said. "She was terrific in helping getting the network back up and running, and she may have some insights to share."

"You know why she isn't here," Austin reminded him. "We can't concentrate all of our key technological talent aboard any single ship. We're stretching the rule as it is by having you and Alan aboard *Pathfinder*. It's necessary, because you've worked together a lot on warp-field issues due to the symbols from the derelict, and Alan has special insights into the other alien symbols that we may be able to put to use. If you two are on different ships, that can't happen."

"If we're talking about key technological talent, you keep downplaying your own, Sam," Yabuno pointed out. "You're actually one of the smartest people I know. Even the aliens couldn't penetrate the security you built into your own network."

"Thanks for the thoughts, but if we start focusing on my alleged technological skills, then we'd have to include me in the rule about ship assignments, and that wouldn't be a good idea," he chuckled. "I wouldn't look forward to having to go a month at a time without being able to talk things over with you guys."

The humor faded from his expression as they got back to business. "We need to consider that they could have anticipated everything we're going to do. While doing that stuff better than they can handle may still be a winner for us, let's keep thinking about whether there's any way to use their technology against them." The images on the displays kept evolving as the discussion went on for hours.

"What do you plan on doing about Harrington?" Liz asked Austin. "One could argue that Courtney Harrington doesn't exist anymore, so there isn't anyone to punish for her old crimes. As far as her more recent actions are concerned, she's now just an extension of the aliens' will, so punishing her won't really mean something."

In spite of the question, Austin chuckled. "J. W. would have liked to have you on his team back when he was preparing for a case. Your comments seemed so reasonable, the answer must be that I shouldn't do anything about Harrington."

It was her turn to chuckle. "You know full well how I feel about her, so you know I don't believe the arguments I made excuse anything she's done. It's still worth asking the question, though."

"Yes, and I've done a lot of thinking about it since she first told us about what had happened to her. First, I have a hard time believing that there isn't enough of her left that she's not the same person she was. Her antipathy for me and the murderous lack of respect for humanity were already a part of her before she met the aliens. Also, her memories are still intact. What the aliens did to her changes none of who she was or what she did.

"The fact that she underwent a gruesome process is unfortunate, but something she brought on herself. It has no bearing on her guilt for the war crimes she committed earlier. While I get it that a new form of compulsion has been embedded in her mind that would be difficult to overcome, I'm not in a position to accept the claim that she has absolutely no control over following orders from her new masters. One look at Powers tells me that it may be possible to resist. By the way, that doesn't mean I think Powers may suddenly turn into a good person; she's still the amoral, lethal person she was before. It means that her dislike of Harrington may be enough to overcome the compulsion embedded in her own mind, at least for a time. There may be other emotional triggers that could have the same impact.

"That's a way of saying that based on what we know currently, I wouldn't let any of them off the hook for following orders from the aliens." He shrugged. "It's a moot point anyway, as I plan on watching their executions for the war crimes they've already been judged to have committed against Citadel. They only need to be hanged once."

———

They were just days away from the end of their journey, and Austin met with Yabuno and Turner. "How sure are you about the location of this complex, Bret?" he asked. "I'd hate to have a large group of ships attempt to move undetected through space while we try to find something that may be far away."

Yabuno chuckled as he stood by a display and nodded at Turner. "I'm pretty sure about my estimate, based on the information that Alan gleaned from their messages and files. I've also matched it with the celestial information you can see in this image of the place. The problem is, we could still be off target by millions of miles, in view of how vast space is."

"Why?"

Turner spoke. "The way in which they used certain symbols makes it difficult to be more precise." He frowned. "The strange thing is, I think they could have been more precise, which leads me to wonder why they weren't."

"Could it have been done for security reasons, in case we got access to their systems for some reason?"

"It's possible," Turner acknowledged, "but they had other options available to keep us away from that information if they wanted."

"What if they still had to make it available for the Phoenix crews? I don't have the sense that being creatures of the aliens has made them particularly brighter, except in a few distinct areas."

Turner shrugged. "All of what you suggested is possible. I'm reacting this way because I've been studying them for a while—their symbols and how they use them—and something doesn't feel quite right."

Austin frowned. "Do you think the information was planted, perhaps to draw us away from Citadel and leave it unprotected?"

Yabuno shook his head. "It's hard to see how that would work. We left several transports there for protection. We rebuilt the defenses in the outer and inner parts of the system, especially near the safe path, and our transports can either take on any invaders or avoid capture by heading out to safety with a normal warp-field move. The transports that are within the inner part of the system aren't in any real danger, since the aliens can't get their ships through the safe path. If they try to send scout ships through, they'll be picked off one by one before they can even finish the trip."

"I can't argue with your instincts, Alan," Austin said, "but we'll have to go as planned and hope that there isn't too much terrain to cover when we arrive."

CHAPTER TWENTY-EIGHT

For the first time in a month, the fleet's ships moved out of their warp bubbles into normal space-time. As Yabuno and Turner had warned might happen, the alien complex was nowhere to be seen. Austin asked the two to check their readings for the location of their target. While that effort was underway, he made contact with the rest of the fleet and confirmed that there were no problems from the journey.

Yabuno and Turner reported back.

"We're in the right place, Sam," Yabuno said. He walked to a display and pointed to a position. This is where they are."

"How far away?"

"Less than ten minutes. We timed it pretty closely, all things considered," he said with a tight grin.

"Good work, both of you," he said. "Get ready for the main show."

He turned to *Pathfinder*'s captain. "Joe, alert the fleet to the position of the complex and our time to arrival. Give them a one-minute countdown to depart as planned."

A countdown appeared on a display, and the seconds ticked away. As usual, Austin stood in his accustomed spot, where he had a good view of everything on the bridge and easy access to the captain and navigator, as well as a link to the chief engineer. Yabuno and Turner were in engineering as well, ready to help make technological magic. Several displays had been arranged for Austin to monitor the course of the engagement; he was set up much like an admiral in command of a fleet. The last seconds ticked away, and the fleet moved out as the reading went to zero. No one spoke as a new countdown appeared, to help carry out their next steps.

———

The transports approached the enemy stronghold in silence. The countdown had been programmed to take into account the distance to the complex, so that everyone would be in the right place at the right time to commence the attack.

The target came into view on the long-range scanners, which magnified and enhanced the image. The place was, to the human eye, misshapen, with architectural choices that at times were unfathomable. The greater scope of the place allowed for a broader range in sizes of the various structures that populated the facility. As usual, their primary colors were shades of browns and blacks.

Austin gazed intently at a display. "Look at the size of that place! Good to see that it matches up with the image from the Phoenix ship. Is there any sign of Harrington's ship, Joe?"

"No," Albretti said, shaking his head. "It could be on the other side, or maybe she showed up and they scrapped her ship as a pile of junk, considering the shape it must be in by now." Austin looked at Albretti with a slightly less grim appearance at hearing Albretti's comment.

"Do we have any ships in place on the other side yet?" he asked.

"Yes," Albretti nodded, "they've just gotten into position. We now have transports all around the target and a complete picture of the place. They can just make out Harrington's ship." A moment later, a familiar image appeared on a display.

"Any sign that ship has been repaired?"

"The holes are still there, but they may have cleared out the logjam in their loader." The dark humor left Albretti's expression. "They may be ready to take us on too."

"How many ships do they have? Are there any empty ports?"

"I count forty-three ports, twenty-four of them occupied. Half of them are still tethered, and half are just holding position. I wonder if the empty ports are where the ships we've destroyed over the years once berthed." Albretti motioned toward the Phoenix vessel. "Interesting that Harrington's ship is the only one not in a port. They probably use shuttles when they need to visit. I wonder if the aliens still want to stay isolated from humans, even ones they control." He looked over at Austin. "They must know we're coming; they're set up to move against us at any time."

"Bret and Alan, any sign they've seen us yet? Any unusual communications traffic by the aliens?"

"No, Sam," Turner replied. "What little traffic we can detect doesn't have anything I can identify as recognition or an alarm."

"Keep your eyes and ears open for any signs of EMP cannons," Austin reminded them. "This time, we won't be able to shield our ships from them by hiding behind the derelict."

Austin looked back at the countdown, which ticked down to below ten seconds. They watched the last few seconds vanish, and they began their moves automatically.

———

Austin didn't expect their approach to be unmonitored, so he wasn't surprised when the enemy began to disperse ships to prevent the humans from approaching any closer without challenge. Numerically, the aliens had the advantage, with Citadel having mustered eighteen transports, plus *Pathfinder*, for the expedition. He decided to interrupt whatever plans the aliens had for trapping them by having several rail guns launch their first rocks. He noticed that even though they'd begun their movements, some of the enemy ships were still tethered in their ports, which meant they weren't facing the full alien fleet yet. He wanted to send a clear message about complacency.

He pointed to several positions on a display. "*KT-3, 6, 14, 15, 23,* and *25,* I want the first three to launch your rocks where indicated, and the second group to launch yours where indicated. Reload right after you launch, because you'll need to have follow-up torpedoes ready to deal with the company. The five-second countdown commences now!"

Seconds later, they were barely able to make out the multiple streaks of massive rocks racing toward the huge ships bearing down on them. The effects were devastating, as Austin had clustered the rocks so that the impacts would effectively rip the ships in half.

At Austin's instructions, *Pathfinder* had already gone into a warp bubble and maneuvered toward both enemy ships in the area, so that it might be undetected even before the rocks reached their targets. The scout ship moved into normal space-time for a moment, and then launched a special torpedo toward the nearest damaged vessel. *Pathfinder* had already begun to shift toward the second stricken vessel before the interior of the first one distorted into a horrific caricature of a ship, spewing energy and materials before explosions took over. By the time the death agonies of the first ship had taken hold, the second one was sent on its way with another torpedo. The smaller ship hovered for a moment as Austin surveyed the scene.

It was already becoming much more difficult to keep track of the action, as repeated bursts from both sides' EMP weapons had degraded visuals significantly.

"We have more company, Sam," Yabuno warned. Austin looked at a display and could make out a long-distance image from the complex. The remaining enemy ships had shed their tethers and were bearing down on the transports at high speed.

Austin grinned fiercely. "I guess this means they've decided to take us seriously after all."

Suddenly, an enemy vessel bore down on two transports at extreme speed, attempting to catch them off guard and prevent the humans from performing a maneuver like the one that had just taken out the other two ships. Austin saw his opportunity and sent a quick message to the transports. *Pathfinder* went into a warp bubble in search of its prey.

Just as the alien ship was within range, it veered sharply to one side, to avoid the expected attack from the transports and catch the scout ship as it reappeared to deliver the death blow. Unfortunately for the enemy, Austin had given a different instruction to the transports. It wasn't until *Pathfinder* reappeared behind the alien ship that it launched a conventional torpedo from close range. The torpedo raced toward its target from an unexpected direction and blasted a hole in the misshapen hull. Because of the direction in which the ship had veered, Austin had been able to select his point of attack so that the resulting hole would be a visible target for the transports. Moments later, the huge vessel found itself ripped apart from multiple angles.

The smaller ship waited for a moment before sending further opportunistic instructions to another cluster of transports and then shifting back into a warp bubble and moving out again.

These encounters revealed a key part of Citadel's strategy. While the main action took place as planned, *Pathfinder* would search for targets of opportunity and set up attacks with groups of transports. To prevent the aliens from simply predicting where the transports and the scout ship would be for each attack, Austin set things up so that either the transports or *Pathfinder* could launch the attacks, with either able to finish things off. Sometimes, Austin wasn't setting things up for that attack, but for another he saw coming down the road. By concentrating their firepower for short periods, they could offset their numerical disadvantage and avoid the drawn-out process of taking out the much larger, tougher ships one shot at a time.

KT-10, commanded by Captain Sara Albretti, was teamed with *KT-2*, commanded by Captain Washington, seeking to take on a single enemy vessel. Captain Albretti faced several displays, one of which had images of all three ships. She pointed to two spots.

"We'll start here, Wash, and you start there. You take the first shot, then we'll do the top-to-bottom and back moves that Joe worked out. If the primary ship shifts out of position, we go to the secondary target and do the same maneuver. If the second ship comes over here, modify the attack sequence as planned. The countdown is in five seconds."

"Acknowledged, Sara," Wash replied.

At zero, both ships vanished and moved toward their target in separate warp bubbles. At least two alien ships were potential targets, so it wasn't clear which one would need to defend itself. As they sought to support each other, *KT-2* appeared and raked an unprotected flank with an intense EMP blast, taking out the lasers on that side. Before the stricken ship could react, *KT-10* appeared under the target, while *KT-2* vanished. The second transport launched a torpedo, ripping open the belly of the larger ship. *KT-2* reappeared behind the enemy vessel as it approached to protect its partner, and blasted its side with an EMP burst. As the target sought to retaliate against the smaller ship, *KT-2* disappeared.

Thoroughly confused, the first vessel was unprepared for the attack by *KT-10* from overhead. The second ship, out of position as it was, could do nothing as a torpedo ripped another hole in the other ship's hull. *KT-10* disappeared, but in a switch, *KT-2* appeared nearby and launched a special torpedo at the new hole. The transport was already returning to a warp bubble as the projectile raced through the entrance to the heart of the target ship.

The other enemy vessel was unable to do anything for its sister ship as it distorted outward and disintegrated in a fiery blast. *KT-2* appeared and launched a rock at the new target, vanishing as *KT-10* appeared and launched another conventional torpedo from the rear. There was no protection from this strike, thanks to the EMP blast from *KT-2* earlier.

As *KT-2* appeared and prepared to finish off the enemy ship, *KT-10* sent an urgent warning: "Wash, watch out! We have company!"

Two alien ships were bearing down on them at high speed, a reminder of the numerical advantage the aliens still possessed. As Wash barked an order to vanish into the safety of a warp bubble, the ship was bracketed by powerful blasts from two EMP weapons. Systems failed, and the degraded image on the display still showed stars, a sign that they hadn't been able to make their escape.

The attack eased, to Wash's surprise and relief. He made out an image of *KT-10* targeting the EMP weapon directly with a rock from its rail gun, obliterating the weapon completely and inflicting major damage on the alien ship. The transport had to back off as the other ship plus the two damaged ships sought to trap it.

"Can we support them, Chief?" Wash called out, determined to return the favor.

"The rail gun is offline, Wash. We took quite a pounding, and it'll take a while to get it back online."

"What about maneuvering?"

"We can still maneuver, but don't count on generating any warp bubbles either, for a while."

"Damn!" he said, worried about his friend and colleague. A moment later, he grinned as he watched a display. Sara had stayed calm, allowing the enemy ships to overrun her position while she vanished into a warp bubble. Her transport then reappeared behind her pursuers and launched another special torpedo into a breach in the ship she'd intended to finish off originally. The other two ships scattered as their sister ship erupted in fire; in the confusion, *KT-10* vanished into another warp bubble and went after the other damaged ship.

Captain Shaw, with *KT-22*, and Captain McKinley, with *KT-5*, prepared to take on an enemy ship. They worked out quickly on their displays the choreography they would use for the attack and noted the starting point for each ship. They had a brief window of opportunity before other enemy vessels would be able to support their sister ship. Neither transport headed straight on toward the enemy, forcing it to split its attention between two attackers.

The vessel moved at high speed toward *KT-5*, and *KT-22* obliged by pursuing in normal space, deploying its rail gun as it closed for a shot. *KT-5* waited until the alien ship was in range and then launched a conventional torpedo, which was intercepted by lasers. *KT-5* then vanished into a warp bubble as *KT-22* launched a rock at its target. An instant later, the enemy ship shuddered from the impact, which gouged a hole that the transports prepared to exploit. *KT-22* remained in normal space as it made ready to follow up with a special torpedo.

Suddenly, *KT-22* was rocked by the impact of a small asteroid that smashed into it at high speed. Shaw was shocked. "Chief!" she called out, as alarms blared. "Where the hell did that come from? Is one of our transports taking shots at us?"

In response, the chief put an image on a display. To their surprise, the Phoenix ship was bearing down on them with another rock ready to launch. *KT-5* appeared and sent a torpedo racing toward the new enemy, hoping to prevent the rock from reaching its target. The projectile detonated slightly off target, causing little damage, but the ship backed away. *KT-22* prepared to escape into the safety of a warp bubble.

Too late, they realized that the alien ships had used the distraction from the attack to gain the time needed to reach them, and both transports were subjected to multiple bursts from EMP weapons. *KT-5* was barely able to stagger into a warp bubble.

Once in their temporary safe haven, McKinley looked at a display. "Where is *KT-22?*" he demanded. The swirl of eerie figures held no answers for them.

———

Three transports formed themselves into an attack group as they noticed an opportunity to engage in another swarm effect to eradicate an alien ship quickly. The target was pursuing a transport and had separated itself from the rest of its fleet. Although the other two enemy ships were too far away to render assistance, they inadvertently provided a convenient shield from anything the complex could launch at them.

The captains consulted their displays and agreed on their attack positions. They set their countdown and vanished into warp bubbles. They reappeared, all out of range of the target's EMP weapon, and launched rocks that pounded the ship with ruthless efficiency. The transport that the enemy ship had pursued then reversed course and launched a conventional torpedo, which passed easily through the shattered hull of the enemy ship, blasting apart much of the ship's interior.

As they prepared to finish off their target, they were rocked by a massive EMP burst from the complex. The ships that had provided the shield had moved away, and the aliens had decided their damaged ship was doomed anyway. Three of the transports managed to escape into warp bubbles, while the fourth had to deal with multiple system failures.

As the EMP weapon continued to pound the transport, two of the sister transports reappeared, out of harm's way. This time, they had their rail guns deployed, and in an instant, rocks raced toward the source of the burst that had crippled the transport. Moments later, it was their turn to watch as one of the major defensive weapons of the complex was put out of commission permanently.

Austin had stressed the important of maintaining the initiative, and the transports pursued the enemy ships, while the third one reappeared and gave assistance to the damaged transport.

———

KT-22 continued to be buffeted by EMP bursts, without any effective means of retaliating or any illusions about what was in store for its crew. Shaw was surprised to note from the degraded images on a display that one of the enemy ships seemed to have broken off the attack. She was even more surprised to see what appeared to be *Pathfinder* attacking another ship from a location that shouldn't have been possible.

Austin had noted *KT-22*'s distress and pulled two transports with him in a hastily arranged formation. Incredibly, *Pathfinder* and one of the transports manipulated an alien ship into backing away from the damaged transport, even as the scout ship launched a conventional torpedo through the hole that *KT-22* had blasted earlier. Because of the maneuver, Austin had ensured that the transport wouldn't be consumed by the destruction of the alien ship.

KT-5 had joined the other transport in causing more destruction with the other two enemy vessels. They alternated in attacking from between the two larger ships, making it impossible for either foe to get a clear shot without endangering the other one. *Pathfinder* and the other transport then appeared above and below one of the alien ships and added to the destruction, while *KT-5* and its sister transport turned their attention fully toward the other enemy vessel.

In moments, all three of the alien vessels that had assumed that destroying the damaged transport would be easy were themselves destroyed. Austin dispatched *KT-5* to look after *KT-22*, while the scout ship and the other transports continued with the chase.

CHAPTER TWENTY-NINE

The field was rife with multiple engagements. *KT-10* teamed up with *KT-14* and *KT-15* as they spotted another target. "They'll expect us to attempt to isolate a single ship," Sara said. "They'll try to blast us from their complex while we're exposed, so we'll do a three-on-two approach instead. We'll do it while still inside their fleet so that their own hulls will offer us protection."

The other captains agreed and consulted their displays for their targets and positions. Sara announced the countdown, and the ships headed straight toward the ship that the aliens would assume was being set up for isolation. At the right moment, the transports vanished into warp bubbles and the alien ships shifted position, expecting to trap the attackers when they reappeared.

Because the transports never intended to attack the lone enemy ship, they reappeared where they hadn't been expected. *KT-10* struck at a misshapen vessel with an EMP blast that took out much of the enemy vessel's rear weapons, and then the Citadel ship disappeared. *KT-15* appeared above the other target, and a rock streaked toward the unprepared vessel as the transport vanished. *KT-14* appeared nearby and followed up with a special torpedo that passed through the newly ripped entrance to the heart of the ship. As the vessel's interior distorted into ruin, *KT-10* reappeared near the first enemy ship and raked the starboard side with another EMP burst.

With a field of fire cleared out, *KT-15* appeared and launched a conventional torpedo, which ripped a hole in the target's hull. *KT-14* appeared as the sister transport vanished and followed up with another conventional torpedo, which blew up major portions of the vessel's interior. As explosions erupted through other portions of the hull, *KT-10* appeared and launched another torpedo, adding to the death throes of the ship. *KT-14* and *KT-15* had already vanished, to face the lone ship that had served as the bait. Moments later, *KT-10* followed suit, prepared to join the other transports in the original game of isolating and destroying an enemy ship. The trick would be to do it without exposing the transports to a surprise from the complex.

———

"How are we doing, Joe?" Austin asked. "By my count, we've destroyed ten of their ships, and four of ours are offline in one capacity or another. Fortunately, none of ours has been destroyed. Two of them can still maneuver and have managed to stay out of trouble while they make whatever repairs are possible. The other two are sitting ducks, although no one is paying them any attention while there's fighting underway. That makes things roughly equal, which is a hell of a lot better than when we started."

"I'd still like us to get our hands on that damned Phoenix ship," Albretti grumbled. "That rail gun is the reason *KT-22* is still out of commission right now. We can't tell had badly it's been damaged, although it doesn't look good from here."

"I'd like nothing better than to blast them as well," Austin agreed, "but we can't have the entire battle dictated by our interest in that one ship. That may even be part of their plan, knowing how badly we want to stop Harrington."

"You're right," Albretti acknowledged reluctantly. "I still hope we'll be able to take a shot, though."

Austin looked at a display as Yabuno contacted him. "Sam, we keep getting readings from this spot every time one of our transports gets close to an unprotected engagement with the aliens. There is a similarity with what we saw when they hit us with their EMP cannon from the complex."

"You think this is another one?" Austin asked with interest.

"It stands to reason that they'd have more than one. After all, their other complex had at least two that we know of," Yabuno pointed out. "Something this size may have more than two."

"Is there anything else about the location that suggests an EMP weapon? How does it compare in appearance with the one we've already taken out?"

Yabuno shrugged. "We can't tell any difference, but that's been true with most of their structures. Obviously, they don't follow the rules we use when it comes to how things go together. Since we haven't figured out the rules they use, there aren't the same clues for us to follow. For all we can tell, it could be a command-and-control center, or it could be a latrine." He grinned. "Gives new meaning to the notion of blasting the crap out of it."

Austin rolled his eyes in spite of the moment. "All right," he said, as he looked at another display. He pointed to a group of transports. "Let's move toward this gang before going into a warp bubble. It'll provide camouflage for our move while messing with their plans for dealing with whomever they think the transports will attack. Hopefully, they'll be looking for us in the wrong place." He sent the transports a quick message letting them know the scout ship was just passing through.

Pathfinder made its way toward the complex, ignoring the images of vessels that sometimes raced nearby but never quite touched them. The craft hovered for a moment among the outlines of structures as it made ready with a conventional torpedo. A moment later, the outlines became solid, and the torpedo raced toward its target. The ship vanished as the crew deployed another torpedo, only to reappear nearby. In an instant, the scout ship launched its torpedo, to add to the destruction before vanishing again. Moments after *Pathfinder* reappeared, a special torpedo streaked toward the target, passing through one of the multiple holes that had been blasted in the structure to serve as entry points for *Pathfinder*'s destructive power.

By the time the energy from the destruction of the weapon reached beyond the structure's tortured confines out into space, the scout ship had already vanished. As they moved away from the destruction in the safety of a warp bubble, the crew took a moment to appreciate the ghostly picture on the display.

By the time the smallest craft in the field of battle reappeared in normal space-time at a safe distance, Austin asked, "Was that one of their cannons, Bret?"

"Hell yes, Sam," Yabuno said triumphantly. "That's two down, and who knows how many to go."

"It's that 'who knows how many to go' part that still has me worried," Austin said.

———

Aboard *KT-22*, Shaw was desperate for word that they could reenter the fight, but didn't want to distract the chief with numerous requests for updates. She decided she'd held off long enough. "Sorry for the interruption, Chief, but where do we stand?"

Weary eyes appeared on a display. "The good news, Captain, is that we've brought the rail gun and torpedo launchers back online. The bad news is we can barely maneuver, not much more than using basic thrusters. Also, until we can do a better job of repairing the nasty hole in our hull, we can't go into a warp bubble."

"Are the warp-field generators themselves damaged?" she asked anxiously.

"No," he said with a sigh of relief. "We were dumb lucky in that regard."

An idea occurred to her. "How long until we can get the hull repaired enough to use the generators?"

"Not long, but we still need to have the propulsion back online."

"How long will that take?" she pressed.

"If we're lucky, maybe thirty minutes. If we're not lucky, maybe a lot longer."

"From what you've said, if we could at least get into a warp bubble, we could get around better than in normal space-time."

His expression turned crafty. "I like the way you think, Captain, but it still means we'll move around awkwardly at best. We'll probably still be more a target than a fighter."

"That's OK, we won't have far to go. We have a favor to return, and I'd like to act on it sooner rather than later. Do it, Chief."

———

KT-10, KT-14, and *KT-15* continued to harass enemy vessels with success. With the fleet of alien vessels thinned out somewhat, the Citadel transports now had more opportunities to swarm around one or two ships and use their temporary numerical advantage to take out the enemy.

They approached a new target, a cluster of two ships that was in turn pursuing a transport. Sara sent a message to the transport, and it veered in such a way as to force the pursuing ships to move closer to the other transports. Just as the enemy ships closed on their target, all four transports vanished. When they reappeared, they had bracketed the pursuers and opened fire from multiple directions. *KT-10* launched a rock into one of the ships, tearing a massive gouge clear through to the vessel's interior.

As the transport vanished, to swing over toward the other enemy vessel, *KT-15* appeared and launched a torpedo into the opening, tearing the interior apart further. At the same time, *KT-14* appeared under the other enemy ship and launched a conventional torpedo, which sliced a new gash in the hull. The other transport appeared as *KT-14* vanished, and a special torpedo raced toward the jagged opening.

The projectile was slightly off course and ended up peeling back major portions of the ship's interior, without destroying it outright. *KT-10* appeared a moment later to finish off the job with a special torpedo that couldn't possibly miss the huge, misshapen opening. *KT-14* reappeared near the first enemy ship and launched a rock toward the pathway that had already been opened. With major portions of the interior blasted out of the way, the rock crashed through, obliterating much of the remainder before bursting out of the hull on the other side. As the original transport prepared to launch a final torpedo to complete the destruction, a ragged hole appeared as a rock crashed through it at extreme speed.

Heads turned, to see the Phoenix ship once again having deployed its rail gun. Evidently the crew of the ship drew some courage from being flanked by three alien vessels. They never saw the rock that crashed into the ship's weapons bay, obliterating its ability to repeat its attack. Sara looked back to a display to see *KT-22*, which had somehow limped into the fray and targeted the enemy ship with its rail gun.

KT-10, *KT-14*, and *KT-15* conferred quickly and raced toward the three alien ships, more confident now that the hated rail gun had been removed from the table. Characteristically, the Phoenix ship backed away from the engagement even as its brethren moved to take on the transports. One of the enemy ships broke off from the attack run, heading straight for the damaged transport.

A moment later, a rock crashed into it at high speed. *KT-22* was clearly using deadly force to warn the aliens away. The would-be attackers hesitated for an instant, making a terrible mistake. Before the vessel could shift course, another rock smashed into it, taking the EMP weapon out. With no way to get to either transport, and in mortal danger from staying put, the ship broke off the attack and sought to rejoin the original attack group. Once again, the three transports demonstrated the benefit of concentrating their firepower on a numerically smaller force.

———

As Austin watched the action, he turned to Albretti. "It's time, Joe."

Albretti nodded, and *Pathfinder* vanished. There was no effort made to maintain a careful pace; the ship raced toward the complex as quickly as possible from within the warp bubble. Moments later, they appeared near a major portion of one of the misshapen structures and blasted it with a sustained EMP burst, following up with a torpedo, which Austin thought improved the appearance of the place. The scout ship launched a probe that settled itself within the wreckage.

Pathfinder vanished and moved to another location within the complex. Again, the EMP burst neutralized the nearby weapons, and again a torpedo blasted an opening for a probe that settled within the heavily damaged interior.

The scout ship vanished back into a warp bubble as an alien ship sought an engagement. The vessel found itself having to break off its attack as *KT-5* pursued it, inflicting damage upon the larger ship while on the run.

Austin grinned at the sight, and *Pathfinder* moved to another location. In short order, the scout ship had completed more than a half dozen stops, and a countdown appeared on a display. "We've located something that could be another one of their EMP cannons," Yabuno said excitedly, pointing to a display.

"Why do you think so?" Austin replied.

"The energy signature looks like they're trying to keep something powered up, without giving away everything. We haven't been providing them with many targets," Yabuno said wryly. "Our ships move around unpredictably, they don't stay in normal space all the time, and they try to use the alien ships as shields against any mischief that may be directed from that complex. The problem is that several of our ships are about to enter the area this cannon could cover. It would be a big opportunity to try to even things back in their favor."

Austin nodded. "What's our best approach?"

Yabuno pointed to another position. "We should have a good shot at them from here."

Pathfinder vanished into a warp bubble and moved toward its new target, again wasting no time. The ship had reappeared, ready for its attack, when all hell broke loose. From the effect on the displays, Austin guessed that they'd just received a huge jolt from another cannon. A second jolt hit them, and Albretti swore as the maneuvering controls wouldn't respond.

"Chief! What the hell happened to our controls?" he called on his link. Although there was static, they could still make out the answer.

"They clobbered the hell out of us this time," the chief reported. "Weapons are offline. Communications are still online. We'll have propulsion back online in a moment, though maneuvering may be tricky. They have another cannon, all right, but not where we thought it would be. They set up a mousetrap for us, and we fell right into it."

The navigator pointed at a display in horror. An opening appeared in the structure they'd attempted to blast, and a giant tentacle spiraled out, reaching for the disabled ship.

CHAPTER THIRTY

A moment later, they were in the grasp of the unholy thing and watched as it pulled them inside the complex. Whatever passed for a door in the odd structure in that part of the complex closed behind them as the tentacle deposited them onto an interior deck. The tentacle vanished.

Yabuno called out. "We're receiving a message from Phoenix, Sam."

"Put it on the display."

They watched as an image of Pandora and Diana in a shuttle's control room appeared. Neither woman bothered to hide the triumphant look on her face at the turn of events.

"I'm so delighted to have proof of how easy it is to manipulate you," Pandora crowed. "We may as well have sent a telegram telling you to show up, when we left the files behind on *Firebird* that would lead you to us, and sent the signals through our backers' beacons."

"You're saying you *wanted* us to come here and kick your ass?" Austin challenged in reply. "By my count, that's exactly what we've done."

The look of glee on her face became slightly strained. "While you've taken out more of our vessels than we expected, capturing you has made everything worth the cost."

"Has it? Our people will finish the job shortly, and this place will just be a bad memory," Austin said. "Killing us won't change that outcome."

The look on her face became more malicious. "Who said anything about killing you? Our backers have something much better in mind for you. They're going to take you apart, just like they did to us. If they find you interesting, they may put you back together, although you won't look like you do now. Who knows, you may not even be immortal anymore. Whatever happens, you'll belong to them, just as much as we do. You'll find there's no way to resist any of their suggestions, let alone orders." She brought up images of familiar planets. "How long do you think Citadel, Earth, and the rest of two solar systems will be able to hold out against our backers, with you to help invade those worlds and exterminate the very humans you've claimed to serve all these years?"

"Just because you're weak doesn't mean I am," Austin said grimly.

"Lazarus thought so too," she scoffed, "right up to the point that he was forced to accept that what he wanted didn't matter." Her expression brightened at a new thought. "That reminds me, we'll be sure to explain to our backers that it would be a good idea to have each of you bonded with people other than your spouses. One of the first things that happens is the physical side of being bonded with your new partner, which is terrific, by the way." She looked at Diana. "Even if you've been getting physical with anyone else, it doesn't matter; it's all in the past and will never happen again with anyone other than your new partner." Diana returned the stare in stony silence.

She glared at Albretti. "That will be my final revenge against the Captains Albretti. You will leave the other Captain Albretti behind forever once you've become a different person and bonded with someone else. Your soon-to-be-former wife will know, of course, and may even throw herself at you, but she won't be able to do anything about it, and neither will you. It won't really matter, anyway, since she'll be dead—with your help—soon enough."

Her expression became more businesslike as her gaze shifted back to Austin. "The time for talking is over, Sam. Leave your ship and you'll spare yourself some unnecessary discomfort." A hint of pain flashed across her face. "If you don't leave, then some very unpleasant things will reach out and tear your ship apart as they pull you out anyway. They may not be all that gentle when they do it either. You've already seen a sample of what they can do when your ship was brought here. Back when we all visited the first complex and our shuttles were pulled inside our backers' ships, some of the people actually thought there was safety by staying aboard them, so they refused to leave. It was necessary to make an example of them, and they never left the shuttles alive. I still remember the screams."

Austin nodded at a display. A moment later, everyone on board Phoenix reacted as if under extreme distress. "What did you do?" Pandora screamed. "Everything is falling apart!"

"I just returned a favor," Austin replied calmly. "It never occurred to you or your backers that successfully combating a break-in to a communications network sometimes reveals more about the attacker than intended. We learned what we needed to take your own network down and paralyze most functions for added measure." It was Austin's turn to stare at his old adversary with something less than fondness. "Face it, Courtney, you're the one who's lost." He pointed to a countdown on a display. "Do you know what this means? Do you have any idea what we were doing when we blasted various sites around this misbegotten place?"

"You were trying to destroy every place where there may be another EMP weapon," she replied sharply. "We had no trouble fooling you by sending the false signals to lure you into our trap."

Austin shook his head. "I guess that's a no. We didn't have access to the power of the derelict to wipe out the place, so we had to come up with something else. We were depositing nuclear devices throughout this complex. Since they've been placed inside, with no ability to neutralize them, thanks to our EMP bursts, there's no way to shield against the blasts. There won't be anything left of this place shortly." He pointed again at the display. "Look again. In about five minutes, this countdown will have run down to zero, and this place won't be here."

"Your ships will be destroyed too!" Pandora cried desperately.

Austin shook his head. "Our ships have already broken off their attacks and are heading away to safety. The few ships that can't proceed under their own power are being towed. Now that your backers know what has happened, I'll bet your ships are trying to rescue the population of this place." He gestured outside. "Of course, things aren't working too well right now, so I'll bet five minutes won't be enough for much of anything."

"You'll die too!"

"Do you really think so?" he asked.

Diana spoke. "You're bluffing, Austin. We know your weapons systems are offline. That means you won't have the chance to escape by blasting another hole in a hatch, the way you did with our ship. Face it, if you want to escape, you'll need to deal too. If you need a way to get comfortable with the idea, think of it as living to fight us another day. All you have to do is reset your countdown to ten minutes."

Austin looked at her silently.

Diana said, "Our backers will make it worth your while, by offering you something you want very badly."

Pandora turned in sudden fear. "What are you saying? You've been talking with our backers without involving me!"

Diana didn't hide her revulsion. "You no longer have value to our backers. So long as you were bonded to Lazarus, you had potential value, but you have not realized that potential following his death." She stared at Austin. "Austin, in return for our turning Pandora over to you, you must agree to reset your countdown to an additional ten minutes."

Austin nodded his head toward the outer hatch. "That's still closed."

"It will open with one minute left."

Austin didn't bother to laugh. "You actually expect me to trust your backers? They've lied to us before, and there's no reason to believe they'll be any different this time. I'd just as soon trust one of those tentacles."

Diana considered the notion. "While the 'tentacles,' as you call them, aren't functioning properly at the moment, we can open the hatch partway as a further sign of good faith. The hatch will open the rest of the way with one minute left."

"It still doesn't matter. I don't trust your backers to keep their word."

Diana's expression hardened. "You don't have any choice. We're in a shuttle just outside your location, on the other side of that hatch. It's coming in through the partial opening now. Pandora will be waiting for you."

Pandora began to shriek and fought against her backers' wishes like someone possessed. Diana struck her colleague across the face. As Pandora sprawled across the deck in stunned silence, rough arms took hold of her, and she was hustled out of sight.

The large hatch opened partway, and a shuttle entered, as promised, and approached the scout ship. The hatch closed behind the small craft. Seconds after the shuttle touched down, a figure with a breathing apparatus was sent reeling onto the deck. The craft took off and left through the reopened hatch, which closed rapidly behind it. The process had been so swift that the environment was still intact.

The assassin looked back at Austin. "Well?" she asked pointedly. Austin never looked away as he said, "Have someone bring Harrington on board, Joe."

Albretti spoke quickly into his link. In less than two minutes, Pandora was brought aboard and moved none too gently to the bridge. She faced the display and glared at Diana with a look of hatred almost as intense as the one she reserved for Austin. Austin ignored her for the moment.

"You're cutting things rather closely," Diana warned. "Reset the countdown, as you agreed."

"Joe, please reset the countdown to thirty seconds."

As a horrified look spread across Diana's face, Austin chuckled. "Thanks for making it easier for us to deploy our last nuclear device. Our people took it with them when they went outside to collect Harrington. It's now sitting just a few feet away from our ramp. With this piece of the puzzle covered, there shouldn't be any part of this complex that survives."

"You broke your word!" was all Diana could utter.

"If the situation weren't so deadly, your comment would almost be funny, considering that the aliens have no honor when it comes to keeping deals with humans. However, my honor is still intact, as I never promised anything. Besides, you can keep your hatch, for all I care. We have another way out. Rot in hell!"

At a nod from Austin, the ship moved into a warp bubble. There was a ghostly flash overhead and then eerie images of terrible explosions and chaos, all of which happened in silence. Nothing ever quite touched them, instead distorting around or past their position.

"Get us out of here," Austin said. He looked at a display and saw that it was devoid of any images of enemy vessels. In short order, they reappeared a safe distance away in normal space-time. Austin was pleased to see a cluster of transports nearby. As they moved closer to their sister ships, Austin spoke to the captain. "Find out if any of the alien ships are still in one piece, or whether they all went up with a bang."

Albretti grinned. "The chief has already been in contact with several of our transports. Chief, tell us what you know about the aliens."

"After they pulled *Pathfinder* inside their complex, the alien ships didn't seem able to coordinate with each other or do anything else effectively, which was probably a result of what we did to them when Sam gave us the word. If our ships hadn't been under instructions to break away from the engagement at that point during the countdown, they probably could have wiped out the remaining alien vessels in short order. Anyway, while our ships were heading away, the remaining misbegotten things went back to their ports and hooked up some more-substantial lines to the complex. They were more than large enough to accommodate people, so the assumption is they were there to accommodate whatever the hell they are. It was hard to be sure, but the best guess is that they were trying to get their population out of the facility before everything went up in multiple infernos. Their actions in setting up their lines were clumsy compared to the smooth way their lines have worked in the past, so they were obviously hampered by what we did to them."

"Did any of them escape?"

"No. They didn't get away using conventional propulsion, and there were no signs of warp bubbles forming around their ships before the complex was destroyed."

"What about the Phoenix ship?"

"Right after the aliens pulled us inside their complex, that ship showed up and parked itself outside. There are reports of a shuttle entering the place and returning almost immediately, which would have been when they deposited Harrington with us. No one knows what happened to their ship after that. With the damage it took from *KT-22*, I doubt it could have done much of anything except share the same fate as the alien ships."

"Thanks, Chief." Austin finally turned to acknowledge the presence of Pandora. "Isn't it typical how you had all sorts of vicious, unspeakable things planned for me? My thoughts for you were much simpler. You got to watch the destruction of your world, which you helped to bring about. The other thing that was interesting was how you proved your own claim to be false."

"What do you mean?" she asked testily.

"You were sure that no one who is a creature of the aliens could resist their orders. If that were true, then you would have left the shuttle and walked up our ramp without coercion. You proved, in your weakness, that cowardice and self-preservation would win out after all," he said wryly.

Her expression was wary. "What happens next?"

Austin shook his head. "I'm done answering your questions, Courtney. All you need to know is that you will be locked up during the trip back to Citadel, and you will then face punishment for your war crimes, punishment that is long overdue."

"You're making a terrible mistake," she said.

As Pandora was led out, Austin gestured toward a display and spoke into his link to Liz. "We need to look after any people who need assistance and then do the same for our transports. I'd consider it a big favor if you would help get us organized."

"I'll be right there," she promised.

CHAPTER THIRTY-ONE

Later, Austin, Liz, Yabuno, the Albrettis, and Turner were seated in Austin's stateroom aboard *Pathfinder*. Liz stood before a display while making a report. "We're getting a lot better at this kind of activity, although I'm not sure that's entirely a good thing."

"It isn't a good thing to have to do it," Austin observed, "but it's a good thing to be able to do it and defend ourselves."

Liz nodded. "One thing we've become especially good at is limiting the toll on human lives. It's amazing how few people we lost, considering what they threw at us. Most of the losses resulted from people being battered by those rocks that the Phoenix ship launched. Thank goodness the rest of the injuries are all treatable." She brought up images of several transports. "I'll leave the technical details to the experts here, but we avoided the outright destruction of any of our transports as well as this amazing scout ship. I can't take any credit for the work that's underway; that's something that Bret has been handling."

Yabuno nodded his thanks as he approached a display. "Getting organized, which Liz helped us do, was an important first step. Now that we don't have to worry about weapons, we can concentrate on making sure the transports are in shape as far as life support, propulsion, and the warp-field generators are concerned. We've been doing what we can to patch up *KT-22* and *KT-6*, which took those hits from the rocks, since we need sufficient structural integrity to sustain the warp fields."

"What about all the damage from the EMP attacks?" Austin asked. "Several ships took quite a pounding, including this one."

Yabuno grinned. "Some of what we're doing looks pretty ugly. Several of the chiefs grumbled a bit over what's been happening to their ships, but the grumbling was just something they needed to do. They're now even more ruthless than the rest of us at doing what needs to be done to get us back home in one piece. Curly will have a fit when she sees it," he chuckled.

"That sounds like an understatement," Austin noted. "When will we be ready to leave?"

"Another day, and then we can get the hell out of here."

Austin looked at Turner. "Alan, did you have any luck in getting any information when you broke into their systems?"

Turner shrugged. "Only bits and pieces, so anything I say will be, at best, a guess. One thing I didn't come across was anything about another complex like this one. You may have been right about our having eliminated their infrastructure enough that they can't launch any further expeditions against us or Earth."

He chuckled. "What an irony, that their plan to trap us served our purposes instead—to remove them from this part of space, perhaps for good."

Austin's expression brightened at the thought before fading slightly. "Was there any information about their home world or a point of origin?"

Turner shook his head. "I didn't see anything like that. Remember, though, we only had a brief opportunity to break into their systems, so we probably missed the overwhelming majority of their information anyway."

"Bret, what about the Phoenix ship? Are we sure it didn't survive the explosions?"

"We can't be sure," he replied, shaking his head slightly, "but it's hard to see what it could have done. We know it didn't get away under normal propulsion, and it would have been tough to sustain a warp field, considering the damage it took."

"Weren't they affected by the paralysis to the aliens' systems anyway?" Joe Albretti asked.

"They were certainly aware of what happened, but we know their shuttle still functioned," Yabuno replied.

"What about the fact that their warp-field generators came from the aliens?" Albretti asked. "With their network down, wouldn't those generators have been down too?"

"Good question, but there isn't any way to know for certain. The destruction of the complex also made it pretty damned difficult to analyze any potential energy signatures from warp-field generators, so we can't settle the matter definitively. I tend to lean in favor of the notion that all that's left of those people and their backers at this point is just a few scattered atoms, but I could be wrong." He grinned. "At least this time we know Her Majesty didn't get away."

"It may seem like an unnecessary question, Sam, but what will happen to her now?" Liz asked. "She'll try to argue that the person who committed those war crimes doesn't exist anymore—*literally*, in fact. She'll also argue that as far as any more recent charges are concerned, she's been under an irresistible compulsion imposed by the aliens and is therefore not in control of her actions."

"Decided to serve as her counsel, have you?" Austin asked with a chuckle. "Before we worry about any of her possible claims, we'll have the doctors check her out thoroughly, so we know what's true and what isn't, on the physical side."

Austin looked at the Albrettis with a twinkle in his gaze. "What now for you two? Will you be staying aboard your respective ships for another month back to Citadel?"

Sara laughed as she took Joe's hand. "Things should be quiet on the trip back, and I've had pretty good luck with promoting my pilots. Wash turned out well, and my current pilot should too. I've already spent a month away from Joe and sharing his bed, and I'm not about to spend another month doing the same thing. My place is always with him."

Liz smiled as she took Austin's hand. "I feel the same way about Sam."

CHAPTER THIRTY-TWO

Curly and her people had been glad to have two months' respite from the grueling schedule they'd maintained to support the Citadel fleet. They were now hard at work, "repairing the repairs," as she called it, that the fleet's engineers had made to the transports and *Pathfinder*. She'd marveled over the fact that some of the ships had held out long enough to return home, although she knew Yabuno had been in charge of those repairs and she could trust him like she wouldn't trust anyone else.

Austin was linked in with the same team that had been in his stateroom a month earlier, discussing a disturbing development relating to Harrington.

They watched a display in silence as Austin's recent interview with Harrington was played.

"This has been a long time coming, Courtney," Austin said.

"What did you call me?" she asked.

"I called you by your name, Courtney. If that's too painful for you, then you know the name Pandora."

"My name is Athena, Mr. Austin, and you've made a mistake."

"I'm pretty sure I haven't," Austin replied with a hint of sarcasm. "Are you really going to try the 'I'm someone else' routine?"

"I don't know what that means, but I told you you'd made a mistake a month ago, but you wouldn't listen to me. I know that I'm not the person you claim me to be."

"That isn't what you said when you thought you had us at your mercy," Austin said. "You were very clear about how you'd been taken apart and put back together by the aliens, in a way that altered your physical appearance but didn't change your memories. You may have been given a new name, but you're still the murderous, callous person you always were. *That* didn't change."

The woman shuddered. "Yes, I remember quite well the agony of what the aliens did to me. I also know that I don't look the way I once did. I was given a new name, but it wasn't Pandora. It was Athena."

"Pandora fits you much better than Athena, Courtney. Athena was the Greek goddess of intelligence, handicrafts, and wisdom, among other things. None of those qualities describes you."

"Saying I'm someone doesn't make me that person, Mr. Austin."

"All right, let's see how far you want to take this nonsense. What was your name before Athena?" Austin demanded.

She shook her head. "I don't know."

"That's a convenient answer," he said skeptically. "All of you know your original names, along with what happened to you in your lives prior to meeting the aliens."

"That's not correct. I was called Athena because I used to be a scientist that Courtney Harrington duped into helping her. That's what I was told, but I have no memories of that life."

"I saw you removed from the shuttle where you and Powers, or Diana, were gloating over having pulled a fast one on us, until I pointed out how we'd actually outfoxed you. Diana then had you removed from the shuttle and deposited on the deck outside our ship, where our people brought you aboard. There was no time for any substitutions. You were Pandora then, and you're Pandora now."

"No, Pandora and I share a likeness in appearance, but we are two different women. I was sitting in a compartment when she was brought out of the shuttle's control room. People started to remove my clothes, before she said it didn't matter because we were all wearing the same kind of jumpsuit. I was then made to walk down the ramp of the shuttle, given a breathing apparatus, and pushed off the ship. Your people then picked me up and forced me into your ship."

"How could two people end up looking alike, considering how thoroughly you were all taken apart first?" Austin challenged.

"I don't know, but it is possible that I was a template, which was repeated when it came to Pandora." She shed a tear. "That must make me the imperfect one, since they either didn't know how to put memories back into people yet, or didn't think it necessary in my case."

"Why give you a name associated with wisdom and knowledge, if you no longer had your scientific knowledge?"

"I'm told that many of the names came from Lazarus, who must have known me when I was a scientist. The name that he provided was given to me before he knew about my loss of memories. By that time, it was too late; once a name is given, it isn't changed." She stared at him. "I am Athena."

Austin's expression darkened. "While I don't accept your explanation about your past, you have also committed war crimes in connection with your activities as part of Phoenix. Those crimes include murder and waging war on Citadel."

"I haven't committed any war crimes," she insisted. "I only did what I was compelled to do by those that made me. I cannot do otherwise, any more than you can choose to stop blinking your eyes."

"You still have a human soul, and as such, you are responsible for your actions," Austin countered.

The woman sat before him in silence.

———

"That's quite a performance," Yabuno said. "If I didn't know what a good actress she is, I'd be wondering if we've made a mistake."

"You didn't ask us to watch those images just for entertainment," Liz noted shrewdly. "You have some concerns about what we're doing."

Austin nodded. "I asked the doctors to check her out thoroughly, inside and out, and to compare their findings with Harrington's medical records, which Astrid was kind enough to forward some time back."

"You've had doubts for that long?" Liz asked.

He shook his head. "No, but once we learned about the changes to their appearance, I wanted to be able to confirm through reliable medical or scientific means that we have the right person."

"I guess I don't want to know how she got those records," Turner said.

"She got them because it is a matter of national security that we make a positive identification of a notorious war criminal," Austin said. "Harrington lost her right to privacy a long time ago when she became a war criminal and tried to make war on us, more than once."

"What do our doctors have to say about her?" Turner asked.

Austin turned to a display. "I've asked Dr. Hall to answer our questions about the subject. Doctor, what are your findings?"

They saw an image of their subject on a display. "The subject, whom we'll call Athena for now, is pretty much what she looks like, Sam," she replied. "She's definitely a woman, in her late fifties, natural light-brown hair, brown eyes, five foot four inches tall, has never had children, has no identifying marks or scars, no dental work, doesn't need corrective lens, and weighs one hundred forty-five pounds."

"Does her DNA match her physical features?"

"Yes, although there's a fair amount of variety in physical appearance possible, even with the instructions provided by DNA. Certain environmental factors can definitely have an impact on a person's body and development, as well."

"Have you had an opportunity to compare your findings with the medical records for Courtney Harrington?"

"Yes, I have. The file for Harrington indicates a woman, also in her late fifties, same height, weight, and eye color, never has had children. Although she's a blonde, the hair color is within the range of possibilities for brown hair."

She brought up several images. "However, she has clearly had dental work done over the years, and there is at least one identifying mark on her body, none of which is present on the body of Athena."

"What is the mark?"

"She had a tiny birthmark on her left posterior region."

Yabuno spoke. "You mean she had a mark on the left cheek of her ass."

"That's correct," she said.

"It's clear that their features are not alike," Liz said. "Are there any signs of reconstructive surgery having been performed?"

"No," Hall replied. "As I already mentioned, there were no marks or scars of any kind on Athena's body, nor were there any signs of feature alterations by various chemical methods."

"Were there any DNA results available for comparison?" Austin asked.

Hall shook her head. "There are no reliable DNA samples available. Every place where Harrington was known to stay for any significant period, including her home where she was under house arrest, has long since been cleaned or otherwise contaminated with other substances. She was an only child, and her parents are long dead, with their remains cremated. There were no aunts or uncles, or nephews or nieces."

"You have already performed an autopsy of Lazarus, but it's a different story when it comes to tissue samples from a living donor. Were there any signs of Athena's cells having been pulled apart and put back together?"

"No, and I would expect to see some evidence of trauma, even years later. However, since I can't see how it could have been done in the first place, I may be mistaken in expecting to detect something."

"What does the evidence tell you about Harrington and Athena?"

"If we accept for the moment the possibility of the aliens having somehow taken humans apart as claimed, then without a DNA sample for comparison, I can't confirm one way or another whether Athena is Harrington. However, I can't conclude that it isn't her either, especially since the overall body type is the same. It is reasonable to consider that if a person could be taken apart and reassembled cell by cell, then it could be done without re-creating scar tissue. One could probably also correct any dental issues or at least remove any artificial materials relating to dentistry."

"What's your best guess about what happened to them?"

"Even if one accepts that the aliens did what they are claimed to have done, there are limits to the possible extent of cell rearrangement. You once suggested that their existing DNA may have been manipulated, rather than re-created anew. I agree with that view. While it's possible that DNA from different people was commingled, I think it unlikely. There's no sign of any unnatural arrangements of DNA, which one would expect to find if an alien race with no prior knowledge of humans tried to commingle DNA from multiple people. What we've seen is still entirely human."

"Thanks, Doctor."

After her image faded from the display, Turner spoke. "What are you going to do? You can't keep someone locked up just because you think she may be a murderer, even though you don't have any proof."

"I just thought of something else we can pursue," Austin replied with a determined look. "Harrington shared quarters with Lazarus on board *Firebird*, and that ship has been locked up tight since we captured it. We haven't touched the living quarters, except to search for files and to confirm that no one was still on board. If we can find an uncontaminated sample of her DNA from *Firebird*, we can compare it with Athena's DNA." His gaze grew colder. "If they match, then we know we have Pandora."

"That still doesn't address the question of whether she is truly a new being and not simply someone who has Harrington's memories, but isn't actually Harrington," Turner countered. "She even suggested that she may just be a template. You've made quite a show of wanting us to be governed by laws. Doesn't that mean that they apply to her too?"

"I think there may be a misunderstanding about what it means to be governed by laws, Alan," Austin replied with some heat. "First and foremost, Citadel's laws are for the benefit of Citadel and its citizens. They aren't for the benefit of others, especially not for those who would do us grave harm. Long ago, when I was a boy, a US Supreme Court justice expressed his view that the US Constitution was not a suicide pact. The same holds true of the Citadel Charter.

"However, there may be a way of getting a better answer on the point you raised," Austin said. "There was another member of their team who called herself Georgia. They said she'd been a scientist named Farmer. I'll bet we have information about her. Let's see if we can find any DNA samples from Earth and have them analyzed. We can seek out DNA samples from her quarters aboard *Firebird* and do a comparison. If they confirm that the DNA was simply recombined, then we'll know the transformation wasn't quite as complete as they think. While J. W. is tracking down that information about Farmer, we'll pay a visit to *Firebird* and collect what we need. In the meantime, Athena, Pandora, Harrington— or whoever the hell she is—stays locked up."

CHAPTER THIRTY-THREE

Austin sat across the table from Athena. She noticed that his expression was unreadable.

"You've been here for over two months, and I think it's time we talked again," he said.

"Does that mean you've finally accepted that I'm who I say I am?" she asked.

"Let's say for the moment that you're right," he said with a neutral expression. "What do you propose we do with you? By the admission of everyone from Phoenix, you are our mortal enemy, regardless of whether we accept your claim that you can't help yourself."

"I'm not your mortal enemy, Mr. Austin," she insisted. "Those that made me are."

Austin shrugged. "It comes to the same thing, since you do whatever they tell you to do."

"While it is true that I cannot refuse to do as they instruct me, the fact is that I am no longer in any communication with them."

Austin scoffed. "When did that happen? It certainly wasn't the case the last time you were in this system."

"They had the means of communicating with us then. When you destroyed the complex where I was made, you destroyed whatever link exists between me and them."

"Are you saying you're now a free woman, able to make up her own mind about things like genocide and war crimes?" he asked skeptically.

"Do not misunderstand me. If I received instructions to act against you, I would have no choice but to do so. However, the connection was broken without my having received any instructions to do anything, which means it is up to me to decide what to do."

"Just what would you do, given the chance?"

"I would try live in peace with everyone either here or back on Earth, if that is where you want to send me."

"Don't your previous instructions to kill us all still apply?"

She shook her head. "I never received any instructions like that, not directly; my last ones were to walk down a ramp to be picked up by your people, which I have done. That means I am free to do as I choose." She stared at him. "I would choose peace."

"Before we talk about peace, we need to talk about some information we have uncovered since the last time we talked. Do you remember your colleague Georgia?"

"Of course I do. She too had been a scientist before becoming one of us."

"That's right," Austin nodded. "Her name was Dr. Nora Farmer. An interesting thing is that while we were able to locate plenty of information about her, we couldn't find a single piece of information about *you*."

"I've already told you, I have no memories of my life prior to being made what I am, so I have no explanation for why you found no information about my former self."

"We'll get to that in time, but one of the interesting things we were able to find was a sample of Dr. Farmer's DNA. Unlike some other people, she had relatives, so we were able to confirm that the sample we had was valid. We had the sample subjected to extensive analysis, with the report on that analysis forwarded here.

"While that report was on its way here, we visited *Firebird* and located Georgia's quarters. Since the quarters have been kept undisturbed, we were able to obtain an uncontaminated sample and subject it to extensive analysis as well."

Austin walked over to a display and brought up several images. "Here is a copy of the report on Farmer's DNA, and here is a copy of the report on Georgia's DNA. I'll spare you the trouble of wading your way through it to interpret it, although you're welcome to try it if you prefer. The findings are what're interesting. They conclude that although Georgia and Farmer look nothing alike, Georgia's DNA is merely Farmer's DNA that's been recombined or manipulated."

"What does someone else's DNA have to do with me?" she asked.

"It's the relationship of the DNA from past to present that's important. It confirms that you are not a brand-new person, but a continuation of someone already in existence."

"That doesn't really matter in my case, since I've already told you I have no recollection of my prior life. I am, effectively, a new person."

"So you continue to say," Austin said. "An interesting thing about that claim is that there's absolutely no proof that it is true. Another thing we did was investigate every single scientist who was a part of Harrington's team, focusing particularly on women within ten years of your apparent physical age. We found that there were eight women who were at least remotely close to your age."

Austin made several gestures, and the images of eight women appeared on the display. "*These* women, in fact. It was our good fortune to find relatives for each of them who were willing to provide tissue samples for DNA analysis."

Austin gave Athena a hard stare. "None of their DNA matched yours, not even in a recombined state."

Her voice became testy. "You simply didn't locate all of the scientists President Harrington used."

"Oh, but we did," Austin said with an unpleasant undertone in his voice. "You're mistaking the challenges of tracking all of the slimy operatives that Harrington used to do her dirty work with the challenges of identifying people who live openly. We may never know the identities of every one of her operatives, since they were used to living in the shadows, but scientists are different. They can be such interesting people, especially where egos are concerned. They like to keep records of their activities and talk about their colleagues. Our people were able to piece together a complete list of the scientists involved in the project, thanks in large part to the scientists themselves.

"It was a huge help that there wasn't any time to scrub all of your records when everyone was told to stow away for the journey to Citadel; in addition to communications with loved ones, colleagues, and others, there was actually a lot of information available from within the project itself. In short, our people have done a thorough job identifying every scientist who worked for Harrington."

"I still say you overlooked someone," she pushed back. "You're trying to prove a negative that can't be proved, so you conclude that you must be right anyway."

"That's why we didn't just search for Georgia's DNA when we visited *Firebird*," Austin said. "We also searched for Pandora's DNA. It wasn't hard to locate the quarters she shared with Lazarus, or to find what we wanted."

"Even if you claim to have found my DNA in any quarters aboard *Firebird*, that finding would mean nothing," she replied dismissively. "It was sometimes convenient to meet in quarters to discuss matters."

"Some of the places where we found your DNA were not where we'd expect to find them," he said pointedly, "unless you were doing something with Lazarus that we've been assured could only have happened between Lazarus and Pandora. Are you trying to tell me that Pandora was completely wrong about what it meant for two people to be bonded together by the aliens?"

Athena remained silent.

His expression turned hard. "However, we found one area where you slipped up all by yourself." He turned back to the display, and the image from the Phoenix shuttle appeared. They watched as Diana struck Pandora, who fell to the deck, stunned. The image paused as Austin spoke. "Do you remember telling me that you didn't change clothes with Pandora when she was removed from the shuttle's control room?"

"Yes, I remember. She said we were all wearing the same type of clothing, so it wasn't necessary to change."

Austin nodded. "Take a careful look at this image, Athena," he said, as the display zoomed slowly toward the collar of Pandora's jumpsuit. "What do you see?"

"I don't see anything, except problems with the resolution of the image."

Austin shook his head. "No, you see the same thing we did, after we looked at everything all over again. There's a tiny trickle of blood from where Diana slapped Pandora, and it made a slight stain on her collar. Even a tiny blood sample can provide DNA."

"There's no blood sample, or you would have produced it. You are just making up a story to support the same incorrect conclusion."

Austin pulled up an image of a jumpsuit. "Do you mean the blood sample that was on the jumpsuit we took away from you when we locked you up? We've compared the DNA from that blood sample with what we found in Pandora's quarters, and they are a perfect match. They're also a perfect match with *you*, Courtney."

Austin's gaze was coldly triumphant. "You were just a bit too clever by adding that detail about not changing clothes after Pandora was removed from the shuttle's control room. That's the one thing that you couldn't explain away, because it came from you in the first place.

You knew we'd never believe there was time for the both of you to have changed clothes anyway, and you provided your embellishment in the hopes of making the story seem more natural. Of course, you didn't know about the blood or the full story about what the aliens did and didn't do with your DNA, so you just figured there was no way we'd ever be able to tie you back to her. The playacting was impressive, however."

Austin brought up one more image on the display and gestured toward it. "Take a good look, because that's the gallows where you will finally die as the disgrace you were to the human race, long before you became a creature of the aliens. You once claimed that you would never face the punishment that waited for you on Citadel, Courtney," he reminded her. "It's been years too long in coming, but you will finally end up where the rest of your ilk have been awaiting you."

She was silent, but Austin already had the confirmation he needed.

CHAPTER THIRTY-FOUR

The day was beautiful, which seemed out of character for an execution. As the sun shone brightly, and a slight breeze kept everyone comfortable, Courtney Harrington was escorted across the Town Square to the steps of a scaffold.

It had been years since a similar scene had played out in the Square, involving a former high official from Earth. The last time, there had been multiple gallows to accommodate the members of Harrington's administration who had conspired with her to commit war crimes and try to destroy Citadel and assassinate Austin. This time, a single lonely gallows stood, a reminder that closure was finally at hand.

Harrington never looked at any of the people who had gathered to watch the end of the sordid saga she'd begun years earlier. After a brief pause at the foot of the steps leading to the platform, she began the final part of her journey.

Many of the people watching her had stood there years earlier or watched the proceedings on their displays as her colleagues met their fates. Joe and Sara Albretti were among those, with something else in common as well. Then, as now, Sara was pregnant. Now, as then, she hoped that what she witnessed would finally bring an end to all of the turmoil they'd faced from Earth, especially at the hands of Harrington.

Harrington reached the top of the platform. The defiance had drained from her, as if she'd come to terms with the fact that all of her bravado had won her nothing in the end. Austin had been adamant that she would be called by her given name and not by the make-believe one the aliens had given her. She stared out over the crowd as the charges were read aloud by a volunteer settler. He stated her sentence and asked if she had anything to say. She was silent as her eyes roamed through the faces in the multitude of people below her.

For an instant, her gaze locked with Austin's. There was neither triumph nor mercy to be found there, and she looked away. She looked at her questioner and shook her head. She nodded at the hood that her questioner held and stood still as it was placed over her head. She was determined not to let anyone see her last expression, because she was helpless to control it. A noose was placed around her neck, and her arms were bound behind her. A moment later, the platform was deserted as she prepared to die alone.

There was no need for her to move anywhere, as the trapdoor would not disengage until the system directed it to do so. Someone brought the system online, and it ran a quick check to confirm that the prisoner's weight and other characteristics matched the profile for the execution. Without any further delay, the portal released itself, and she plunged down sharply, her fall and her neck broken before she reached the ground.

It was all over, which a doctor confirmed by examining her body. Like Lazarus before her, her body would be cremated, with the ashes to be dispersed in deep space, to avoid creating any site on Citadel where tradition would require that any part of her would receive some measure of respect for the dead.

The scaffold was disassembled quickly, with the components taken away to serve other, less lethal purposes. People drifted away, glad to get back to their business. In a short time, there was no way to tell that there'd ever been an execution.

CHAPTER THIRTY-FIVE

J. W. Preacher sat in a very comfortable chair in the Citadel embassy as he watched the latest message from Austin.

"Thanks again, J. W., for all the things you, Astrid, and everyone else have done to help us bring closure to this nightmare," he said. "While it would have been a small gesture on the part of Harrington to accept her punishment without complaint, I guess we've learned that she's never been willing to accept responsibility for anything."

Austin's expression darkened slightly. "On Citadel, we have retained a file showing her execution, although I admit I'm not quite sure of the best way to deal with it. On the one hand, it's important to show everyone that she's truly gone, punished for her many sordid crimes. On the other hand, there is a morbid fascination attached to these things, and it would end up being replayed indefinitely within the public sphere. At this point, the file has been kept from the public, and I am leaning against ever releasing it. Consider yourself authorized to certify her death as needed.

"One thing people discovered is that although they thought they were making a copy of the execution when watching it on their displays, they didn't end up with anything," he said with an amused look. "Bret and Melody had disabled the function during the proceedings. The people actually present knew better than to try to make a recording, as it has long been the policy that only an official recording is made, for archive purposes."

Austin's expression turned into something Preacher understood as being completely direct. "We've known each other far too long to need to beat around the bush about some things, J. W., so I'll just say what's on my mind. You've already talked about taking certain steps as they relate to the operations of Phoenix, and I agree with those steps. I want you to do whatever it takes to shut down what remains of Phoenix, without giving anyone the notion that Citadel is prepared to accept responsibility for any claims by any of the victims of Phoenix's actions. As far as I'm concerned, Citadel is by far the innocent victim in this sordid mess, and we have no reason to apologize to anyone if we take ahold of stuff that is toxic to humanity and dispose of it.

"Work with Astrid and Dan to make sure we don't, in turn, become contaminated by exposure to things the aliens touched or that Phoenix touched on their behalf. Anything of a nonalien nature that Astrid and Dan don't believe we can use safely should be destroyed." He shook his head. "There's no way to ever trust anything that they've touched, and if we give it away to others, they may make some mistakes that could create more problems for everyone. If it sounds like I'm describing a scorched-earth policy, I am. Square it with Pete, Amelia, and the AN any way you feel is necessary, but this can't ever happen again.

"What I want to do is give people another practical reason to not mess with us when it comes to visiting other planets in our system. While we've reestablished our scouting laboratory on Shiloh, we've decided to take some measures to prevent future unauthorized visits. I'm pleased to confirm that our people have finally developed an effective vaccination against the Shiloh bug. While we've made it a policy to vaccinate prospective visitors to Citadel against the nasty surprises we've found on Citadel itself, we are taking a different approach with respect to other planets in our system. For now, other than the Citadel population itself, the only people who will receive vaccinations against the Shiloh bug will be the people who have a need to be there in the first place. That means no one from Earth will receive the vaccine, not even people from the Citadel Group, so people will need to assume that visiting Shiloh without permission will be like playing Russian roulette with their lives. We will also monitor traffic to and from that planet for now, to ensure that we have sufficient protections in place against what could end up as a biological nightmare.

"Please make sure that everyone in that solar system knows this, so that any enthusiasm for unauthorized visits on habitable planets elsewhere in our solar system is curbed. It goes without saying that visits to New Harbor will be even more tightly monitored for now, and only people with invitations from Citadel will be allowed to visit as we set up a scouting laboratory there."

He sighed. "While we've tried to stay out of local politics, that policy hasn't served us well. I agree with your assessment about the end of Pete Lee's career as president, but I want to make sure that it actually happens that way. I'm not willing to place our security at risk, or the security of your solar system at risk, for another four years due to his indecisiveness and general lack of sound judgment. It was only because our people were there and willing to spend our own blood and treasure that there's still a planet there without the kind of devastation that hasn't been seen since the Bio War.

"I've included a private message for Pete that you should review in advance. You'll see for yourself that it is blunt and brutal. Don't leak the message, but find a way to make the points about my displeasure known publicly so that Lee can't try to tie himself somehow to the success of fending off another attack. I expect that he's already been under fire for his actions, so adding our own displeasure to the rest of the criticism should help move him into early retirement.

"We need to open more lines of communication between Citadel and people who are currently or are likely to be leaders there. I want you to take note of these people and help me to establish those lines. At some point, I'll need to visit Earth anyway to refresh my own contacts, so I should plan on meeting some new faces as well."

Austin and his friends were hard at work, enjoying the run of his home, as they put the events of the past months behind them.

"Care to share with us the details of your new personal defenses?" Yabuno asked while nodding in the direction of the restored weapons complex. "I assume that you have another rail gun in place, although there are rumors that you have some other surprises set up."

Austin chuckled. "That's one of the benefits about rumors. I don't have to confirm or deny them, but people come away with the notion that they shouldn't mess with me."

"They've already figured that one out, after hearing about the wreck of your old complex and how you took out Lazarus with your bare hands," Albretti noted. "It's kind of a shame that you didn't have a chance to do the same with Powers. She managed to avoid being on a scaffold next to Harrington, when she was guilty of plenty of crimes in her own right."

Austin's expression remained relaxed. "One thing I've tried to do is to avoid thinking too much about people like Powers, Flynn, and Harrington once they've been dealt with. There probably aren't more than a couple of her atoms still attached to each other at this point, so I don't worry about Powers having cheated the hangman. At least she didn't cheat death any more than Harrington or Flynn did."

"Any thoughts on Citadel, going forward?" Sara asked.

He paused for a moment, as if savoring a glass of fine Citadel wine. "Yes, I have a few thoughts. The first is to continue to extend our network further out into space, both for the scientific value from any data we obtain and as an early warning system.

"I'd also like us to continue to improve upon our warp-field technology. I believe that one day our transports will be able to move into and out of normal space-time as easily as *Pathfinder* can now. What a notion—to no longer be at the mercy of an adversary that can wait us out and predict where our transports must appear and maneuver accordingly. When that day arrives, we will have put in place an amazing defense against practically any intelligent intruder."

"Those ideas have a strong defensive feel to them," Liz noted. "What about other areas?"

Austin grinned. "I haven't forgotten about those things. While we're nowhere near that point yet, a day will come when Citadel may find itself being both a community and a starting point for further exploration."

"Are you talking about Planet Shiloh?" she asked.

"In part," he replied, nodding. "For now, we'll continue with having observational stations set up in several locations on the planet where we can keep collecting and analyzing data. While I believe the steps we took were reasonable ones to evaluate whether there were any biological problems as far as humans were concerned, there's no reason not to investigate the planet's biology in much more detail, to make certain there aren't any other surprises waiting for us.

"At some point, we'll probably decide that the population on Citadel needs room for expansion, and Shiloh is the logical place to use for that expansion. Somewhere down the road, we'll do the same for New Harbor, which is why we're setting up observational stations there as well. In fact, after we have some good data on the New Harbor climate and other key factors, we'll probably want to begin with any terraforming that's needed to bring up the temperatures a bit. It won't be as useful to evaluate the microbial environment there while things are a bit colder than they are now, since we'll want to know about any problems that are likely to show up in a modified environment. In time, the stations for Shiloh and New Harbor may serve as the starting points for new settlements.

"We still have plenty of places to explore in this solar system, and we'll probably have a hell of a lot of fun doing it. However, one day we'll face the question of whether we've explored everything we want to explore here and what it means for us going forward."

He looked toward the sky. "Of course, that depends on where we want to go. It also depends on what we can learn from things closer to home."

"Speaking of things closer to home, Alan, are you ready to throw in the towel where the derelict is concerned?" Albretti asked.

"Not at all," he said. "In fact, it feels like something is getting ready to become clearer, although I've said that before."

Austin laughed sympathetically. "I know I've had that problem plenty of times. Anyway, as I was saying, eventually Citadel may be a starting point for exploring things we can't even imagine now."

"I can imagine aliens," Turner said. "What you're saying is that eventually we'll have to deal with them again."

"Not necessarily," he replied easily. "There are plenty of places to go that wouldn't take us anywhere near them, although I refuse to rule out approaching a particular area just because they may show up sometime. That would be the same as just conceding immense areas of space to them that they've sought before but couldn't take. We've demonstrated that we can take care of ourselves in a way that wasn't possible when we first came here from Earth. Besides, we'd end up making plenty of stops before ever reaching them, wherever they may be."

"Maybe, maybe not," Turner said. "That depends on what kinds of distances are involved in reaching stars with habitable worlds. If we go in that direction, I hope meeting the aliens doesn't happen within our lifetimes," Turner said. His expression became more somber as he looked at Austin. He didn't add that anything was possible within Austin's lifetime.

PROLOGUE CITADEL

The story continues in the next novel by Robert Adrian, *Prologue Citadel.* Sam Austin and Sara Albretti regain consciousness aboard a shuttle. The last thing they remember is maneuvering the small craft near the giant alien derelict that had drifted into the Citadel system years earlier. Bret Yabuno had made an unsuccessful attempt to use a remote probe to gain access to the ancient vessel, based on Alan Turner's interpretations of ancient alien symbols. Instead, the ship had come to life, with cold blue fire surging throughout the Citadel system, causing massive damage. The energy reached but somehow didn't destroy the shuttle.

As they recover their senses, Sam and Sara learn that their shuttle has been damaged, with most systems offline. They are surprised to find no trace of the derelict. As they study the stars more carefully, they are disturbed to learn that they aren't even in the Citadel system. Somehow, they have ended up in Earth's solar system. Something else doesn't seem right, which they confirm when they realize that they have been hurled more than a hundred years into Earth's past.

Somehow, they have to land their crippled ship on Earth without being detected and find a place to hide. While they search for a way to return to their own time and loved ones, ancient memories return to Sam from his time as the United States president. He knows about the assassination that will propel him into a role he never wanted, as well as a horrific biological war that will extinguish more than half of the planet's population. He also knows about a savage attack on his home that will leave a loved one dead. Should he run the risk of extinguishing the future he knows by alerting President Sam Austin and others to the dangers? The longer it takes for him to find a way back to his own time, the more likely it is that he will slip up and change something that can't be undone. The stakes become even higher when he reviews the data from the accident and learns some disturbing implications for his own time, assuming he ever returns to it.

Robert Adrian is the pen name of an attorney with more than two decades of experience working primarily with Silicon Valley technology companies. He grew up reading Robert Heinlein, Isaac Asimov, Ray Bradbury, Andre Norton, and other giants of science fiction. Now, as the author of the *Sam Austin Chronicles*, he blends his passion for science fiction with other interests, such as historical and futuristic writing. Book four of the series, *Countdown Citadel*, is the sequel to the series that includes *Destination Citadel, Target Citadel,* and *Checkmate Citadel*. Adrian enjoys completing projects in his workshop and participating in local music events, which is how he met his wife. They live in the San Francisco Bay Area with their three children.

www.ingramcontent.com/pod-product-compliance
Lightning Source LLC
Chambersburg PA
CBHW071212250626
47159CB00001B/293